Woman on the Other Shore

Woman on the Other Shore

Mitsuyo Kakuta

Translated by Wayne P. Lammers

KODANSHA INTERNATIONAL
Tokyo • New York • London

TRANSLATOR'S NOTE: Events in some chapters of this book make reference to the Japanese school year, which runs from April to March, with only a short spring break between years. Summer vacation falls between the first and second terms, starting around July 20 and lasting between four and six weeks depending on the region. Junior high goes from seventh to ninth grades, high school from tenth to twelfth.

This book has been selected by the Japanese Literature Publishing Project (JLPP), which is run by the Japanese Literature Publishing and Promotion Center (J-Lit Center) on behalf of the Agency for Cultural Affairs of Japan.

Originally published in Japanese in 2004 by Bungei Shunju, Tokyo, under the title *Taigan no kanojo*.

Distributed in the United States by Kodansha America, Inc., and in the United Kingdom and continental Europe by Kodansha Europe Ltd.

Published by Kodansha International Ltd., 17–14 Otowa 1-chome, Bunkyo-ku, Tokyo 112–8652, and Kodansha America, Inc.

Library of Congress Cataloging-in-Publication Data

Kakuta, Mitsuyo, 1967–
 [Taigan no kanojo. English]
 Woman on the other shore / Mitsuyo Kakuta ; translated by Wayne P. Lammers.
     p. cm.
 "Originally published in Japanese in 2004 by Bungei Shunju, Tokyo, under the title: Taigan no kanojo"—T.p. verso.
  ISBN-13: 978-4-7700-3043-6
  I. Lammers, Wayne P., 1951– II. Title.
  PL855.A3T3513 2007
  895.6'36—dc22
                                2007001381

www.kodansha-intl.com

Woman on the Other Shore

1

When am I ever going to stop being the same old me?

With a start, Sayoko Tamura realized she'd been absentmindedly turning the same question over and over in her mind, and a crooked smile came to her lips. The very fact that she was thinking such thoughts meant one thing hadn't changed since she was a little girl. She'd spent practically her entire childhood wondering what it would be like if she were somebody else. *What if I were everybody's sweetheart Yoko? What if I were super-whiz Nitta?*

Sitting on a park bench under a canopy of tree branches, she turned her gaze toward her three-year-old daughter playing in the sandbox. There were many children Akari's age at the park, and they had all found at least one or two other kids to play with. But as usual Akari was shoveling all by herself off in the corner. When she got to be a little older, would she be asking herself the same question: *What if I were somebody else?*

With a sigh, Sayoko pulled her cell phone from the hip pocket of her jeans. The log showed no missed calls, so she dialed her home phone to check for messages there. Nothing. The call she was expecting had not yet come.

Akari had been born three years ago in February. About six months later, Sayoko followed the advice of the parenting magazines she read and began taking her daughter on outings to the park closest to home—at the suggested hour, and dressed according to form. She got to know other mothers with children Akari's age, and even arranged to meet with them to go for their babies' periodic checkups and vaccinations together. But as time passed, Sayoko began to notice a certain cliquishness among some of the young mothers who came to the park. She saw that they were following the lead of one woman in particular, and although they were careful not to be too open about it, avoiding any obvious snubs, they were in effect ostracizing one of the other mothers. Being over thirty herself, Sayoko was noticeably more advanced in age than most of the women, so she could accept that they might think she didn't fit in. It didn't mean they thought she was a bad person. They would naturally assume that someone as much older as she was would have different perspectives and be harder to open up to. It was an entirely understandable response, really.

Even so, once she realized what was going on, Sayoko found it depressing to go to the park, and she gave up the daily outings for a while. But then it wasn't long before she started feeling guilty about keeping her daughter cooped up at home all the time. She worried that without the park and its opportunities for meeting other children, her little girl might never develop the social skills she needed.

And so Sayoko and Akari had spent the last two years slowly making the rounds of every park within walking distance of their condominium. Once they'd been going to Park A long enough for Sayoko to identify the social dynamics of the mothers who gathered there, they moved on to Park B. Fortunately, there was no shortage of parks large and small within range of their building.

Sayoko learned that people who wandered from park to park this way were known as "park hoppers." *But it's not like we're hopping around by choice,* she muttered as if making excuses to someone as she left the house with Akari in search of each new park. *We're just trying to find a park where we can feel at home.*

This particular park, about a twenty-minute walk from their building, was the largest they'd found in their travels, and it drew a more mixed crowd than the communities of young mothers Sayoko had found so characteristic of the smaller parks. Here she saw fathers walking their babies, or older folks playing with their grandchildren, and even the mothers were much more varied in age and dress. Not only that, but, as a matter of courtesy, all the grownups ignored each other; nobody ever tried to talk to anyone unless it was absolutely necessary. Deciding she preferred it that way, Sayoko had been bringing her daughter here for nearly six months now.

Of course, even if the grownups kept to themselves, the little ones usually made friends. While their parents buried their noses in books or fiddled with cameras nearby, the children thrown together in the midst of all the play equipment gradually gravitated toward one another and began playing with kids they'd never seen before. Now and again tears would flow in a dispute over a toy, but even then the grownups tried hard not to get involved. It seemed to be an unwritten rule at this park.

Digging in the sand with her plastic shovel, Akari paused to watch two girls her age playing house in the middle of the large sandbox. One of them wore a red T-shirt, the other a sunflower-print dress, and they were giggling and chattering over a set of colorful plastic dishes, their voices ringing crisply into the air. A little boy tottered up from the far side of the sandbox and eyed them as if wanting to be included. At first they just stared back, but then the girl in the sunflower print picked up a fork and handed it to him, affecting what must have been the mannerisms of her own mother.

While pretending not to watch, Sayoko kept a surreptitious eye on the threesome in the middle of the sandbox and on Akari shoveling all by herself in one corner. Every so often she saw her daughter cast a glance toward the others, then quickly go back to her digging.

Sayoko often marveled at how much the daughter took after the mother. No matter how badly the girl wanted to join a game, she was too shy to simply walk up and ask if she could play, so she waited timidly nearby, hoping to be invited. Of course, children seldom noticed such things, and by the time Akari cast her next sidelong glance the others might have run off to play somewhere else. As Sayoko watched Akari's eyes dart back and forth, she invariably recognized in them the movements of her own eyes. This was exactly how she'd looked at the mothers in all those other parks, where she'd found it so hard to fit in. And each time she realized this, it gave her a deep sense of failure as a mother. If only she were a more self-confident and outgoing parent who could strike up easy conversations with whomever she met, pretending not to notice the walls that cliques tried to erect, then surely Akari would be growing into a more self-confident and outgoing child as well.

Sayoko had considered going back to work before this. She'd thought about it during the first two years of her marriage, before Akari was born, as well as in the three years since. Instead of fretting all the time about which park to go to, maybe what she needed was to find herself a job and put Akari in nursery school. Her daughter was bound to make more friends there than she made as a "park hopper." She would probably learn to be more sociable. Yet Sayoko had continued to hesitate. *What kind of mother chooses to work when her child's at such a precious age? The poor girl, being torn away from her mom like that!* She made excuses for her inaction by repeating the refrains she'd heard from other stay-at-home mothers at the park. But the real reason for dragging her feet lay elsewhere. When she saw cliques forming among the young women at the parks, it reminded her all too well of the office politics she'd had her fill of before she got married.

After college, Sayoko had taken a job with a film distributor, a company known for giving new hires a great deal of freedom and responsibility from day one. She enjoyed the work itself, and she also liked the easygoing company culture in which subordinates weren't expected to be so formal with their superiors. But as the years went by, tensions that had been indiscernible at first rose to the surface. Certain members of the permanent female staff were caught in an endless cycle of petty charges and counter-charges with the contract workers—about who was supposed to make sure coffee and iced tea were available; about what time workers could leave at the end of the day; about the dress code; about personalizing the ladies' room. If you tried to stay out of the fray, whether by being nice to everyone or ignoring everyone, you could soon find yourself being picked on by both sides. It required a tremendous effort to maintain the right distance from the opposing parties, and in fact Sayoko expended huge amounts of energy attempting to do exactly that. Fortunately, just when she was becoming completely fed up with the toll this was taking, her boyfriend, Shuji Tamura, conveniently popped the question. She quickly said yes, and almost as quickly submitted her resignation to the company. Shuji was obviously none too happy about the latter—he had assumed Sayoko would continue working even after she got married—but she pretended not to notice.

It was about a month ago that Sayoko had finally broached the subject with her husband.

"I've been thinking I'd like to go back to work."

"Sure, why not?" he replied absently, not even bothering to ask what might have prompted her decision. Sayoko realized he must think she wasn't serious, she was just sounding out a momentary whim.

But Sayoko was dead serious. She bought recruitment magazines and scanned the job listings, looking for anything that said *No experience necessary. Homemakers welcome.* She'd gone to a number of interviews and been turned down every time, for whatever reason. For each appointment, she had to leave Akari with her mother-in-law, who invariably had a snide remark or two to offer. But Sayoko refused to let the repeated jabs get to her; if anything, she became more determined than ever as she searched the ads and sent in applications.

Now she glanced at the display one last time before shoving the phone back into her hip pocket. She leaned her head back and looked up at the sky. Beyond the leaves swaying gently overhead stretched a flawless expanse of cerulean blue.

The woman she'd interviewed with two days before had told her she'd get back to her today. Despite her perfect string of rejections so far, Sayoko hoped this time might be different. In fact, she was secretly counting on it. Not only was the woman Sayoko's own age, but they'd gone to the same school. Since it was a megaversity with a huge student body, it wasn't actually all that unusual to run into fellow alumni, but this woman behaved as if she'd found a long lost friend.

"Can you believe it?" she beamed, sounding very much like she was still a student. "Just think how many times we must've walked right past each other! Under the ginkgo trees coming in from the gate, you know, or in one of the dining halls."

The children who'd been playing house in the middle of the sand-box were now playing store, calling out to the shopkeeper with a bit of a nasal twang.

"I'd like just half of that cabbage."

"Could you clean this fish, please?"

Sayoko saw her daughter keeping a close watch on the action out of the corner of her eye. All of a sudden Akari was looking her way, a plea in her eyes—obviously hoping Mom might step in. Sayoko hastily averted her eyes. It tore at her heart, but she wanted Akari to learn to make friends on her own.

Several minutes later, the girl rose slowly to her feet, sand clinging to her skirt. With an expression of grim determination, she stepped toward the children playing store. The three seemed to be busy dividing things up and deciding what would be what in their game.

"Okay, so we'll use these for money," one of them said. "But not those. Those aren't money."

When Akari reached the spot where they were playing, she held out her shovel and sand-filled bucket as if to get their attention. But whether because they didn't notice or were deliberately ignoring her, none of them even glanced up. She lingered there for a while, but when it sank in that they weren't going to ask her to join them, she abruptly threw down the shovel and bucket. As the bucket tumbled toward the ground, sand spewed onto the little boy's head. He burst into tears.

"Oh dear," Sayoko said, rushing to the boy's side and brushing the sand from his hair. "I'm sorry, I'm so sorry."

Akari watched from a few steps away. She was on the verge of tears herself.

A young woman in a hat approached with a smile. "That's all right. He'll be fine," she said, then turned to her boy. "Settle down, now, Shin. Stop being such a crybaby. You're frightening your friends."

His two playmates gave each other looks and turned to go.

"Come over here, Akari. You need to apologize," Sayoko said sharply. "What got into you anyway—throwing your bucket down like that?"

She regretted the tone of her voice even before the words were out of her mouth. Why did she keep letting this happen? She knew it wasn't fair to Akari, but somehow she couldn't help herself. It so exasperated her to see her daughter having trouble making friends that an unintended harshness crept into her voice.

"Don't be upset, sweetie," she said more gently. "Let's just tell your new friend we're sorry, okay?" She turned toward the boy and his mother, but they were already halfway across the sandbox heading in the other direction.

"Well, maybe it's time to stop by the supermarket and get on home. Mommy just remembered she forgot to do the laundry."

Gathering up the bucket and shovel, Sayoko took Akari's hand and started back toward the bench.

At the supermarket, Akari rode in the front of the cart as Sayoko wheeled up and down the nearly empty aisles. Ground beef was marked down, so she decided to make hamburger steaks for dinner. Checking prices as she went, she added spinach, carrots, and eggs to the cart, then remembered she was out of fabric softener and headed for the laundry aisle.

"Do we have Mil Mil, Mommy?" Akari leaned back to ask about her favorite yogurt drink. "Did you buy Mil Mil?"

"Yes, dear," Sayoko said absently as she checked prices on several brands of softener. She selected the least expensive refill pack she could find, even as her gaze lingered on a name-brand product that cost three times as much.

A month ago, when she'd finally made up her mind to go back to work, the push had come from an utterly trivial thing: a blouse on a rack in a department store. While shopping in Kichijoji, she'd lifted the tag on a top that caught her eye, and found it marked ¥15,800. As she stood contemplating the tag, she realized she had no idea whether that was high or low. Of course, it was a lot more than she paid for Shuji's dress shirts, and it would certainly blow a big hole in their monthly budget. But how did it stand in the typical thirty-five-year-old woman's wardrobe? What did women her age expect to pay for a well-made blouse these days?

It stunned her to realize she didn't have the first idea. And as she thought about this, everything seemed to fall together: her park hopping, to escape the young-mother politics she wanted no part of; her exasperation at Akari for following her own unfortunate example and playing by herself; and her inability to name the going price for a woman's blouse. Didn't they all have a common thread? If she started working again, she would soon learn the price of clothes, she would no longer have to worry about outings to the park, and she would have fewer occasions to snap at Akari. Sayoko became convinced that going back to work would solve everything.

"There. We're done shopping, and now we just need to hurry home so Mommy can start the laundry," Sayoko said in a sing-song voice as she picked up the grocery bag in one hand and took Akari's in the other. If she didn't hear about that job by the end of the day, she decided, she would buy another recruitment magazine tomorrow.

Swinging their arms in a wide arc between them, Sayoko and Akari started on their homeward trek.

It was a little after eight that evening when the phone finally rang. Shuji was home, watching a ball game, but he made no move to get up from the table.

"Mo-o-ommy, the phone!" Akari called from her high chair, and Sayoko hurried in from the kitchen to pick it up.

"Hello?"

"Oh, hello, Mrs. Tamura," came the voice of a woman sounding very relaxed. "Aoi Narahashi here, from Platinum Planet. Thanks for coming in the other day."

Sayoko was caught by surprise. She had pretty much given up on getting a call.

"N-not at all," she stammered, bowing deeply at the phone. "It was my pleasure."

"I'd like to offer you the job. I hope you'll accept."

"Oh, my goodness! Yes! Do you really mean it?"

Shuji glanced her way.

"Actually, though, before anything else, I think I need to fill you in a little more on exactly what the job is. I'm a little worried I might have given you the wrong impression the other day. If you decide after you know all the details that it's not for you, please don't hesitate to say no."

Sayoko could hear loud music playing in the background, and then a raised voice trying to be heard above the din. She imagined

15

that loud background voice ringing out in the cramped offices she had visited two days before.

"I'm sure there won't be a problem."

"In any case, could I ask you to come to the office again? Tomorrow if possible, or the next day if that's better. Whenever's convenient for you."

"Tomorrow will be fine," Sayoko said eagerly. "I could be there a little after noon."

"Great! I'll see you then," the woman said, and hung up.

Sayoko very deliberately placed the handset back in its cradle before letting out a whoop. "I did it!"

"What?" Shuji turned to ask. "Who was that?" His eyes were already back on the TV.

"Who was that, Mommy?" Akari echoed, holding up her kiddie fork in a hand covered with rice.

"Remember what I was saying last month about going back to work? I just got offered a job! I was actually starting to worry I might never find anything. Anyway, the boss is the same age as me, and it turns out we even went to college together, though we didn't know each other. She's real down-to-earth and friendly, and it's only a tiny little company but I liked the relaxed atmosphere. I've been away from work for five years, so I'm thinking a small place like that might be the best fit. Especially since I felt like I hit it off with the boss."

Giddy with excitement, Sayoko rattled on as she carried the salad to the table and set out plates for it.

Platinum Planet's offices occupied what was once a two-bedroom apartment on the fifth floor of an old mixed-use building near Okubo Station on the Sobu Line. One bedroom was filled with desks for the staff; the other, a traditional tatami-mat room, had a plaque over the doorway that somewhat grandiosely declared "President's Office." These connected directly to a larger room of about four meters by five, the original living-dining area. There was clutter everywhere, but curiously, in spite of the mess, Sayoko had felt very much at home during the interview. The boss struck her as a forthright person, and while they talked frequent bursts of laughter spilled from the staff office, where several women worked at their desks. *This is perfect*, Sayoko remembered thinking. *I wouldn't have to worry about cliques and confrontations and childish backbiting here. Not with so few people, and such an easygoing boss.* The atmosphere was by far the brightest of any place she'd been.

Shuji cast another glance her way. He seemed taken aback by the intensity of her enthusiasm. "Sounds great," he said tepidly as he turned back to the TV. "But what about Akari?"

Akari perked up at the mention of her name. "What about Akari?" she echoed.

"She can go to nursery school."

Shuji said nothing as he put some salad on his plate.

"I've given it a lot of thought," Sayoko went on. "I know some people say they feel sorry for kids who have to go to nursery school, including your mother. But I don't see how it can be anything but good for Akari to get to play with so many more kids her own age. Plus we're going to have all kinds of new expenses as she gets older. Even now, in fact—"

"What exactly will you be doing?" Shuji cut her off.

"The ad said cleaning."

"Cleaning?"

"But they're actually a travel agency of some kind."

"So what does that mean?"

"I guess I'll find out more tomorrow. Oh, oops, I'll need your mother to babysit again. Could you call her, dear? I'll switch once you've got her on the line."

Shuji had been keeping his eye on the game as they talked. "All right!" he exclaimed to the crack of a bat.

Great, thought Sayoko, *he cares more about the game than about me going back to work after five years off.*

"Well, whatever," Shuji said distractedly. His eyes remained glued to the TV. "But it's been a long time, so be sure to take it easy at first."

"Hooray for Mommy!" a smiling Akari cheered—though she could hardly have understood what her mother's excitement was about.

"Thank you, sweetie. Here's a great big kiss for you!" Sayoko wrapped her arms around Akari's neck and smacked her on the cheek. The girl squealed with delight.

Sitting across from the president of Platinum Planet in a rather seedy-looking Chinese restaurant in Okubo, Sayoko glanced back and forth between her new boss and the name Aoi Narahashi printed on the business card at the edge of the table.

The moment she'd arrived at the office, the woman had hustled her right back out the door, saying, "Let's get some lunch." As she followed, Sayoko wondered giddily what sort of fancy restaurant someone who owned a whole company might take her to—especially since she hadn't been to a restaurant of any kind in a long time. But when they arrived, the place proved to be a run-of-the-mill neighborhood eatery with a faded, handwritten menu plastered on the wall. It was after one o'clock, so they had the upstairs seating all to themselves.

The waitress came with some beer and two glasses. Aoi lifted the bottle to fill Sayoko's glass, then her own.

"Cheers!" she said grandly, raising her glass. "Welcome aboard."

They clinked glasses and drank.

"What school were you in at the U?" Aoi asked with white foam clinging to the corner of her mouth.

"The Faculty of Letters. I majored in English literature." Instinctively, Sayoko used the courteous forms of speech expected when speaking to superiors.

"Oh, please. Let's not stand on ceremony. After all, we're exactly the same age," Aoi said. "I was in philosophy. It took me an extra year, but I finally did manage to finish. You know, I actually had a couple more interviews scheduled, but I made up my mind on you as soon as you left."

"Do you mind if I ask why?" Sayoko said in surprise.

"There's that formal language again," Aoi said, throwing her a disapproving look as she poured herself some more beer. "But why should you be so surprised?"

"I just wondered what made you so sure about me. I mean, everybody else kept turning me down. The ads would say 'Homemakers welcome,' but I'd get to the interview and they'd be afraid I was going to call in sick all the time because I have a little girl and kids are always coming down with something. Or they'd lecture me that majoring in English was no guarantee I was actually any good at it, and I'd better not try to claim so. Stuff like that. To be honest, I was really getting discouraged."

Aoi threw her head back and laughed. "When interviewers say things like that, you know there has to be some serious disgruntlement swirling around beneath the surface. They're taking their own frustrations out on the applicants. I don't have that kind of negative stuff weighing me down, so I can be a better judge of character. That's all."

The waitress approached bearing a tray crowded with two full lunch specials, watching her every step. Today's entrée was a stir-fry with eggplant and ground meat. When the waitress was gone, Aoi drew two pairs of chopsticks from the holder on the table and handed one to Sayoko.

"Now, I need to be sure you understand what you're getting into," she said, her face turning serious. "What you'll mostly be doing is cleaning people's houses. At the film distributor where you worked before you got married, you said they had you choosing Japanese titles for Asian films and handling spin-off merchandising, right? Well, this job isn't going to let you exercise your creativity or offer you the sense of satisfaction a job like that gave you. It's a service job—basically just plain old manual labor. Are you sure you want to sign up for that kind of work?"

"Absolutely. I'll do anything. I just want to be working again." To herself she added, *Not "want to," actually, but "have to." For Akari's sake. And for my own sake as her mother.*

"Glad to hear it. That takes a load off my mind," Aoi said and promptly started in on her meal. Sayoko pulled apart her chopsticks and turned to her food as well.

Between bites, Aoi filled Sayoko in on the Platinum Planet story, scarcely raising her eyes from the food in front of her. The company was sort of an odd-jobber for the travel industry, she explained. Their main business was putting together and operating travel packages to various resort destinations, mainly in Asia, both for individuals and corporations; in some cases they sold these packages to other travel agencies as well. But they also took on a variety of contract work from other agencies—acting as a purchasing agent, gathering information about overseas locations, arranging transportation and lodging, compiling customer surveys, and pretty much anything else an agency might ask them to do.

"That's why I describe us as an odd-job service," Aoi said. "Like I said, I took an extra year to finish college. Then as soon as I graduated, I started my own business. Not that that's saying much, since at first it wasn't a whole lot different from being a student for hire, you know. Basically I just did whatever people asked me to do. As it turned out, that soon became what the company was all about. And one great benefit was that I developed a really wide network of contacts."

Aoi paused to take a sip of beer. She wore no makeup or jewelry. She certainly dressed modestly for the president of a company,

Sayoko thought, realizing how laughably off the mark her image of a woman who ran her own business had been. The picture she normally conjured up for that sort of a person was of someone dressed to the nines in designer clothes and weighed down with quantities of flashy jewelry, her face painted to elegant perfection. She was too nervous to notice at the time, Sayoko now recalled, but Aoi's appearance at their initial meeting had been much the same—a far cry from the stereotype she'd pictured beforehand.

"Five or six years ago a bunch of hotels in southern Sri Lanka formed a consortium called the Garden Group. This was in towns on the Indian Ocean like Weligama and Tangalla that hadn't really been developed yet for the tourist trade. We won the contract to be the group's exclusive sales agent in Japan—all hotel reservations from this country would now go through us. That put our business on a much stabler footing for a while, but then the whole terrorism thing blew up, along with the wars, you know. I suppose we were lucky in a way, since our core business was with travelers who didn't let that sort of thing bother them so much, unlike the big agencies, but we still took a hit. Then came SARS. You'd think the gods were out to get us. A lot of small companies catering to the overseas traveler like us bit the dust."

Sayoko worked on her entrée as she listened, nodding from time to time. If they were in the travel business, how exactly did cleaning people's houses fit in, she kept wondering, as Aoi alternated briskly between talking and eating.

"Anyway, what with all that, I've been thinking we need to diversify," Aoi went on. "Like one obvious thing might be to break into domestic travel as well, you know. But I've been mulling over some other things, too, and one idea I had was to start up a housekeeping service."

She had finished her food. Pushing her bowls aside, she leaned forward and propped her elbows on the table.

"I know, I know. Why housekeeping, of all things? But I have a long-term vision here. Living in Japan, we pretty much have to get on a plane no matter where we want to go, plus we really don't get all that much vacation time. Even so, in spite of all the obstacles, everybody's always going on trips, all over the world. You'd be hard pressed to find a country we don't visit. It was when I ran into some seventy-two-year-old Japanese tourists in Paraguay that it hit me like a flash: our love of travel isn't going away. In fact, it's probably going to grow. And I suppose this may partly be wishful thinking, but I'm willing to bet that workers will start getting lots more vacation days as time goes on. That's where the housekeeping service comes in. The idea is to look after people's homes when they go off on extended vacations— water their shrubs, weed their gardens, bring in their mail, air out their rooms, make sure the house is clean. Going away on vacation could be a whole lot more relaxing if you didn't have to worry about all those niggling chores while you were gone, don't you think?"

Aoi was leaning animatedly into her words.

"I suppose so," Sayoko nodded rather tentatively. To someone who hadn't traveled anywhere at all since her daughter was born, it didn't sound like a particularly lucrative venture.

"Of course, things like this don't take root overnight. For one thing, right now, not that many people go on such long vacations that they need someone to come in and take care of their house. But in any case, I don't have to make it pay right away and I think it's important to get started, so I decided to work with a housecleaning service a friend of mine runs and broaden the target market to include other people too, not just travelers. That's where you come in.... Whew! All this talking is making me thirsty," she said, and gulped down the rest of her beer.

Sayoko finally finished her food and put down her chopsticks. Most of Aoi's explanation had gone right over her head, but she gathered that Platinum Planet was experiencing financial difficulties, and it sounded like Aoi had decided to turn it from a travel agency into a housecleaning service. But to avoid the stigma of admitting failure, or maybe because of a legal catch of some kind, she was forcing it into a "housekeeping for travelers" mold. It was probably something like that, she concluded vaguely.

"About the hours," Sayoko spoke up, finding her chance now that Aoi had paused. "I think the job description said three or four days a week, but I was wondering if there's any chance I could work five days."

Aoi's eyes widened. "My, my, aren't you fired up!"

"Actually, it isn't that. The thing is, I'll need to enroll my daughter in nursery school, but they might not accept her if I'm only working three days a week. Admission decisions depend a lot on the mother's hours and other work conditions."

"Oh, right, of course. You said you had a daughter. Then how about we do this? I really only need you three days a week for now, but eventually it'll be five, so we'll go ahead and classify you as a regular, full-time employee instead of a part-timer. You probably need some kind of letter to that effect, right?"

"Are you sure it's all right?"

"Of course, of course. It's no problem at all. Except I won't pay you for five days."

"Heavens, no," Sayoko replied a little too forcefully.

"I'm just teasing," Aoi said with a guffaw.

"You know, this reminds me of the student cafeteria," Sayoko said, gazing out the large picture window. Sunlight flickered through the leaves of a tall tree overhead just like at the dining hall she'd frequented on campus.

"Oh, right, you mean the newer one," Aoi nodded, squinting a little as she looked through the glass. "I ate there quite a bit, too. I even went back after I graduated. It was so cheap."

"Then we might really have bumped elbows sometime."

"Remember the marinated tuna bowl? Only ¥580—except that was way more than I could spend in those days. All I could do then was drool."

"Sure, I remember. I drooled, too. Curry and rice for ¥170 was my mainstay. The cheapest item on the menu."

"Right. And good luck ever finding any meat in it!"

They looked at each other and laughed. Talking about their student days like this, it was hard to believe they'd only just met. It felt like they must have eaten lunch together in the student cafeteria dozens of times, moaning about the out-of-reach tuna bowl or meat-challenged curry.

"All right, then." Aoi reached for the check and got to her feet. "Can you come back to the office once? I'd like to introduce you to the others." Sayoko hastily rose to follow.

As they started down the narrow stairway, Aoi looked over her shoulder to say, "I'm so glad I found someone like you for this job, Mrs. Tamura."

"That's very kind," Sayoko said, bowing.

Sayoko caught a bus when she got off the train in Ogikubo, but traffic was backed up and it was going on four by the time she reached her mother-in-law's house in Iogi.

"What took you so *long*, dear? I suppose you just *had* to see what was new at the department store? How *nice* to be so young at heart."

Grandma Tamura looked up from the TV in the living room sounding a little put out, her words dripping with sarcasm. "For your information, I kept Akari going until just a few minutes ago. You said not to let her nap, so I did everything I could to keep her awake, I really did, but when you didn't come home and didn't come home, and she kept getting fussier and fussier, I had to give up and let her lie down."

To hear Shuji tell it, this was simply the way his mother talked

24

and she didn't mean to be snide or sarcastic. Sayoko wanted to think he was right, but somehow she'd never quite learned to shrug it off with a smile.

"I'm sorry. The traffic was stop and go, and the bus hardly got above a crawl."

"Do you really have to go back to work, Sayoko? Is it so hard to make ends meet on Shuji's paycheck?"

"It's not that," Sayoko said, smiling vaguely as she started for the tatami room upstairs.

Akari lay with arms and legs flung wide on a guest futon in the middle of the floor. Lifting her daughter's limp body like a heavy wet blanket, Sayoko slid her off onto the tatami floor, then folded the futon and put it away in the bedding closet. When she was finished she gathered Akari into her arms and descended the stairs. She could hear her mother-in-law busy with something in the kitchen.

"I'm sorry, Mother," Sayoko called from the front hall, "I need to be going right away. I'll come again some other time when I don't have to rush off in such a hurry. Thank you so much for taking Akari today."

Grandma Tamura appeared carrying a paper bag. "Can you take this?" she said. "It's some organic vegetables, and also some dried fish from Odawara. They were gifts, and I wanted to share with you and Shuji."

Sayoko groaned inwardly at the extra weight, but she could hardly say no.

"That's nice of you. Thank you," she said with a bow. "Well, I need to be going." She bowed again as she closed the door behind her.

Sayoko made her way toward the bus stop with the sleeping Akari clutched in one arm and the heavy shopping bag dangling from the other. A hint of orange had come into the light over the city as the sun sank lower in the sky.

"No *wanna*," Akari mumbled in her sleep right next to Sayoko's ear.

25

First I'll need to visit all the nursery schools nearby, and then there'll be applications to fill out, and then...

On the bus, Sayoko's mind began to spin as she made a mental list of all the things she would need to do. A whole new life awaited her tomorrow. No, it had already begun today. How often had she awakened to rain and rejoiced that she could skip the park that day, only to have her joy displaced a moment later by pangs of guilt? But that person was now fading rapidly into the distance, like the view outside the bus window.

2

"What a hick town!" Aoi Narahashi muttered as she gazed out her bedroom window. Filling her entire field of vision was a vast expanse of rice paddies, giving way in the distance to mulberry fields, and beyond that to bamboo groves.

It was an assessment she had come to when she first arrived in town, the moment she got off the train and noticed that every high school girl in sight was still wearing her skirt long. Why were they in uniform during spring break anyway?

"Aoi! Are you up?" she heard her mother calling from downstairs. "Time to get moving!"

Aoi quickly reached for her school uniform on its hanger. She slid her arms through the sleeves of the brand new blouse, pulled on the pleated skirt, and headed downstairs with the jacket and ribbon in her hand.

Her mother stood at the table lifting scrambled eggs from the fry pan onto her plate.

"It won't do to be late on your first day, dear, so hurry up. You want to be sure to get out the door in plenty of time."

"I know, I know."

Aoi sat down and stuck a fork into a breakfast wiener. With her other hand she reached for the television remote and changed channels from the morning drama her mother had on to a news show. Shots of Tokyo Disneyland came on screen: it was apparently one year ago today that the park had opened.

"Hey, I was watching that," her mother grumbled as she came back from the kitchen and set a plate of toast in front of Aoi. Even so, she stood watching the Disneyland coverage with apparent interest.

Aoi said nothing and bit into her toast. The breakfasts her mother made for her hadn't changed in the slightest way since their big move. It made her feel like she was still in the same old town, getting ready to go to the same old school. She turned away from the TV to look out the window. The sight of the rice paddies beyond the curtains reassured her that, no, she wasn't in that detested place anymore.

"Don't dawdle over your food, dear. Think how embarrassing it'd be to show up late on your first day of school. Oh, your ribbon. There were some special instructions for tying it, weren't there? I remember getting a handout. Where did I put that?"

She shuffled over to the buffet and started opening and closing drawers. Aoi didn't know why, but she felt a surge of irritation come over her as she watched her mother search.

"Relax, Mom. I'm not gonna get picked on again just for being a little late. And even if something does happen, I promise not to insist we move again."

Her tone was facetious, but when her mother turned around she was fighting back tears.

"You really needn't worry, dear. This is a proper girls' school, and the students all come from good families. They won't be going around bullying each other. I'm sure they're too mature for that."

Mrs. Narahashi's attempt at being comforting only fueled Aoi's aggravation. *Oh, sure. A girl whose father drives a cab and mother has to look for work the minute they move into this poor excuse for a home is gonna get along real well with all those fine princesses from good families.* The sarcastic comment was on the tip of her tongue, but she shoved the words back with a forkful of scrambled eggs. No point in upsetting her mother. Buying a house even as old and beat up as this one had to have been a pretty big stretch for her parents.

Her father used to eat breakfast with them at least every other day, but he was driving longer hours since the move; now they were lucky to see him at dinner once in three days. And it wasn't for jollies that her mother spent most of her days pounding the pavement in search of work.

"Thanks for breakfast, Mom," Aoi said as she finished tying the dark red ribbon into a bow under her chin. She stood up and faced her mother. "Does this look okay?"

Her mother carefully compared Aoi's bow with the instruction sheet she'd found. "Yep, looks good," she said, gazing intensely at her daughter. She followed Aoi to the door.

"See ya later," said Aoi.

"Bye-bye! Have a nice day, dear! Daddy'll be home for dinner, so I'm planning to make something really yummy."

She was trying a little too hard to sound cheerful and flapped her hand wildly in an exaggerated wave. You'd think she was a newlywed seeing her husband off to work for the first time, thought Aoi with a smile as she closed the door gently behind her.

A short distance up the street toward the bus stop, Aoi turned to make sure her mother was no longer watching, then reached under her jacket and rolled the waistband of her skirt over and over on top of itself until the hem was above her knees. Once she had her skirt at the right length, she quickly ran the rest of the way to the bus stop.

Aoi and her family had moved here from Isogo Ward in Yokohama less than a month before, right after Aoi finished ninth grade and graduated from junior high. It was a move prompted by bullying. Somehow, Aoi had failed to learn the secrets of friendship. She didn't know what she had to do to get along, nor what made things go sour. All the way back through grade school, she'd never had anybody she could call a close friend. Even when she thought she'd finally made a friend, that person would invariably drift away after a few weeks and start hanging out with someone else. Or worse, she and her new pals would snub Aoi and whisper mean things behind her back. Aoi never understood what she could be doing wrong. She was still trying to figure it out when she moved on up to junior high.

In grade school the problem was simply that no one would be her friend, but once she started junior high it escalated to outright bullying. Her books disappeared, her indoor sneakers acquired legs, and her gym clothes were stolen. The entire class openly shunned her, and soon she began finding her desk and chair moved out into the hallway each morning. No matter how many times she returned them to their place, they'd be right back out in the hallway when she arrived at school the next day.

By the end of eighth grade, she was refusing to go to school most of the time. But she never felt any ill will or bitterness toward the ringleaders because she always assumed it was her own fault. What other explanation could there be? She must rub people the wrong way somehow. She must deserve to be blackballed.

When the school warned her in ninth grade that she might not graduate, she started attending a little more often even in the face of the bullying. But she spent the entire day staring at the floor. She soon knew the patterns on the linoleum better than the faces of her teachers or classmates.

Aoi's parents worried about her missing so much school, but for the most part they seemed to be telling themselves that the problem would go away when she got through junior high. Things would be different in high school—especially if the school was far enough away that none of the students knew her from before. At least that was what they decided to place their hopes on.

It was in fact exactly for this reason that Aoi had first told her parents she wanted to move. As long as she lived here, she could never stop being the same old Aoi. She would always be bugging people and provoking their hostility; she would forever be branded a loser and a pariah. Even after she finished high school and went on to college or joined the working world, she still wouldn't be able to leave that person behind. She needed to move away now, to a place where no one knew her faults, or she would never be able to change her destiny.

When Aoi first expressed these thoughts to her parents, they tried to persuade her she was wrong, but disturbing stories in the news soon made them change their minds. Three junior high girls leaped to their deaths, and a junior high boy was charged with the murder of a homeless man. Both incidents took place right nearby, in Yokohama.

Aoi's mother had grown up in Gunma Prefecture and her grandmother still lived there, so her parents decided that was the place to go. Plans for the move took shape with dizzying swiftness, and the next thing Aoi knew she was being sent to stay with her grandmother so she could take the entrance exams to several girls' schools in the area. When she made the cut at an institution of marginal academic standing, they completed their move in a whirlwind rush.

Aoi's mother sorely missed the comforts of her life in Yokohama. There weren't any decent supermarkets or department stores, having to be neighborly with the neighbors was tiresome, good jobs were nonexistent no matter how hard she looked, and the people who lived here were all such boorish busybodies. These were exactly the reasons she'd left Gunma in the first place, back when she was young. She seemed to be trying not to air her complaints about their new environs in front of Aoi, but she did this with a certain obviousness that Aoi became convinced was deliberate. She couldn't help thinking it was her mother's underhanded way of getting back at her for forcing them to move.

The auditorium was a solid sea of girls, girls, and more girls. Which was no surprise, of course, since it was an all-girls' school, but this was the first time Aoi had seen so many teenagers exclusively of her own gender gathered in one place. On the platform, sporting a light green suit, the headmistress was addressing the assembly at great length, stressing the importance the school placed on English education. Japan was entering an age when a genuine command of the English language would be increasingly vital for every individual, she declared, punctuating her words with repeated emphasis.

Aoi looked across the rows of heads seated in front of her. It surprised her how few were bleached or permed or buzzed short up the side. She'd expected a school of underachievers to be crawling with disaffected misfits, but maybe the students here were more straitlaced than she'd imagined. She hadn't seen anybody else with a short hem on her way to school either. It'd probably be a good idea to lower hers again the first thing she had a chance, she decided as she returned her gaze to the sixtyish woman still holding forth at the podium. She'd hiked it up because she didn't want people to think she was a dweeb, but if nobody else was modifying her uniform, she might only be singling herself out for unwanted attention.

"Psst. Did you have that done somewhere?"

Hearing a sharp whisper nearby, Aoi put these thoughts on hold and glanced around her. The girl two seats over on her right was leaning forward and looking straight her way. Her hair was cut short like a boy's, and she had a boyish face as well. Like a boy of maybe five or six.

"Hunh?" Aoi didn't immediately understand what the person was asking about.

"Your skirt. It's short," the boyish girl hissed impatiently. "Where'd you have it done? I know Seiyodo won't do it."

"I just rolled my waistband, that's all," Aoi breathed. She had no idea what Seiyodo was.

"Really? And it won't come undone?"

"Probably not."

The girl sitting between them cast annoyed glances at them as they talked across her. She straightened up and leaned back in her chair to stay out of the way of the conversation.

"Show me later, okay? You just roll the band?"

"Uh-huh."

"Cool. When I went to Seiyodo—"

"Quiet there!" a teacher standing nearby hissed in their direction, cutting the girl off. Aoi turned her attention back to the front of the hall.

"Take the English word *the*, for example. T-H-E," the headmistress was saying. "Because we don't have the corresponding sound in Japanese, all the other schools teach you to pronounce it *za*. But here we teach you to say *the*," she enunciated in what was presumably the correct pronunciation. "*Za* is made-in-Japan English. I call it Japanglish, and if you go to an English-speaking country and say *za*, no one will know what you're talking about."

Listening to the headmistress's interminable discourse on English, Aoi thought she must have come to a really dumb school. But at this particular moment, she couldn't have cared less if the school was dumb, or all the students were below average, or they taught her to say *the* instead of *za*. All that mattered to her right now was that the girl who'd asked about her skirt didn't seem the least bit put off by her.

As everybody started from the auditorium toward their classrooms, the girl from two seats over jostled up to Aoi. "What's your name?"

"Aoi Narahashi. *Aoi* like the flower, then *nara* as in the trees and *hashi* as in bridge."

"I didn't know the trees in Nara were anything special."

She'd mistaken *nara* for the place name instead of a kind of tree, but Aoi didn't want to rub her the wrong way by correcting her so she just smiled.

"You?"

"Nanako Noguchi. Nanako is 'fish child,' and Noguchi is like Goro Noguchi the singer."

"Fish child?"

"Uh-huh. You write 'fish' plus 'child' and together they're read 'Nanako.' Because my family's always been from around here."

How did that explain anything, Aoi wondered. This was an inland prefecture, no water on any side. At a loss, she simply said, "And your family name's Noguchi?"

"Never mind that, Aokins," the girl said playfully. "Just call me Nanako." With a hard slap on Aoi's shoulder, she went skipping off toward the front of the procession. Watching her go, Aoi felt a sudden twinge of doubt. Maybe she was some kind of weirdo. "Fish child," she whispered quietly to herself, barely moving her lips. Was it only a matter of time before this girl stopped talking to her, too? Would she point at her and jeer the first time Aoi made a mistake? Would she tip her lunch box over and hold her nose? Would she throw Aoi's gym clothes on the floor and stomp on them with her shoes?

By the time Aoi looked up again, Nanako Noguchi had disappeared into the crowd.

The classroom windows looked out on a wide expanse of low-slung roofs with a fringe of mountains rising beyond. Aoi gazed out at the blue-gray silhouette of the distant range, barely listening to the fluid cadences of the teacher reading from their English language textbook.

Over the weekend she'd gone to Hayakawa Farm with her mother. Her father had dropped them there in his off-duty cab. The previous weekend they'd explored the Snake Center, and during the break before school started they'd all visited Mount Haruna together. Aoi had little interest in any of these places, and she could tell her mom and dad weren't especially excited about them either. None of them particularly enjoyed sightseeing. But her parents put on a show of having a great time, bubbling constantly with suggestions to go here or go there, and Aoi understood that they intended it entirely for her benefit, so she did her best to pretend she was as enthusiastic as they were. *I wanna try the place that serves pork cutlets with the special sauce*, she suggested, or, *How about we check out Yabuzuka Hot Springs next weekend?*

With two full weeks gone by since school began, the girls in Aoi's class had divided themselves up more or less into distinct groups. There were the jocks who all seemed to have more energy than they knew what to do with; there were the bookish girls whose banter seemed a bit too earnest; and there was the faster crowd that raced straight for the nearest bathroom to slather on makeup as soon as they were dismissed at the end of the day. Aoi herself had gravitated toward a bunch of perfectly ordinary girls—a nondescript group brought together not by common interests or personalities but by the proximity of their assigned seats. In spite of this relatively weak group identity, everyone seemed to live in mortal fear of becoming separated and left out in the cold, so they bonded during class breaks with exaggerated chatter and squeals of laughter.

Nanako Noguchi remained unaffiliated. She flitted back and forth among the various tribes during lunch or when moving through the halls to classes held outside their homeroom—spending the noon hour, for example, learning how to polish her nails with the girls in the fast crowd, but then whooping it up with the athletes as they all headed off for gym class. The great mystery to Aoi was how Nanako managed to do this without being snubbed by anyone.

So far, so good, Aoi breathed in relief as school let out each afternoon. She'd made it through yet another day without drawing scowls for something she'd said, blending smoothly into the conversations that sprang up around her. The lunch her mother packed for her had had sufficient color to spare her any embarrassment, and she'd avoided any spills that left ugly brown stains on her texts or notebooks. She'd laughed in the same places as everybody else, and she'd jumped right in when the others badmouthed their teachers.

As she headed down the hill toward the bus stop reflecting on her day, she felt a light tap on her shoulder. Turning to see who it could be, she found Nanako smiling back at her with a large, non-regulation yellow bag slung across her chest. They hadn't spoken again since opening assembly.

"I've been wanting to ask. Why'd you put your skirt back down?" she said as she fell in beside Aoi. The diminutive Nanako barely came up to Aoi's shoulder.

"Hunh?"

Nanako doubled over with laughter. "You do that every time I ask you something," she said between guffaws. "Go bug-eyed and say 'Hunh?'"

Several of their classmates came up behind them and hurried on by. A few paces ahead, they turned to wave. "Bye! See you tomorrow!" they called, then raced on down the hill with their pleated skirts flouncing and their black hair flickering in the sunlight. Aoi followed their progress through narrowed eyes, as if gazing at something wonderful.

"You told me the other day you just rolled your waistband, so I tried it," Nanako said as she lifted her jacket and began turning the narrow strip with both hands. "But it gets all puckered up. See? Looks weird, right?" Tucking her jacket back under her elbows, she showed Aoi the unsatisfactory results. Aoi laughed. Nanako's entire manner reminded her of a toddler who has yet to learn the concept of doing things neatly.

"Seriously. It's weird, right?" Nanako frowned.

Aoi reached around Nanako to undo the crudely rolled waistband and start over, this time carefully smoothing out the puckers as she went. The smell of Nanako's perspiration held a faint scent of citrus. A large truck roared by in the roadway next to the sidewalk, kicking up dust in its wake.

"There, how's that?" said Aoi. "It helps if you make sure to fold it evenly and smooth the wrinkles out as you go."

Nanako looked at her reflection in the window of a small grocery they were passing and turned a pirouette. "You're right," she said, amazed at the difference.

Aoi gazed at Nanako's legs extending straight as pencils beneath her raised hem. On the first day of school, as soon as she realized she was the only one wearing her skirt short, Aoi had hurried to the bathroom and returned it to normal so as not to attract attention. The midcalf length prescribed by the school was so yesterday, plus she was convinced it made her legs look fat, but better that than being different and calling unnecessary attention to herself.

"How'd you do on the math quiz we got back today? I got a two— can you believe it? A two! I asked Naomi, too, but she refused to tell. She just kept insisting it was the worst, it had to be the lowest in the class. But there's no way it could've been worse than me. I'm such a total pea-brain, it's not even funny."

Nanako prattled on about one thing and another as they continued down the dusty sidewalk. Clumps of tall, spindly weeds grew here and there along the roadside. Something about the way Nanako talked reminded Aoi of women her mother's age. Women who took no interest in most of what went on in the world and, within the one tiny little slice of the world they did care about, refused to believe that a single shred of ill will or distrust or any other troubling sentiment could exist. The kind of woman she'd seen strike up conversations with her mother in train stations and tourist spots as if they were sisters or something. They were friendly as could be, and they'd overwhelm you with kindness. But let anything go wrong, Aoi reminded herself, and they would coldly shove you away almost every time.

The students already waiting at the bus stop were strung out in several small groups, each engaged in its own heated conversation.

Aoi fell in line, and Nanako halted next to her, still prattling on. *She must go the same way I do,* Aoi thought, listening vaguely. *I wonder where she lives?*

Directly across the street from the bus marker with its badly rusted timetable stood a shelter barely big enough to hold half a dozen vending machines ranked side by side. Several students went whooping across to buy canned drinks, then came racing back. Cars and trucks kept zipping by at high speeds, but there was still no sign of the bus. As they waited, Nanako skipped incongruously from one topic to another: from their pop quiz in math to their choice of electives, from their choice of electives to the latest movies, from the latest movies to the best way to make French toast. About the time Aoi was wondering how they'd gotten onto French toast, two buses came along one right after the other.

Pressed tightly together in the center aisle jammed with fellow students, Nanako looked up at the taller Aoi.

"You don't mind if I come to your place, do you?"

"Hunh?" Aoi popped her eyes wide.

Nanako buried her face in another student's back and laughed. "You did it again!"

"Aren't you going home?" Aoi said.

"As if. My house isn't even this direction. I only came this way because I wanted to go home with you." She was grinning as if it were the most natural thing in the world.

No one was home when they arrived. Mrs. Narahashi was either out on the job hunt or shopping for dinner. A yellow shaft of sunlight cut through the dimness of the dining room as Nanako followed Aoi in and plopped down at the table. The chair she chose was the one Aoi's father always used. It gave Aoi an extraordinary sensation to see a classmate she barely knew sitting at the dining table in her new house where she didn't even feel entirely at home herself yet.

Aoi went into the dimly lit kitchen and opened the refrigerator to see if they had any juice. All she found to drink was milk and Cal-pis. She got out two glasses and started to add ice. One of the cubes slipped from her fingers and clattered across the floor. She realized for the first time how on edge she was.

Nanako waited at the table with chin in hand. "Yippee, Calpis!" she exclaimed like a child when Aoi set one of the glasses in front of her. Lifting her drink, she gulped it down all at once, then wiped her mouth with the back of her hand and broke into a big smile.

As sunlight poured into the dimness of this still vaguely unfamil-iar room where a girl with short hair sat smiling at her, Aoi expe-rienced a feeling of déjà vu. But she knew it was not any actual event that she recalled; it was a scene from her daydreams. She was remembering a scene she had pictured countless times in her fanta-sies: a kind and not unattractive girl, someone well liked by everyone in her class, had said she wanted to be Aoi's friend, had come to visit her home without needing to be begged, and sat there looking at her with a warm smile. Over and over and over again, Aoi had dreamed of the day she would be part of this utterly ordinary scene.

After holding her new friend's boyish gaze for several moments, Aoi quickly turned and stepped back into the kitchen. She couldn't let Nanako see that her eyes were beginning to fill.

"You know, Aokins," Nanako called after her, stretching the words out in a bit of drawl. "There's something really relaxing about your house. Can I see your room, too? Later on?"

"Sure," said Aoi, twisting the tap and splashing water on her face.

"Ahh, Calpis is so good!" Nanako exhaled with satisfaction. "Say, Aokins, you're new here, so you probably don't know very many places yet, right? Maybe one of these days I can show you a special place I know. It's been my secret hideout ever since I was in grade school."

Nanako jabbered on without pause in that manner that re-minded Aoi of women her mother's age who refused to entertain the slightest suspicion or wariness toward other people. From the kitchen, Aoi put in the occasional "Uh-huh" as she continued splashing water on her face. The water came out of the tap much colder here than at the apartment in Yokohama.

Why had this girl befriended her? Why had she asked to come to Aoi's house? Why did she want to show Aoi her secret hideout? Why had she picked Aoi? What did she want?

Aching to ask these questions but unable to, Aoi simply went on grunting "Uh-huh, uh-huh" as her diminutive friend rattled on. Finally she reached for the faucet and twisted it tight. When she straightened up, drops of water rolled down her face and fell to the kitchen floor like tears.

3

Training for the new housekeeping venture was slated to begin on June 2, which would be Sayoko's first day on the job. Aoi instructed her to wear clothes she didn't mind getting dirty and to be in front of the Bank of Tokyo-Mitsubishi branch across from the south entrance of Nakano Station at 9:00 A.M.

Sayoko was so determined not to be late that she arrived twenty minutes early. She stood with her back to the bank's closed shutter as she waited, gazing out at the gently falling rain and thinking about Akari. She'd dropped her daughter off with Grandma Tamura only a short while before. Might she already be in tears?

Other mothers she knew had warned her how hard it could be to find a place in a licensed nursery school, and she remembered reading the same in her parenting magazines, but somehow it hadn't sunk in that this would apply to her. She imagined blithely that all she had to do was submit an application, and the facility of her choice would immediately welcome Akari with open arms. So she spent the weeks before she started work visiting every nursery school within walking distance of her building, carefully inspecting each facility's surroundings and the size of its playground as well as observing what the children were like and how the childcare staff interacted with them. But then when she decided on her top three picks and got her applications in, she was told by her first choice that they had ten people on their waiting list; and although the lengths of their lists varied, none of the schools could take Akari immediately. The best Sayoko could do was to put Akari in line. With her starting date

41

at hand, she'd been forced to ask her disapproving mother-in-law to babysit until one of the schools called with an opening.

Aoi had said a white van with an "At Home Services" logo on its side would come to pick her up. Watching the rain drip from her umbrella as the minutes ticked by, Sayoko felt like a homeless day laborer waiting in the park for a job broker to show up. Even though this was her first day of work in five years, her heart wasn't beating any faster. She wasn't especially fired up, nor was she particularly nervous. She was filled instead with a defiant resolve that, damn it all, she was going to do this, come what may. Shuji's mother had agreed beforehand to take Akari, and yet when Sayoko went to drop her off that morning, she couldn't resist getting in one of her digs. *I never wanted to be the kind of mother who wasn't there when her children got home*, she declared even as Sayoko was hurrying back out the door. *It's beyond me how a woman can abandon her child just so she can go to work.*

Sayoko spied the "At Home Services" logo at about five past nine as the white van of Aoi's description turned into the plaza in front of the station. Moving quickly from her spot in front of the bank, she trotted forward toward an opening in the curb beyond where the buses stopped. The van pulled up and the front passenger window slid down. A middle-aged woman with a dry complexion peered across from the driver's seat.

"Hop in the back," she said curtly in a deep, masculine voice without bothering to ask her name.

"I'm Sayoko Tamura. I look forward to working with you," Sayoko said with a polite bow, then opened the back door. Several women already seated there nodded vaguely in her direction.

"Good morning. I'm Sayoko Tamura from Platinum—"

"Get in, get in," the driver growled impatiently, and Sayoko climbed hastily aboard.

She settled into the seat behind the driver, next to a young woman with bleached blond hair. Suddenly she felt a tap on her shoulder and turned to find Aoi sitting in the middle of the next seat back.

"Miss Narahashi!" she exclaimed. "What are *you* doing here?"

"I have to learn the ropes too," she said in a low voice, flashing Sayoko a peace sign.

On Aoi's right sat an older woman with graying hair gathered at the back of her head; on her left was a baby-faced woman who wore no makeup but looked like she must be pushing forty. Neither of them said a word, and Aoi offered nothing further either. This apparently wasn't the moment for the greeting Sayoko had rehearsed last night in the bath. Only the rhythmical *fwump-fwump* of the windshield wipers cut through the silence in the car. Soon the blurry red light through the water on the glass changed to green and the van moved forward. Nakano Station receded into the distance beyond the screen of raindrops.

A job broker picking up homeless day laborers. Sayoko recalled the image that had gone through her mind as she waited for the van to arrive, and nodded to herself that she'd had it right. The driver was the broker, and Sayoko and the others were housewives with no means of earning their own keep who found themselves adrift. Sayoko quickly pushed aside these self-abasing thoughts by repeating to herself emphatically that she was going to forge on, come what may.

After about twenty minutes, the driver called out three names, and the blonde, the grayhair, and the babyface got out to follow her into an apartment building. When they were gone, Sayoko turned toward Aoi, but found her dozing with her mouth agape. She sat quietly and waited.

Soon the driver returned and pulled the van back into traffic without a word. Another twenty minutes later, she stopped in front of a building with a white tile façade and announced, "Everybody out."

Sayoko and a bleary-eyed Aoi got out of the van. The rain was about the same as before, neither lighter nor heavier. Their driver unloaded some cleaning supplies from the back and locked the car.

"Follow me," she said brusquely, and started toward the building with a bucket in each hand. She entered the code for the security door and let them inside, then led them to the elevator and pressed 5. Sayoko and Aoi followed shoulder to shoulder, walking in silence. Aoi widened her eyes and made a funny face each time their eyes met.

They proceeded in single file down the well-polished fifth-floor hallway to a door marked 506. From the building's elegantly appointed exterior, Sayoko expected to find a suite of luxurious rooms, but what she saw when the woman unlocked the door and pushed it open made her want to recoil.

"Come on in," the woman said, entering.

Sayoko stepped nervously into what turned out to be an empty studio apartment with just one main room of approximately four meters by five. The breath of its former occupant seemed to linger faintly in the air, as if the premises had been vacated only moments before. Compared to what they had passed on the way up, the interior of the apartment looked old and dated, and Sayoko's skin went cold at the astonishing filth she saw everywhere. Too many stains to count discolored the carpet, which was visibly matted with fallen hair. Strewn across the entire room were small, white, gravel-like pellets that presumably came from a cat's litter box. A heavy film of nicotine had turned the wallpaper the color of the setting sun, and a sticky substance of unknown nature and origin clung to the walls in spots as well.

The state of the two-meter-square kitchenette was no less shocking. The exhaust vent was covered so heavily with blackened grease, Sayoko doubted its blades would respond to the switch. The gas range was likewise caked with a thick black veneer of grease and dust and baked-on food scraps across the entire top. What would it take, Sayoko wondered as her eyes roamed about the room. How long would you have to let things go for a place to get this bad?

"Good grief!" Aoi gasped as she entered behind Sayoko.

Sayoko stiffened, half expecting Aoi to be scolded for her outburst. Instead the woman turned to look at her with a wry grin on her face.

"What're you so shocked about? Your place is pretty much the same."

Sayoko was secretly pleased to note that the woman did know how to smile.

"Give me a break. I never let it go this far," Aoi said.

"Well, I hope you're both ready to put in some serious elbow grease. Don't expect any mercy from me," the woman said. She turned to look at Sayoko. "Your first assignment is to get this entire place looking spick-and-span again," she declared. "Here. Take this." She handed her one of the buckets filled with cleaning supplies. "You'll start in the kitchen. Aoi, you get the bath and toilet. The main room comes after that. Now remember, this is different from cleaning your own home. You don't necessarily have to do the bathroom and the kitchen and the entryway and everything all by yourself. One of you can start by doing only kitchens, while the other can do baths. In other words, the aim is to make yourself into a kitchen specialist or a bathroom specialist. Of course, during your training period, I'll be going over kitchens and bathrooms and balconies and everything else with each of you, but your ultimate goal is to develop a specialty where you can say no one does a better job on this than me. Got that?" Then like a schoolteacher addressing her class she added, "What do you say?"

"Yes, ma'am," Aoi said, sounding very much like one of those schoolchildren, and Sayoko quickly followed suit.

The woman turned to Sayoko. "I never introduced myself," she said. "My name is Noriko Nakazato and I'm the owner of At Home

Services, which is a housekeeping company. I'll be working with you over the next couple of months. Welcome aboard." She flashed her a warm smile.

Sayoko went into the kitchen as directed but wasn't sure where to begin. Somewhat tentatively, she filled her bucket with water and began sprinkling some scouring powder in the sink.

"Hold it right there. Isn't there something else you should do first? You've got a head on your shoulders, so I suggest you use it."

Sayoko turned to find Noriko standing behind her, arms akimbo.

"Don't forget you have hot water, too. See this, and this, and this? Anything that comes off, you want to get it into hot soapy water right away, to soften up the grime. Then clean something else while those things soak. Got that? What do you say?"

"Yes, ma'am," Sayoko said weakly. She stopped up the sink and started the hot water. As the sink filled she turned to look for some rubber gloves in the caddy of cleaning supplies she'd lifted from her bucket a few moments before. She rummaged through the jumble of rags, cleansers, and assorted tools but failed to find what she was after.

"I suppose you're looking for gloves," Noriko's voice rang out behind her again. "Sorry, but you won't find any. In cleaning, your two bare hands are your most reliable friends. With bare hands, if there's any dirt left, you feel the roughness right away. When the dirt's all gone, you get nothing but smoothness. Wear gloves and you'll never feel a thing. Don't worry, our cleansers are all-natural, so they won't mess up your hands. The ones that do nasty things to your hands may be tough on dirt, but if they're that hard on your skin, you know they have to be toxic. It's just that people these days try to cut corners by choosing the most powerful chemicals they can find."

When Noriko first started in on this harangue, Sayoko stopped what she was doing and turned to listen, but she was promptly told "No, no, keep working while I talk," so from then on she just nodded

or put in the occasional "Uh-huh" or "I see" as she went about removing the grates from the range and the fan from the vent. Everything
she touched was tacky with grease. She dropped the detached items
into the hot water in the sink.

She'd been convinced, all those weeks ago, that going back to
work would solve everything. But now, as she lowered the grease-
encrusted fan into the water, she was no longer so sure. The day she
told Shuji her job description, he'd responded with what could only
be taken as a put-down.

"Oh, so basically we're talking cleaning lady."

That had stung, but in point of fact, here she was, a cleaning lady.
She was scouring some unknown stranger's kitchen sink and range
while gritting her teeth over her mother-in-law's snide remarks and
worrying that even at this very moment her daughter might be bawling her head off. How was this supposed to solve anything?

"Stop! Easy does it!" Almost as soon as Sayoko attacked the range
top with her scouring pad, another admonition from Noriko interrupted her thoughts. "Try going at it more gently, and in circles," she
urged.

Sayoko eased up on the pressure and began moving the pad in
circles. Sure enough, the resistance of the grime against her strokes
began to melt away.

Once she was satisfied that Sayoko had the hang of it, Noriko proceeded to the bathroom and started issuing directions to Aoi. Sayoko
craned her neck out to see what Aoi was doing, but the half-open
door blocked her view. She could only hear their voices.

"Ugh. It's like slimy strands of seaweed."

"We don't need the commentary. Just scrape it all out with one
of those chopsticks. When you've cleared it, sprinkle some of this
around, and let it sit while you wash out the tub. Got that? What do
you say?"

"Yes, ma'a-a-am. Ooof. This is so foul!"

"I said you may dispense with the commentary."

It almost sounded like a comedy routine, and Sayoko had to stifle a laugh as she turned her attention back to her own task. Working her way slowly across the range top, she got so she could predict with almost gleeful accuracy when the last speck of grime would come away. The resistance of the caked-on grease diminished slowly, bit by bit, until *poof*, she could feel the precise moment when the last trace of friction faded to nothing—as if her pad had suddenly entered a small, circular void. She drew the scouring pad aside and stroked the bare stainless steel with her other hand. The polished surface slid smoothly beneath her fingers, exactly as Noriko had said.

Once Sayoko learned to read the progress of the retreating grime, scrubbing the grease-spattered floor on hands and knees and stretching deep into the cabinets to wash off a shelf turned into unexpected fun. Her soap-filled sponge described endless circles on the floor, round and round and round, and as she felt the layers of grease gradually peeling off beneath it, she could also feel her crowded mind steadily emptying out. Her mother-in-law's sarcastic voice fell silent, the nursery school waiting lists vanished, her doubts as to whether work was the answer melted into thin air, and a wide-open blankness spread in their place. It was a blankness that she found so serenely relaxing she wanted to remain in its hold forever.

There was still a good bit of work left to do, but they wrapped it up for the day a little before five. Back in the van, Noriko retraced the route they had come that morning, continuing toward Nakano Station after stopping to pick up the women they'd dropped off on the way. Fatigue showed on everybody's face.

Sitting behind the driver's seat, Sayoko glanced repeatedly at her watch. Aoi wanted her to stop by the office and start a work diary, but she'd told Grandma Tamura that she would pick up Akari by six. At the rate they were going, it would already be after six when they got back to the office, which meant it would probably be at least six-thirty before she finished writing up her daily report and started home.

"Would it be all right if I made a phone call?" Sayoko asked timidly in the quiet van.

Aoi turned to look at her from the front passenger seat. "To who?"

"I left my daughter with her grandmother, and I need to let her know I might be late. Otherwise I'll never hear the end of it."

It was depressing to think of the biting remarks Grandma Tamura would have in store for her, so she tried to lift her spirits by saying it in as light a tone as she could.

"Actually, in that case, why don't you plan to do your diary at home? You can just go straight home from Nakano."

"Would that be all right?"

"Sure, you can write your report anywhere. This is your husband's mother you're talking about, right? Is she one of those mother-in-laws from hell?"

Still turned around in her seat, Aoi asked it like a child who can't wait to hear what happens next in the story.

"I don't know if I'd say that, but she likes to make snide comments, and she can lay it on pretty thick sometimes."

Self-conscious in front of the other women, Sayoko leaned close to Aoi and lowered her voice to say this. Aoi showed no such restraint.

"Oh, great! She makes snide comments. What people like that need is a punch in the nose!" she said, shaking her fist.

The other passengers, all silently gazing out their nearest windows up to now, looked at each other uneasily for a moment and then burst out laughing. Noriko quickly joined in, doubling over on top of the steering wheel. Suddenly the weariness that had hung so heavily in the air dissipated, and a fresh breath of cheerfulness blew in to replace it.

"She's right. You should give her a good whack," Blondie said between guffaws.

"Oh, if only we could," said Babyface.

"No, really, you youngsters today are a lot stronger, so why couldn't you do it?" Grayhair put in. "In my day, all we could do was grin and bear it, no matter what they dished out," she added as she launched into a personal tale of woe.

In the driver's seat, Noriko couldn't seem to stop laughing. Her shoulders kept shaking as she drove.

Sayoko got out of the car with the others at Nakano Station, bowed her good-byes, and started for the ticket gate. When she heard Aoi calling after her, she stopped and turned.

"Good job today! Don't let Granny give you grief!" she yelled, shaking her fist again as she did so. The three women whose names she couldn't remember were smiling warmly and waving to her. Sayoko bowed deeply once more and turned to go through the gate.

Rushing up the stairs to the platform, she hopped on the west-bound train and dabbed at the sweat on her forehead. Aoi's voice urging her not to let Granny get her down still rang in her ear, and she smiled. Much as Sayoko had simplistically assumed a woman who ran her own company would wear designer outfits and fancy jewelry, Aoi had no doubt called to mind the stereotypical standoff between mother-in-law and daughter-in-law portrayed in soap operas and cartoon gags—playing on tired old clichés for easy laughs.

She gazed at her own disheveled reflection in the window and murmured quietly to herself, *Don't let Granny give you grief.*

The next morning, a woman she thought looked familiar was already waiting in front of the bank when Sayoko arrived. She quickly recognized her as one of the people she'd met at the Platinum Planet offices on the day she went to accept the job, but she couldn't immediately recall her name. She was surprised how disappointed she felt on realizing that Aoi wouldn't be coming.

"Good morning. I look forward to working with you," Sayoko said, bowing formally to her "senior" colleague, whom she guessed to be ten years her junior in age.

The younger woman quickly sidled up. "Tell me, tell me," she said as if they'd known each other for years, "you went yesterday, too, right? What was it like? Was it hard work?"

Under overcast skies, the van pulled into the turnaround again at 9:05, and Sayoko climbed into the back with her younger colleague. Already seated there was an entirely different crew from yesterday. The young woman sat next to Sayoko and prattled endlessly in her ear. As she listened, Sayoko finally remembered that her name was Junko Iwabuchi, and that she'd had a temporary position at a publishing company before coming to Platinum Planet.

Noriko drove them to the same work site as the day before. There, she instructed Sayoko to continue with the kitchen while she started Junko on the main room. The younger woman was soon getting the same treatment Sayoko had received the day before.

"You can't get the dust off the ceiling just by thwacking it with a duster. Use your head. You do have one, don't you?"

"It's not enough to sweep the carpet, you have to beat it! Got that? What do you say?"

Sayoko listened from the kitchen while attacking some stubborn patches of grease on the vent fan with a scraper.

At the fast-food restaurant where they went for lunch, Junko began squawking the moment they sat down.

"Man, am I beat! This totally reeks. Nobody told me about anything like this. I really don't believe it. I mean, it's like, are you serious? Look at me," she said, thrusting out a cheek for Sayoko's inspection as she continued her bellyaching. "I'm having a makeup meltdown, aren't I? Hey, wait a minute! You're not even wearing any. Sheesh, you could have told me. How was I supposed to know I was in for hard labor?"

Her facial cream was indeed starting to break up, but Sayoko just nodded vaguely as she pulled at the wrapper on her hamburger with wrinkly fingers.

"Seriously, I've got to talk to the boss about this. She's gonna have to send Mao or somebody instead of me. I mean, my back can't take it. And I'm not just saying that. I have a bad spine. It's congenital. The problem with Miss Narahashi is that she has no head for details. She never did give me a proper job description."

When Sayoko first met Junko Iwabuchi at the office, the woman hadn't struck her as the sort to prattle on and on like this. But now, about the only time she fell silent was when she paused to take a fresh bite of her hamburger; otherwise she managed to keep a constant stream of chatter going even while she was chewing and swallowing. The words kept coming like steady rain, and Sayoko merely nodded or grunted now and then to show she was listening.

"Maybe that just means she doesn't have much faith in me. But when I look at her, I don't see a person who's very good at planning for the future. It's kind of like she's still trapped in a student mindset or something, you know? Without Yuki Yamaguchi to stay on top of the finances, we'd never survive from one month to the next. Somebody says, 'What do you think of this, boss?' and she hops right on board without even thinking. Maybe I shouldn't talk about my elders like this, but she's just so totally haphazard. I think in the end it comes down to never having had a proper job. I know because I spent five years working for a big publisher. I see stuff all the time where it's obvious she doesn't have a clue."

Sayoko noticed their reflection in a mirror on the wall. Her small but sturdily built companion sat across from her with dark stains under her arms and her makeup blotchy from perspiration. Sayoko herself had stringy locks of hair clinging to her scalp like strands of seaweed, and her bare face looked wan and sickly.

Seeing that Sayoko's attention was drifting, Junko leaned across the table and lowered her voice almost to a whisper.

"You wouldn't know this, but there's actually a lot more to Miss Narahashi than meets the eye."

"More than meets the eye? You mean like she's some kind of slick operator or something?"

"No, nothing like that. I'm talking about her history. They say she was in all the papers."

"Was she a child genius or something?" The tone her companion was taking irked Sayoko, but curiosity got the better of her.

"Oh, please. Does she look like a genius to you? Let's just say she's had an eventful life," she said, sounding smug. She paused to lick some ketchup from her finger. "When they say someone's been in the papers, they have to be talking about a major incident or scandal of some kind."

Sayoko was about to ask for further elaboration, but before she could open her mouth she noticed the clock on the wall.

"Looks like it's time we got back."

She stood and quickly began gathering cups and hamburger wrappers onto their tray. Junko let out a long, heavy sigh.

Back scrubbing grease and nicotine stains from the kitchen walls, Sayoko thought about how women like Junko Iwabuchi were the very reason she sometimes became convinced nothing was ever going to go right, and grew so depressed she could hardly bring herself to step outside. She'd encountered people like this before, in college as well as earlier, going all the way back to when she was a little girl—and, of course, at the film distributor where she worked before getting married, too. Coming up to you like they were your best friend and you shared all your confidences, they would start running people down right and left, expecting you to agree with everything they said. But then the next thing you knew you'd see them cozying up to somebody else and making *you* the target of their smears. As Sayoko thought of this, the doubts that had finally begun to subside reared up again: Was it really so important for her to work even when she had to waitlist her daughter for nursery school? As this question began echoing louder and louder in her head, she tried to smother it by focusing her mind solely on the circular motions of her sponge. The grease resisted the sponge, clinging stubbornly to the wall, and the more lather the cleanser produced, the heavier the sponge grew.

Every now and then she would hear Noriko impatiently correcting Junko in the main room.

"What did I tell you? You'll never get those fat fingers of yours in there. Use a chopstick. Got that? What do you say?"

Noriko dropped them off at Nakano Station and they took the train back to the office in Okubo. Junko straggled up the stairs after Sayoko, moaning repeatedly about her poor back and wanting to know why their building didn't have an elevator.

Sayoko glanced at her watch. It was half past four. She could probably get her report written and leave by around five, so she'd be picking Akari up at five-thirty. She was still preoccupied with these thoughts when she bumped into someone coming the other way on the third floor landing.

"I'm sorry," she said, raising her eyes. The young man looked familiar.

"Oh, hi, Takeshi!" Junko called out from behind. Sayoko remembered that this was someone else she'd met on the day she came to accept the job. Aoi had introduced Takeshi Kihara not as a member of the staff but as someone who helped out when they were busy.

"Hi! You guys just getting back?" he said with a friendly smile, coming to a halt. "You must be pretty wiped out."

"That's an understatement if there ever was one. It was the absolute worst!" Junko shrilled. "How can she do this to us?"

Takeshi turned to Sayoko. "What kind of work is it exactly—this thing you're doing?" He settled himself against the cement banister.

Before Sayoko could open her mouth, Junko was answering for

her. "Would you believe housecleaning? And let me tell you, it's heavy labor. I mean, totally." She sat down on the steps.

"So Mrs. Tamura's supposed to be heading up a new housekeeping team, is that it?"

"The boss went yesterday herself, so she knew exactly what I was in for, but she never said a word. And I have a bad back!"

Sayoko glanced between the two of them and her watch as their exchange continued back and forth. They appeared to be settling in for an extended chat.

"I'm sorry, I need to be going," she finally said in a low voice, moving on up the stairs. Takeshi called after her, and she paused to look back.

"You'll have to tell me more about this housekeeping thing sometime," he said with a smile and a wave.

For some reason this show of friendliness rubbed Sayoko the wrong way. She gave a perfunctory nod and hurried on.

"I can tell you *aaaall* about it," she heard Junko declare below.

Aoi was alone in the office when Sayoko came in, busy at the dining table. She looked up from what she was doing.

"Hey, there! How'd it go?" she said, sounding like one student greeting another.

"Um, is there a particular desk I should use?" Sayoko asked, standing uncertainly in the dining room.

Aoi motioned to the empty chair across from her. Piles of CDs and videotapes, magazines, postcards, and the like were strewn all over the table. Taking a seat, Sayoko pushed a few things aside to make some space, then reached into her bag for the notebook she'd broken in the day before as her work diary. She spread it open in front of her and started writing. Silence filled the room. Aoi put a cigarette between her lips and picked up her lighter as she watched Sayoko write.

"So, did Noriko play the same fearsome taskmaster today?"

"That's the word for it all right," Sayoko said with a laugh. "Fearsome."

"Believe it or not, that scary lady used to be a meek little housewife. I originally met her when I was on a trip overseas. She somehow got separated from her tour group, and I happened by—I was traveling by myself—so she asked me for help. She was in a total panic."

Aoi paused to light her cigarette, and then continued.

"For years, she couldn't get pregnant, and she was so miserable, but finally she gave up on having kids and decided to start a housekeeping business with a friend. Then *boom*, the next thing she knew she had a baby on the way. When I first met her she was the typical self-effacing housewife, but once she started her business, or it may have been after she became a mother, somewhere along there she turned into a real ball of fire."

Sayoko looked up from her notebook. "Mrs. Nakazato has a child?"

"Two, actually. One in first grade and one in kindergarten. After the first one, the next came right away."

"That young?" Sayoko said in surprise.

"Uh-huh. Because she had them so late. She says to me, if you don't want kids, then fine, but if you do, have them while you're young, the sooner the better. You just don't have the same energy in your thirties as you do in your twenties, she says, and it gets even worse in your forties. Her kids were born when she was almost forty, and it was also right after she'd started up a new business, so for a while there she had a pretty rough time of it."

"I can imagine," Sayoko said. She'd stopped to listen, but looked at her watch and hastily resumed writing.

"You know, I've been meaning to ask. Once a month, our staff gets together with people from other companies to network over drinks. Could you come? We'll make it your welcome party, too. I just need to know when would be good for you."

Sayoko looked up. "I'll have to ask my husband," she said. It struck her that in the three years since Akari was born, she had yet to leave her daughter in Shuji's care while she went out anywhere but the grocery store. Would she actually be able to do it?

"Right. Of course. Just let me know if you can come. A Saturday is fine too, if that works best for you."

Aoi started gathering up the CDs and videotapes piled on the table before putting them in a corrugated box.

Maybe if it was a Saturday, Shuji would say okay. Especially if she asked them to schedule it relatively early and didn't stay too long. As her pen raced across the page, Sayoko realized with surprise that she was already calculating how she might make it work. There'd been a time when she would have promptly run the other way if invited to go drinking with people she didn't even know, but now she felt her heart quickening with anticipation. Aoi Narahashi was the same age as she was and ran her own company, Noriko Nakazato had reinvented herself as a fireball of a working mother, and Sayoko was eager to meet others like them both. She wanted chances to talk with women of every stripe. She wanted someone to reassure her once and for all that she'd made the right decision to go back to work.

"Oh, it's raining," Aoi said.

Sayoko turned to look through the doorway of the "President's Office." Aoi's tatami desk was as usual piled high with papers and books teetering on the verge of avalanche. Raindrops spattered against the large window above the desk and ran down the glass.

4

"Hot chocolate with cinnamon, and crepes filled with vanilla ice cream," Nanako said.

"Shakey's seafood pizza," Aoi countered.

"Sazaby handbags," Nanako came right back.

"In that case, dresses from Flandre."

"No, no, no! I said let's name our *favorite* things, not just things we might want," Nanako objected. She tore off a tuft of grass and threw it at Aoi lying on the ground.

"Ack! Stop!" Aoi screamed good-naturedly, rolling away.

"Okay, it's my turn," Nanako said. "Raw egg over steamed rice." She was hugging her knees, with her underwear in full view.

"Um, let me think," Aoi said from where she lay. "*The Little Prince.*"

"You're such a baby," Nanako snorted, tearing off and tossing down long blades of grass one after the other. "I say David Bowie."

"Motoharu Sano."

"Ga-a-aag! Not even! You're hopeless, Aokins. That Niagara guy beats Motoharu any day." Nanako stretched her legs out flat and fell back onto the grass.

"But one thing you have to agree, the Southern All Stars totally rock."

"Yeah, sure. I like SAS."

"I wish they'd come to Tsumagoi. That's close from here, right?"

"As if," Nanako scoffed. "You don't know anything, do you? Tsumagoi's way far away. That's the trouble with you big-city folk. You think anything in the same prefecture has to be close. Kusatsu, Minakami, Kita-Karuizawa—you just lump them all together."

She tore off another tuft of grass and threw it at Aoi. Aoi laughed as the slender blades of grass rained down on her face.

When they both fell silent, the sound of the river rose in her ears. She'd never really thought of her old Isogo neighborhood as the big city, but she rather enjoyed the way Nanako said "the trouble with you big-city folk…" It made her feel like someone special, someone very important.

Lying there on her back, all she could see was sky. A bank of clouds was slowly starting across her field of vision, advancing with almost imperceptible deliberation.

Nanako let out a loud sigh. "It's not fair," she said.

Aoi rolled her head toward her. Prickly blades of grass tickled her ear.

"What?"

"Tsumagoi's a long way away, Kita-Karuizawa's a long way away, Maebashi and Takasaki are a long way away, and Tokyo's even farther away." It came out sounding almost like the chorus to some song.

"Not really," Aoi disagreed. "Once you get to Takasaki, it's just one quick hop to Tokyo."

Nanako turned to look at her, and for several moments they held each other's gaze through the overgrown grass.

"I'm hungry," Nanako finally said, looking away and starting to get up. "Want to get something to eat? Octopus balls? Or maybe ramen at Yasumaru's?"

She briskly brushed off her hiked-up skirt. Dust and bits of dead grass scattered into the air, flickering in the light of the sun.

"I've got a sweet tooth. How about cake and tea at Hasegawa's?" Aoi said as she also rose to her feet.

Before them the river twisted gently down the middle of the wide riverbed. Blue sky reflected off the face of the flowing water.

"This little girl doesn't have that kind of cash, I'm afraid. Three-fifty's my limit."

"Wow, you're really hard up."

"Your treat?"

"No wa-a-ay. Let's do octopus balls then. I'll at least spring for a lemon soda."

"Yippee!"

Nanako skipped down the road along the levee, her yellow shoulder bag slung across her chest. Aoi followed close behind, listening to the constant rush of the water. Farmland spread out beyond the river, and in the distance a cluster of buildings rose against the horizon. None of the buildings was very tall—no more than four or five stories at most.

After school, they'd ridden a bus going the opposite way from Aoi's home for about ten minutes before getting off at a stop along the main highway. Walking on in the same direction, they soon came out on the Watarase River. There was a levee and a breadth of dry riverbed, and beyond that flowed the river, with large rocks jutting out of the water here and there.

To Aoi, it looked like any other river, but this was the spot Nanako called her secret hideout. Other schoolkids hardly ever came here, she'd explained the first time she brought Aoi, and almost no one else did either. If it rained, a bridge was only a three-minute dash away. And most importantly of all, she gushed, this was where you could see the biggest sky. But what Aoi found she liked best about the place—even more than the bridge or the big sky—were some old, abandoned railroad tracks that ran along the far side of the river, choked with weeds. Nanako declared the abandoned rails depressing, but walking the overgrown tracks made Aoi feel like she could go anywhere she wanted to go.

Aoi followed Nanako along the levee, eyes fixed on her back. A winged ant briefly buzzed her ear, then flew away before she could even wave it off. An old man walking his chestnut-colored dog came from the opposite direction and passed on by. She could faintly hear Nanako humming a song under her breath.

When the second term started up after summer vacation, the groups that had begun to take shape in April became set in stone. Even the nondescript bunch Aoi belonged to, brought together by the accident of seating, was showing signs of surprising cohesiveness. The members had different tastes in music and books, they didn't dress or wear their hair alike, and they had almost nothing in the way of mutual interests to talk about, yet for some reason they clung to doing things together as if their lives depended on it. Aoi herself took great pains to avoid getting bumped from the group. She listened attentively to Keiko Nozawa's incomprehensible babble about anime, she feigned interest in Kana Hirabayashi's favorite fanbook even though she didn't like the star, she borrowed and read the girls' comics Natsue Shimodaira brought in, and she nodded in sympathy to the dreary health problems Mamiko Takano was always going on about.

Nearly every day, Aoi and Nanako met somewhere after school, and they often exchanged notes or called each other on the phone, but they never spent time together during the day. As in the spring, Nanako remained unaffiliated with any one group, freely talking with anyone and everyone, mixing and laughing with whatever group the circumstances called for. For her part, Aoi would have liked to hang out with Nanako at school as well, but she was convinced it would be courting danger. She suspected it was only a matter of time before their classmates began turning against Nanako, calling her a people-pleaser and a phony and a weirdo. Being linked to her could put Aoi in the line of fire, too, and she definitely didn't want that.

She cringed at her own small-minded calculating, and she hated herself for it. She sometimes even wished Nanako would blow up at her—come right out and call her the weasel she was, or tell her *she* was the phony and refuse to have anything more to do with her. But Nanako never approached Aoi when she was doing things with her group at school, and she never accused her of being two-faced for meeting her only in a different location after school.

"Guess what," Nanako said, turning back toward Aoi with a smile. "We switch pretty soon to winter uniforms, right? Well, I've been thinking I definitely want to get my hem raised. Properly, I mean—at a shop somewhere."

"Then maybe you should get your jacket shortened a bit, too. Though I have no idea what that sort of thing costs."

"Really? I always thought the jacket looked better long. I actually asked my parents to get me a size bigger, but they wouldn't listen. They insisted this one's still perfectly okay."

Thinking she'd heard someone call her name, Aoi stopped for a moment to glance over her shoulder. Nanako walked on without noticing. A taxi was driving at a crawl thirty or forty meters away. Aoi saw instantly that it was her father. He had his window rolled down and was waving as he called her name. *Oh, please,* she thought, pretending not to have recognized him. She didn't want Nanako to see her father driving a cab. He kept getting closer and closer.

Just then she spied the top of a bus coming into view down the highway, far ahead of where Nanako was now walking.

"The bus is coming!" she shouted. "Run!"

Summer was officially over, but the bus shimmered gently in the heat as it approached. "Aoi!" she heard her father call again from behind, but she ignored him and dashed after Nanako, grabbing her hand as she went by and practically dragging her the rest of the way to the bus stop. Apparently realizing his daughter was ignoring him on purpose, Aoi's father stopped shouting after her.

The two girls plopped down on the seat at the back of the bus, their shoulders heaving. Aoi watched her father's cab glide by outside the window.

"Whew! We made it," Nanako said, breathing hard beside her. "You sure run fast, Aokins."

Turning to look out the rear window as the cab drove away, Aoi wondered what she was trying to hide. What exactly was she worried about? What did she expect Nanako to say if she met her father? She knew very well Nanako wasn't going to say anything—neither about the man who drove a ridiculously overdecorated cab in a ploy to attract customers, nor about Aoi's own small-mindedness. And that wasn't all, she realized as she turned to face forward again, took a deep breath, and finally began breathing more easily. The fact was, Nanako never said a bad word about anything. Of course, she did make fun of teachers she disliked, and she could sometimes really get going about what a stifling place this was. But she said "I like" instead of "I hate," declared "I wish I could" instead of "I can't," and if you ever heard her say "That makes me sick," it was always in a way that made you laugh. Yet somehow you never got the feeling she was trying to be a Miss Goody Two-shoes. Since she seemed to do all this without even being aware of it, Aoi imagined that she had grown up seeing nothing but happy things. Someone must have gone to great lengths to remove any sign of corruption or ugliness or cruelty or anything harmful along the path her life had led her.

What helped Aoi realize that Nanako never looked at things negatively was in fact the transformation that had come over her mother since moving to this town. They'd been here six months now, and Mrs. Narahashi had found work that occupied her from nine to four every weekday. Yet to Aoi she seemed like a completely different person from the one she'd known in Yokohama.

Mrs. Narahashi was preparing dinner in the dim light of the unilluminated kitchen when Aoi arrived home from school.

"Isn't this awfully late for you to be getting home?" she said, but went on immediately as if not really expecting a reply. "Wash your

63

hands when you're done changing. I want you to help me."

"Okay!" Aoi said in her best cheery voice and hurried up the stairs. Closing the door to her room behind her, she replayed in her mind the image of her mother standing in the kitchen with the light of the declining sun coloring everything orange, and she heaved a deep sigh. She got out of her school uniform and hung it up, then pulled on a sweatshirt and jeans and headed back downstairs.

"All right! It's gyoza night!" she said as she went to wash her hands at the sink. "Thanks, Mom. Seems like we've been having a lot of boring, old-folks food lately."

Her mother still hadn't turned on the lights in the kitchen, and the room had taken on a deeper shade of orange.

"I'm sorry, dear, but you've seen the meat and fish they sell at the co-op. All brown and disgusting. I'm amazed anybody ever buys the stuff. You may complain about our food, but it's hard when everything else is half-spoiled and all I have to work with is vegetables. And sometimes even the vegetables are bad. Like today's chives. Completely limp. Ready for animal feed as far as I'm concerned. Doesn't anybody around here care? Do you suppose maybe that's all they've ever seen, so they don't know any better?"

Her mother spoke in fits and starts as she held the bowl with one hand and kneaded the meat mixture with the other. Now she paused and looked at Aoi, standing in the middle of the kitchen with nothing to do.

"If you'll get the tray from the cupboard, you can start filling the skins."

As Aoi took a seat at the table with the tray, her mother set the bowl of filling in front of her. Aoi spooned a dollop of meat onto a skin and folded it into a gyoza.

"Mom, do you know any place around here that does alterations, like to shorten skirts? Would Iwahashi Cleaners do something like that?"

She realized too late that this might not have been the best topic to bring up, but her mother was already off and running.

"Alterations are the same story. You can't find a decent seamstress around here either. Forget Iwahashi's. They have that old geezer basically running the place by himself, and their dry cleaning rates are sky high, too. What do they take us for? Back in Yokohama we could always rely on Hakuyosha, remember? Weren't they the best? Great workmanship, and always so polite. Of course they're a name brand, so . . ."

Whatever her reasons for invoking "name brand" now, it wasn't the sort of thing Aoi's mother had ever paid attention to before their move. She'd only gone to Hakuyosha because they happened to be located nearby, and she used to crow about the bargains she got by dashing into the supermarket just before closing time and grabbing packages of beef on last-minute markdown.

Aoi got up from the table to switch on the overhead light. The orange glow filling the room vanished in a blink. *I saw Dad a while ago. Will he be home for dinner today?* She was on the verge of blurting the question out when she stopped herself. This wasn't a topic she wanted to bring up either.

"Would you rather have macaroni salad or potato salad, dear?"

She thought for a moment. "Macaroni, I guess. With cucumber."

"All right," her mother answered, but then went to the refrigerator and started taking out some potatoes. Aoi said nothing and went on filling gyoza skins.

Gloomier and crabbier and all but completely drained of the almost manic cheeriness she had displayed before: this was how Aoi would sum up the change that had come over her mother. But what she found most disturbing of all was her blatant fabrications of memory. Listening to her, you'd think she must have lived the life of a corporate president's wife back in Yokohama, buying nothing but brand-name fashions from trendy department stores, cooking with only the finest brand-name ingredients from foreign-owned super-markets, traveling by taxi on all her shopping trips, dining at famous restaurants with her family every weekend, enriching her mind at the Cultural Center and lunching with her housewife friends on week-days. Her mother spoke of these things so often that Aoi wondered in all seriousness if she didn't have a screw loose. But every time she brought up one of these rose-colored memories, it was invariably followed by a comparison with the present, and so Aoi had come to understand it as part of a mechanism that, however precariously, helped her mother keep a grip on her sanity. She would shrink from no fantasy or delusion if it served to diminish the town in which they now lived.

Her father had not returned by the time dinner was ready, so the two of them sat down to eat without him. The room felt oddly quiet in spite of the television blaring at an almost painful level.

"How's work at the hotel?" Aoi said, unable to bear the silence. "Getting into the swing of it?"

Mrs. Narahashi's first job after their move was at a country club, but something about the work there disagreed with her and she had quit after three months. A month ago she'd found a new job at a business hotel.

"What can I say?" she shrugged with her eyes glued to the TV. "It's not really my kind of work, but there's not much I can do about it, is there? A town like this, you can't really insist on finding office work, or accounting. The ladies I work with are such hillbillies. They never stop yakking. So-and-so did this, so-and-so did that. All the lat-est gossip. They're so unsophisticated."

Aoi put down her chopsticks with a small sigh, which she took care not to let her mother hear. Darkness had crept up against the dining room window. A commercial blasted from the TV.

"Goodness, are you done eating already?" her mother said, glanc-ing at Aoi's rice bowl, still half full. "I hope you're not trying to diet.

You'll only wind up stunting your growth." Without bothering to put down her chopsticks, she reached for the remote and changed the channel.

"Can we go skiing during winter break?" Aoi said. "I heard it's close if you go by car. You know how to ski, right, Mom?"

Aoi stacked her dishes and carried them to the sink.

"It's only September and your mind's already on winter break? Is this your way of telling me you can't stand school, Aoi?"

She had a vacant look on her face, staring at the TV with her chopsticks poised in midair. The opening theme to a suspense thriller came on.

"Whatcha been doing?" Aoi said into the handset. In her room upstairs, she was leaning against the door with the cord from the phone in the hallway stretched as far as it would reach.

"Just now? Reading," Nanako replied.

Aoi never heard any sounds in the background when she talked to her friend on the phone. She'd never seen Nanako's house, but she pictured a large, spacious home that was always quiet, and parents who were gone a lot. She didn't imagine that Nanako had to talk with her phone cord stretched to the breaking point just to get it into her room, nor that she had to sit against the closed door because the cord wouldn't reach her bed. But Aoi considered herself lucky to have gotten a phone put in upstairs at all.

"Reading what?"

"The book I borrowed from you. *Hey There, Little Red Riding Hood.* I expected it to be a takeoff on the fairy tale, but it's about some guy going to Tokyo University."

"But it's good, don't you think?"

"Well, I guess I don't like books that are all words. I need pictures," Nanako said with the candor of a small child.

They'd said good-bye only a short while before, but Aoi already ached to see her friend again. She longed to escape from this dreary house, where she never stopped feeling her mother's mournful sighs eating away at her spirits, and to slip away somewhere bright and gay and free of negativity where she could talk and laugh with Nanako to her heart's content.

"So anyway, Aokins, where shall we meet on Saturday? Hanazawa Bookstore?"

"Yeah, that's as good a place as any. I can't afford to buy anything, but we can browse all we want."

"Who cares about buying. It's fun just looking."

They both fell silent. This wasn't unusual. They'd call each other for no reason in particular, and then they'd sit there for long periods of time without saying anything. But Aoi never felt awkward about the silence that flowed between them. There was no pressure to fill the dead air. She just sat and listened to the sound of Nanako's quiet breathing coming over the telephone line, drawing pictures in her mind of the room Nanako was in, of the things Nanako must have around her.

"There's something I wanted to ask you, Aokins," Nanako said, breaking the silence. "Did you ever watch *Anne of Green Gables* on TV when you were little? The cartoon?"

"No, I never saw that," she said. "I read the book, though."

"Then at least you know about Diana, right—Anne's best friend, the pretty one? Their houses are way far apart, but their rooms face each other, and since they didn't have phones in those days, there's this scene where Anne and Diana stand by their windows at night with oil lamps, and they hold books in front of the lamps to send signals to each other—you know, to make it look like they were flashing on and off."

Nanako's voice was soft and steady.

"I don't remember that."

"Well, I don't know about the book, but they did that on TV. Anne

68

and Diana stood by their windows watching each other's lamps flash on and off in the distance."

"Hmm," Aoi grunted, falling silent again. Nanako was quiet too. Nothing but silence traveled back and forth between them for several moments. Aoi looked up at the window of her unlighted room. Beyond the window she could see only the darkened sky. Several stars glinted in the blackness.

"I wish we could do that between our houses," Aoi finally said. "Like with flashlights or something."

"Now we have phones, silly," Nanako said, laughing.

Suddenly Mrs. Narahashi was yelling up the stairs: "I wish you wouldn't tie up the phone, Aoi."

Aoi quickly covered the mouthpiece, but not before her friend could hear.

"I guess I'll see you tomorrow, then. After school, at the usual place. Bye-bye," Nanako said lightly and promptly hung up.

Aoi listened to the beeping line for a few moments, then opened her door and returned the handset to its cradle. She could hear a man and a woman arguing furiously about something in the thriller her mother was watching downstairs.

In October the entire student body switched to their navy blue winter uniforms, and about that same time Aoi sensed a subtle change in the atmosphere that had hovered over her classroom since April. She couldn't tell how many of her classmates might also have noticed, but her own sharp sensors had picked up a disturbing vibration. It gave her a bad premonition.

And then it happened.

One day at lunchtime, Kana Hirabayashi went to the school store to find something to eat, and while she was away Haruka Shindo approached Aoi's group.

"Don't you think Kana's kind of weird?" she said. "When she

found out I had Ozaki's new record, she asked to borrow it, but that was a long time ago and she still won't give it back. I mean, if she's such a big fan, why doesn't she just buy it herself?"

Haruka belonged not to Aoi's inconspicuous circle but to a group of five or six considerably more outgoing girls. They ignored the ban on colored lip creams, used band-aids to hide their piercings, and tinted their hair just enough not to draw attention; they'd recently shortened their skirts en masse, and made a habit of changing into navy blue knee socks as soon as they left the school grounds each day. Just being approached by someone from this crowd set off a series of nervous glances between Keiko Nozawa, Mamiko Takano, and Natsue Shimodaira in Aoi's group.

"Her parents are cheapskates," Keiko said, and Aoi looked at her in disbelief. Her face was flushing, but this didn't stop her from going on with uncharacteristic vehemence. "They won't even get her new sneakers." She let out a scornful titter.

"So that's why she keeps wearing those ratty shoes. Their smell'll take your nose right off. My shoe cubby's right over hers, so I know all too well." Fiddling with a lock of her hair, Haruka glanced toward the door. "Oh, here she comes. Just say something to her, okay? Tell her I want it back. Since you guys are her friends."

She rejoined her own circle at the back of the room, and a moment later a burst of laughter rose among them. Keiko and Mamiko and Natsue exchanged uneasy looks again. For a brief second Aoi had the illusion that everything in her field of vision was rapidly receding into the distance.

"Crap," Kana said as she approached with a bag of potato chips in her hand. "The filled buns were all sold out, and the only thing left was chips. Boo hoo." She laughed.

Aoi expected someone to pipe up right away that Haruka had come to ask for her record back, but no one said a word. Kana seemed to sense a certain awkwardness in the air.

"Is something wrong? Sorry I kept you waiting. Let's eat," she said breezily and sat down.

"You suppose they were really sold out, or she just didn't have the money?" Keiko muttered out of the corner of her mouth. Aoi could scarcely believe her ears. "Come on, girls, we'll eat in the courtyard today." It had the sound of a command, and Keiko immediately started for the door, ignoring Kana. Mamiko and Natsue followed as if this had been planned all along. Aoi stood gaping for a moment, but then shook off her astonishment and hurried after the others. Glancing over her shoulder as she passed through the doorway, she saw Kana sitting alone at her desk looking stunned.

This was exactly what she had feared, thought Aoi, staring blankly at the blackboard during fifth period. Even so, the abruptness of Keiko's transformation had been a shock. This was the girl who had done nothing but talk blissfully about anime all these months. It made Aoi wonder if she hadn't experienced the sting of ostracism before. Feel that sting once, and you would do anything to avoid a repeat. Like Aoi herself making sure never to speak with Nanako at school.

Aoi looked away from the blackboard toward Nanako, seated a little behind her next to the window. Nanako was gazing out the window with her chin in her hand, staring intently at something Aoi could not see. Aoi studied her profile as if she were looking at a painting or a photograph, admiring its purity of line. The sound of their teacher reading a passage from a novel came to her from somewhere far away. Then, perhaps sensing Aoi's gaze, Nanako turned and looked at her. Their eyes met. Nanako playfully crossed her eyes and stuck out her tongue.

"Things have been kind of touchy in class lately, don't you think?" Aoi said.

They'd spread a beach mat on the grass by the river, and Nanako was laying out the packages of yakitori, octopus balls, doughnuts, chocolate bars, and other goodies they'd picked up on their way.

Aoi's ominous premonition had come true. In the days following the lunch incident, no one would talk to Kana anymore. Haruka's group made fun of her to her face, while the other students snickered from afar. Her former friends stopped including her in anything they did and acted as if they'd never even known her.

But this treatment lasted only about ten days for Kana, after which Keiko was labeled a sourpuss and became the new target. Their classroom's notorious bad-girl group, who signaled their membership by wearing their skirts extra long, started bullying her viciously, cutting up the hem of her skirt with scissors and sticking duct tape in her hair.

Aoi trembled in fear. First Kana, and now Keiko—both from her own group of friends. Might she be next? But to her great relief, the focus shifted a few days later to Masako Aihara of the bookworm crowd. Aoi was almost ashamed of how relieved she felt.

"Why? What do you mean?" Nanako said, reaching into the brown paper bag from the small general store by the bus stop where they got off and pulling out two cans of beer. Nearly everything in the store had been covered in a thin layer of dust. She looked at Aoi. "If you're talking about all that dire stuff Hitomi's been saying about colleges, forget it. She just likes to hear herself talk. Tenth grade is way too early to be worrying about entrance exams." She flashed Aoi an innocent smile and handed her one of the beers. The can was wet with condensation.

"Tell me," said Aoi, making no effort to hide the irritation in her voice. "Do you do that deliberately?"

She was in fact annoyed with Nanako. No one could have remained oblivious to the malignant atmosphere that had taken over their classroom ever since the Kana Hirabayashi affair. Yet Nanako continued to flit from group to group as if nothing had changed, neither attaching herself to any single clique, nor turning her back on them altogether and going it alone.

"Do what deliberately? Oh, let's have a toast. *Hap*-py birthday! Oops, I guess that's not for me to say," she bubbled, thrusting her can at Aoi's.

"Happy birthday," Aoi echoed, pulling on the pop top. The warming beer pushed foam from the opening, which Aoi hastily covered with her mouth to take a sip. "That's nasty," she grimaced, and it was obvious from Nanako's look that she shared the sentiment.

"Happy ice cream!" she said nonsensically.

They slapped each other on the shoulder and burst into gales of laughter.

"Nobody told me beer tasted so bad."

"I was sure it'd be good. I guess we should've gotten can cocktails instead. Those are supposed to be sweet."

"We must be late bloomers—getting our first taste of beer at this age."

"And sneaking down to the river to do it."

They laughed some more.

"Let's eat, let's eat," Nanako said. Tearing open the package of yakitori and removing the lid from the octopus ball tray, she began tossing the bite-size pieces into her mouth, one after another. "Yummy-yum-yum," she yelled wildly, throwing herself back on the mat and flapping her legs. Her white thighs flashed beneath her skirt and Aoi quickly looked away.

"Lately it's been like the whole class is playing a game of who can we pick on next," Aoi said between bites of yakitori from a skewer sticky with sauce. "You can't tell me you haven't noticed. It started with Kana, and now it's Masako. Everybody treats them cold and mean, and sometimes they really cross the line. Like when they cut up Keiko's skirt. People are going around terrified, wondering if they might be next, whispering stuff behind each other's backs like they're the secret police or something."

The river flowed ceaselessly before them, mirroring the tall blue sky. The grass that had grown so wild and thick during the summer was now withered, stirring drily in the passing wind.

"We're in high school, not kindergarten!" Aoi cried in exasperation. "Talk about infantile. It's ridiculous. I guess I was right. It really *is* a dumb school. This'd never happen at a proper prep school, that's for sure." In an odd sort of way, her own words were emboldening her, and she went on. "Just look at Kazuyo Ube and her gang. Wearing those long skirts in this day and age—they look like peasants. Some nerve they have, thinking they can make fun of others. At the junior high I used to go to, they'd be the first to get the cold shoulder."

"Of course it's a dumb school!" Nanako erupted. "I got in, didn't I?" She let out a shriek of laughter.

"I'm trying to be serious," Aoi said icily, her irritation rising again.

"Well, if you don't like it," Nanako said, suddenly turning serious herself, "then just don't be part of it. It's as easy as that. Kazuyo and Masako are both perfectly nice people, in case you didn't know." Still on her back, she stabbed an octopus ball with a toothpick and dropped it into her open mouth.

Aoi heaved a deep sigh and fell back onto the mat with a skewer of yakitori in her hand. The blue expanse overhead was interrupted by only a few scattered wisps of cloud. "You're so lucky, Nanako. You're totally fearless. I bet you had a totally happy childhood, didn't you. You probably never had anyone take a dislike to you, always got along with your sister, your mother was a complete angel, and everything always went the way you wanted."

Nanako neither confirmed nor denied this. She wrinkled her nose and let out a little chuckle as she sat up and took another sip or two of the beer she'd practically spat out before. Raising her knees, she wrapped her arms around them and hugged them to her chest.

"From the time I was in kindergarten...," Aoi started to say, but then fell silent for several minutes as she tried to decide whether she really wanted to go on. If she did, she might turn Nanako against her. But if she didn't, the gulf between her and her friend who'd lived such a charmed life would just keep growing wider and wider. "From the time I was in kindergarten, I was always getting picked on, and I never had any friends. Never." She felt herself choking up, but desperately held back the threatening tears in order to continue. "In junior high, I couldn't face school anymore. It was just way too scary. I suppose you can't even imagine. The thing is, I knew there was something wrong with me. I knew that. But nobody would talk to me, so I could never figure out what I had to do to fix it. That's actually why we moved here. So I wouldn't have to go to high school in Yokohama. My mom really didn't want to come, but I insisted. No way was I going anywhere I might run into my old classmates."

Aoi paused as what she'd said only moments before about her new school and classmates went through her mind. She stared at Nanako's back, realizing that if she was going to do like her mother and look down her nose at their new town just to make herself feel better, she deserved every bit of abuse and ill will people heaped on her.

"You know, all those people that picked on you?" Nanako said without turning around. "They were probably just jealous. Because you had something they didn't have. Because you had so much."

"That's okay, you don't have to say that. I know perfectly well there's something wrong with me."

Aoi held a doughnut up and peered through the hole. A thin wisp of cloud was crawling slowly across the sky. Then suddenly the patch of blue was replaced by Nanako's eye in the doughnut hole.

"Ack! You startled me!" Aoi cried, and Nanako rolled back onto the mat in a fit of laughter.

Nanako raised a doughnut in front of her eye like Aoi. "Well, anyway, you can't really judge things like that by yourself," she said. "But in the end, I'm glad they picked on you. Otherwise we'd never have met."

She paused a moment before continuing in a flat, measured voice, almost as if reading from a prepared script.

"I want you to know, Aokins, that you don't have anything to be afraid of at school. Even if you're right, even if they keep passing the icy treatment from one person to another like you say and it comes round to you, I'll always be your friend, and I'll do everything I can to stand up for you. Even if everybody else turns their back on you, if you always have at least one person to talk to, then you've got nothing to be afraid of, right?"

Aoi continued peering at the sky through her doughnut and said nothing.

"And I don't mean this to be some kind of deal or exchange. I'm not asking you to do anything for me if I'm the one that gets shut out. In fact, I'd rather you brushed me off like everybody else. It's safer that way. 'Cause none of that stuff scares me. Seriously, let them turn their noses up at me and chop up my skirt and say bitchy things and hide my sneakers all they want. None of that can hurt me. None of that stuff matters to me."

Aoi lowered her doughnut to her mouth and took a bite out of it. Then she raised it back in front of her eye to peer through the C-shape that was left. It looked to her like the blue inside the C was melting and pouring out into the wide-open sky.

"Oh, I've been meaning to ask you. Did you ever hear what they say about silver rings?" Nanako said, abruptly changing the topic.

"What? I don't think so."

"If somebody gives you a silver ring on your nineteenth birthday, then happiness will follow you the rest of your life."

"Really? The rest of your life? You mean somebody like a boy-friend, right?"

"If we don't have boyfriends when we turn nineteen, how about we give each other silver rings? That way we'll both be happy the rest of our lives."

"Well, I'm sure you won't have anyone, so I'll give you the ring," Aoi cracked, "but I intend to have a boyfriend who'll give me mine." She let out a guffaw.

"So says the girl who got me one measly package of yakitori this year," Nanako sniffed. She took a sip of beer. "Don't you see I was giving you a gentle hint to start saving now so you could give me a proper present by the time I'm nineteen? You should be more grateful!" She pedaled her feet as she laughed.

Their laughter echoed along the riverbank, mingling with the rustle of the flowing water. When Aoi raised her head to peer at the river, it looked to her again like the sky was melting and pouring out onto its surface.

5

A place opened up for Akari near the end of June. It was at Sayoko's second-choice school, but the opening came much sooner than she had expected. An aging complex of company housing nearby was slated for demolition, and several young families had moved away in quick succession, creating a rare string of vacancies.

Both in the days before Akari started and during her phase-in week, Sayoko thought she might go nuts from all the things she had to do. Getting her daughter properly registered was only the beginning. She needed to make Akari a school bag, prepare several towels with her name stitched to them, and take her shopping for sneakers to use as indoor shoes as well as extra changes of clothes to have on hand. She rode her bicycle from home to the nursery school and from there to the station and back, exploring alternate routes, and she discovered several shortcuts as well as a convenient place to do some quick shopping on her way home.

Meanwhile, work had yet to become a matter of simply showing up and getting down to business each morning. Noriko Nakazato had more things for her to learn with each new job site they went to.

"Lime scale forms when calcium and magnesium salts react with the air and precipitate to form a film on surfaces in contact with water. Agents for removing the scale contain abrasives, surfactants, acids, alkalis, and solvents."

Every so often Noriko would rattle off some such tangle of information, and Sayoko diligently scribbled it down in her notebook like a student, adding to her growing collection of notes on different cleaning tasks and which cleanser was best suited to each.

It was supposed to be for the sake of her job that she was putting Akari in nursery school, but there were days during this frantic preparation period when some requirement from school kept her up most of the night and she went to work half asleep. She sometimes found herself spacing out and losing track of what she was doing, but at least she no longer agonized over whether going back to work had been the right decision. She simply didn't have the time. All she could do was take care of the task in front of her, one thing at a time.

I have to consider myself lucky, Sayoko reminded herself over and over as she scrubbed tiles in the bathroom of a vacant condo unit. The young mothers she'd met at the nursery school assured her it was practically unheard of for anyone to find a place in less than a month. And now, for the last two weeks, Aoi and Noriko had generously allowed her to work five short days instead of three full ones. Even after the phase-in week was over, she was required to pick up Akari at four for a while.

Each day continued to be like Sayoko's first. She rode the At Home Services van to a job site and set to work cleaning a vacant apartment. Either Aoi would go with her, or it would be one of two other Platinum Planet employees—Misao Sekine, who dyed her hair brown and wore trendy-looking clothes in an effort to shave years off her age; or Mao Hasegawa, a younger woman with her short-cropped hair dyed red, officially classified as only a temporary employee. Junko Iwabuchi had presumably followed through on discussing her alleged back problem with Aoi, for she did not come again.

Sayoko marveled at Noriko's consistent ability to turn up empty apartments that required such astonishing amounts of elbow grease one after the other. From kitchen vent to stove to toilet to bath, the fixtures were of every imaginable type, but the thick layers of grime encrusted on them were always pretty much the same.

Today's studio unit had apparently been treated with a bug bomb by the movers several days before. The entire place was littered with dead cockroaches when they entered, and Sayoko's first task became to dispose of the corpses. After that she was sent to the bathroom, where she got down on all fours and mutely scrubbed at the black and pink fungus that had taken over the tiles of the washing area next to the tub.

I really do have to count myself lucky, Sayoko told herself again, not bothering to wipe away the bead of sweat that rolled from her temple down to her chin. This was already Akari's tenth day at school, but she had still kicked and screamed that she didn't want to go. Even in her bicycle seat on the way, she sat with her tiny head thrown back, bawling to the heavens. Although Sayoko no longer second-guessed her decision to work, it tore at her heart to see her daughter in such distress. *Poor little thing. It's such a pity...* Her mother-in-law's constant refrain threatened to fall from her own lips.

But her mother-in-law had to be wrong, Sayoko told herself adamantly as she scrubbed at the grout with a toothbrush, anticipating that moment when everything in her head would go blank. This very day, Akari could be making new friends and having the good time Sayoko could never provide for her at the park. Where was the pity in that?

Noriko came for her with the van at exactly two o'clock. Sayoko hopped into the front passenger seat and they headed for the nearest station.

"I really appreciate your letting me work short days like this."

"Don't mention it. You make up for it by coming five days anyway." The woman often joked and laughed with Aoi, but she remained strictly business with Sayoko.

Sayoko eyed the sky as they drove. Murky gray clouds hung low overhead, but so far the rain was holding off. The silence in the van started to feel awkward.

"I understand you have children too, Mrs. Nakazato," she said.

"That's right," Noriko told her with a single deep nod.

"Did you put them in nursery school when they were little?"

This time there was no reply.

Wondering if perhaps she'd said something wrong, Sayoko hastily continued. "I never imagined how much trouble the school was going to be. Though I suppose it's mainly only now, at the beginning. I had to sew a tote for her things, and a second bag just for her sneakers, and then they want you keep a diary of all her activities. The other day when I was writing my work diary, I started to put down the time Akari got up that morning and what she had for breakfast."

Noriko let out an amused snort, and Sayoko breathed a sigh of relief.

"The thumb-sucking drove me bananas," Noriko said with no obvious connection, and it took Sayoko a second to realize she was talking about her own children. "For me, it was my own mother bugging me, not my mother-in-law. She was convinced that the stress of me working all the time was what made my boy suck his thumb. Plus I got plenty of grief from the public health nurse, too, lecturing me up and down about the thumb-sucking like I better jump when she says jump. Believe it or not, I'm actually kinda thin-skinned. I thought I was going to have a nervous breakdown."

Sayoko gazed at Noriko in the driver's seat. Something maternal had suddenly come over the stern-faced woman who never wore any makeup and was such a taskmaster on the job.

"Then one day Aoi said something to me. She said, 'Relax Nori, did you ever see a grown man sucking his thumb?' I knew right away she was right, of course. I had to laugh."

The station was coming up less than a hundred meters away. Sayoko wanted to hear more and hoped against hope that the light between them and the station would turn red.

"These days it's 'Poopy!' and 'Pee-pee!' all the time. Blurting it out anywhere he pleases—in a restaurant, in a department store. Makes me want to give him a good whack on the head sometimes. But you know, to paraphrase Aoi, you never hear grown men shouting 'Poopy!' or 'Pee-pee!'" She laughed.

The light did not turn red, and the van sailed right on into the turnaround in front of the station.

"Here we are."

"Thanks so much for the ride. I'll see you tomorrow."

With a quick bow, Sayoko jumped out of the car and hurried into the station.

Akari came bounding over like a puppy as soon as she saw her mother at the gate. Only a few short hours had gone by, but to Sayoko it felt like she'd been separated from her daughter for a week, and she squeezed her tight in her arms.

Just then a woman pushing a bicycle came up to them with a smile. "Hi, there! It's Akari, right? Did you see my Chiemi in the yard?"

Akari stopped smiling and eyed her classmate's mother warily as she worked her way around behind Sayoko.

"I'm sorry," Sayoko said. "I'm not sure she's learned everybody's name yet."

"Oh, right, she's still pretty new, isn't she? I read your little article in the Cypress Flier."

"Are we expected to write something every month? It's been so long since I had to write anything, I got a serious case of writer's block."

"I know what you mean. You tense up and forget how to write some stupid kanji. But I don't think you need to worry. Once every three or four months should be plenty."

Sayoko stood and talked with Chiemi's mother for several more minutes about the school's newsletter, which introduced the month's birthday boys and girls and printed other brief articles submitted by mothers. She could hardly believe herself. Here she was, standing out in front of the school on a cloudy day, carrying on a perfectly normal conversation with a woman whose name she didn't even know, without being at the slightest loss for words. Yet it was now even harder for her to believe that just two or three short months before this she'd been utterly incapable of striking up conversations with the women she met at the park.

"Well, see you tomorrow." With a wave of her hand, Chiemi's mother headed on into the schoolyard to look for her child.

"Bye," Sayoko waved back, then quickly lifted Akari into the child seat attached to the handlebars.

Pedaling toward the supermarket, she thought about what to make for dinner and started a mental list of what she would need to buy.

"Who'd you play with today, sweetie?" she asked Akari. She'd been asking her daughter this same question every day, praying for the day when Akari would finally respond with the name of a new friend she'd made.

Akari ignored the question and instead began singing a song of some kind under her breath. It was a tune Sayoko didn't recognize. One of her daughter's favorite tunes was from an anime series she watched on TV, so she thought at first it might be that, but quickly realized it was something else.

"Is that a new song you learned today?" she asked.

Without turning in her seat, Akari gave a single small nod.

"I thought so. You know what, sweetie, I want you to know that even when Mommy has to go to work, Mommy's always going to be right beside you in my heart, watching over you. No matter where I am, I say to myself, I wonder what Akari's doing now, and I look and see, Oh, she's having lunch, Oh, she's learning a new song.

Every day, even when you can't see me, Mommy's always there with you, okay?"

Staring straight ahead, Akari gave another small nod.

"Can you sing it louder, so Mommy can hear?"

Sayoko pushed harder on the pedals. A moist breeze stirred the leaves of the trees all up and down the street. She'd been putting off asking Shuji about the party, but she was definitely going to do it tonight.

"Is it okay if I stay out a little longer?" Sayoko pleaded into the cell phone pressed to the side of her face. She had slipped out of the noisy tavern into the quiet elevator lobby ahead of the others to call her husband.

"Hunh?" came Shuji's voice from beyond a haze of static. Sayoko wasn't sure whether there was a note of irritation in his voice or it was just the poor connection. She glanced at her watch. Only a few minutes past eight.

"I mean, it's my own welcome party, you know, and they set it up on a Saturday just for me. I feel kind of awkward saying all of a sudden that I have to leave early."

"Now watch me get this foisted on me every weekend."

"Foisted?"

He had probably meant it as a joke: she could hear it in his voice. But the reply had slipped out before she could bite her tongue.

"Akari went down a little bit ago," Shuji said. "She made me read the same book five times in a row." He'd apparently caught the edge in Sayoko's tone and changed the subject to avoid a confrontation.

The tavern's automatic door slid open and the rest of Sayoko's group came pouring out after settling the bill. Aoi hurried toward her.

"Sorry. I have to go," Sayoko said quickly into the phone. "And thanks. I promise not to be too late." She hung up.

"So? What'd he say?" Aoi asked with a hopeful smile, the smell of alcohol on her breath.

Sayoko smiled back and flashed her a V. "He said okay."

The Platinum Planet staff—Misao Sekine, Junko Iwabuchi, Mao Hasegawa, and Yuki Yamaguchi, who handled the accounting—along with several others from the party, trooped across the street yelling out suggestions for their next watering hole. Takeshi Kihara held back, standing next to Sayoko. Was he coming to Aoi's place, too, she wondered with a measure of dismay. She'd hoped for a chance to talk with Aoi alone, and besides, she'd never really gotten a very good impression of Takeshi. It wasn't that he had a particularly unpleasant manner, but he made her feel ill at ease somehow.

When Takeshi stepped into the street to hail a cab, Sayoko quickly whispered in Aoi's ear: "Is he coming, too?"

"Hardly," she said. "He lives in the same direction, so we're dropping him off."

Sayoko breathed a quiet sigh of relief. Takeshi turned to shout that a cab was stopping.

"Promise not to be shocked when you see my place," Aoi said to Sayoko as she slid into the back seat.

"Should we have him go to Shimokitazawa first?" Takeshi asked from the front.

"Now don't get any ideas about tagging along. Sangubashi first is fine."

"Oh, sure. Like I'd want to do that. Give me a break," he said, then turned to the driver. "First to Sangubashi, and after that it'll be to Shimokitazawa."

The car started up. Sayoko stole a glance at Takeshi in the rearview mirror. She could only see one of his eyes.

The networking-slash-welcome party held in Shinjuku had started at five with about twenty people attending. It was a mixed crowd in both age and profession—a retail shop producer, an event coordinator, a management consultant, an aspiring actor, and so forth—but Sayoko was struck that they all seemed very much like Aoi in spirit: completely open and unguarded, quick to laugh, and easy to talk to. They'd immediately started treating her like an old friend. She spoke for a time about child rearing with a woman who published a free paper. She and Yuki Yamaguchi together offered some love advice to the young actor. She compared notes with Misao Sekine on the apartments they'd cleaned, each of them trying to trump the other's tale of the worst filth they'd encountered.

Except for her own colleagues, Sayoko still couldn't attach names to faces three hours later, but she felt as if she hadn't had so much fun laughing and talking with friends at a drinking place in a hundred years. Several times during the evening she had looked across the tatami-style banquet room for a chance to talk with Aoi, but Takeshi remained ensconced at her side every time. Not until the gathering was breaking up and they found themselves slipping into their shoes side by side had they been able to exchange any words at all, and it was then that Aoi had invited Sayoko to come to her place for some more drinks.

"Look, Takeshi," Aoi broke the silence in a serious tone of voice. "That stuff you were saying before, about a personal guide of some kind who's not an interpreter or escort? I can't help thinking it'd be the same as turning people over to a local host. You're really only looking at the bottom line."

"I figured you'd say that. But you can't deny there's a real need. It's a damn sight better than letting people fall into the clutches of some smooth-talking gigolo who hits on Japanese tourists."

Sayoko gathered that they were discussing a new business idea. Feeling rather like a child excluded from grown-up conversation, she watched the buildings drift past outside the window. The cab soon put the neon lights of Shinjuku behind them. 8:18 P.M. On a normal Saturday, she would be cleaning up after dinner, pausing now and then to look out at the inky blue sky beyond the glass doors to the balcony. Tonight she'd learned that the sky over Shinjuku at this hour glowed a bright purple.

"I just don't see what it accomplishes. You still write off any possibility of the chance encounter they might have otherwise."

"That sounds typical, coming from you. But if you don't mind my saying, I think it makes a whole lot more sense than something completely unrelated like housekeeping."

"Sense? It's hardly your place to be telling me what makes more sense. It's my company, and besides, travel and housekeeping aren't unrelated at all."

"Well, maybe not, but..."

Takeshi turned in his seat to look at Sayoko sitting directly behind him and flashed her an enigmatic smile. She squirmed, wondering what he could possibly mean by this gesture. *I wish you'd hurry up and get out, you creep!* she muttered to herself, still feeling like that excluded child.

After dropping Takeshi off, they drove on for a time before the cab pulled up in front of an aging ferro-concrete apartment building. The rest of the quiet residential side street was lined with a mixture of private homes and wood-frame apartment buildings. Emerging from the car first, Sayoko tried to hand Aoi a share of the fare when she slid out behind her, but she refused to take it.

"This is the place," Aoi said in the silence that descended after the cab drove off. She raised her arm in a sweeping gesture toward the building. Leading the way inside, she stopped at a bank of rusty mailboxes to insert a key and remove her mail. The building had no security door at the entrance, and the elevator was such a relic Sayoko had to chase anxious thoughts from her mind as they ascended. They got off on the fifth floor and proceeded along the exposed walkway to Aoi's door.

"Please come in," Aoi said as she hurried to switch on several lights around the main room. A soft yellow glow lit up the walls and ceiling of a one-bedroom apartment. There was stuff piled here, there, and everywhere.

The main living area measured about four meters by five, and the bedroom was a six-mat tatami room. Sayoko was taken aback to discover that Aoi lived in an apartment so much smaller than her own—though she supposed it was in fact ample space for a single person living alone.

"I knew it," Aoi said with a little laugh. She was starting to prepare something in the kitchen. "Everybody who comes here reacts the same way. They just gape. First the building's so antiquated, and then my place is always such a shambles. One person who came for drinks had the temerity to say she shuddered for the future of the company after she saw the state of my apartment. Well, I'll have you know, we may be in a bit of a slump at the moment, but we're not doing so badly that we can't meet the payroll. Oh, please sit down right there. Don't mind that stuff."

Sayoko moved a heap of clothes carefully to one side and sat down on the sofa. The curtains were open and she could see lights from the skyscrapers on the business side of Shinjuku shining in the darkness far in the distance.

"Wow! You have a great view!" she exclaimed.

"Yeah, that was what sold me on the place," Aoi said with obvious pleasure.

Sayoko looked about the room. A 25″ TV. A synthetic leather sofa. A large potted plant with dust-coated leaves. An abstract painting heavy on blue tones hanging on the wall. An assortment of magazines strewn about the floor. A vintage air conditioner that looked so old you wondered if it really worked. Some ebony furnishings and a grab bag of other items from across Asia. On the one hand, exotic figurines and fabrics brought back from trips overseas accented the room, along with the abstract painting, while on the other, stacks of cardboard boxes stood in the corner and fax printouts crammed with tiny numbers littered the floor.

As she took it all in, Sayoko found herself wondering *What if?* What if she had gone on working at the film distributor instead of getting married? She would probably be living today in an apartment not so different from this one. All by her lonesome, or sometimes with a friend, she would come home drunk to a room like this, pour herself a nightcap, and gaze out at the city lights in the distance.

Aoi brought two wine glasses and a cheese plate to the coffee table and sat down cross-legged on the floor.

"What's your place like?" she asked.

"Three bedrooms," Sayoko replied. "About a twelve-minute walk from the station. Having a toddler means the place is always turned upside down."

"Wow, I wish I had that kind of space. Is it a condo?"

Aoi poured the wine.

"Uh-huh. Complete with thirty-five-year mortgage."

In recent days, Sayoko had finally followed Aoi's urgings and dropped the customary honorific forms of speech she had initially used with her boss—though she still didn't feel comfortable addressing her by her first name. On the days when she left work early, she always went straight home and simply reported back to Aoi by phone. Once Sayoko had finished describing her day's activities, Aoi would ask how things were going at the nursery school, or how Sayoko was faring with the "old bag" and her snide remarks. Sayoko would get caught up in Aoi's easy manner and say more than she should, and as the days went by she realized that she'd also stopped using the formal speech forms.

Sayoko took a sip of her wine. "You know, I feel really relaxed here. Maybe I'll come here with Akari if things get bad at home." She meant it as a joke, but as the words left her lips she could hear Shuji saying "foisted" in her ear.

"Sure, anytime. Come right ahead. We can put down futons in the tatami room and sleep all in a row. On second thought, forget holing up in this tiny dump. If you're gonna run away from home, let's head for a hot springs somewhere. Soak in open-air tubs. Feast on fancy meals. Really live it up!"

Aoi lit a cigarette and laughed.

"Ooh, a hot springs. That's tempting. I haven't been to one in years."

"Then let's do it. Seriously!"

"I cringe to think what my husband might say. I'm so disgusted with him. Know what he said a while ago—of all the nerve? He said I'd 'foisted' Akari on him, can you believe it? As if he thinks spending time with his own daughter is some kind of tiresome chore, like the laundry or the dishes."

Her tongue loosened by alcohol, Sayoko let the words flow without restraint. She had discovered only recently how good it felt to spill. Whether it was the grief she got from her mother-in-law or the unguarded word her husband let slip, sharing it with someone brought out its funny side, and she could laugh and forget. On the other hand, even the tiniest little thing could take on exaggerated weight and start to feel like a major tragedy if she kept it bottled up inside. With Aoi, she'd found that she could talk about anything without the slightest hesitation.

"Oh, boy. I think you just reduced any desire I might've had to get married by at least seventy percent. That's why so many more women these days are saying forget marriage, forget kids. The true cause of plummeting birthrates isn't women who work, it's the grievances of happily married housewives."

"It's different for you, because you can take care of yourself just fine without a man. But going it alone was way too scary for me. I never believed I could make it in the working world."

"Really? That's the exact opposite of me. I never believed I could make it as a wife and mother. The working world is easy: you just do whatever comes up. Take care of business one thing at a time, and pretty soon the day is over. Repeat tomorrow."

Aoi paused, and silence filled the room. The smoke she exhaled wafted slowly toward the ceiling. Far beyond the window, tiny lights flashed on and off atop the skyscrapers of Shinjuku.

"Do you happen to have a snapshot of your daughter with you?"

Sayoko took out her cell phone and flipped it open to show Aoi the picture of Akari she used for her standby screen.

"Wow, what a sweetie! I think maybe she has your eyes," Aoi said, then without looking away from the screen asked, "Wasn't it scary when you had her?"

"Scary?"

"For me, it's absolutely terrifying. Fear's a real bugaboo, isn't it? Here I am, a grown woman, supporting myself in my own business, happily making cold calls, confident I can take on men with twice my experience and come out on top, but the thought of bearing a child sets me quaking. Kind of pathetic, isn't it? But I can't help it. I imagine the child I carried inside me growing up and getting hurt or breaking her heart over something I don't have the slightest clue about, and it scares the daylights out of me. I suppose it's because I never told my parents anything when I was young. What if my kid turned out like me? I'd hate that," she said with a chuckle as she handed the cell phone back.

"Actually," Sayoko said, looking at her daughter smiling back at her from the phone, "that's exactly what I think sometimes—that Akari's getting to be like I was. And I hate it, too. I want my daughter to be brighter, more outgoing, more sociable, you know, but when you consider what a terror she is at home, it's almost sad how timid she is outside. A lion at home but a mouse abroad, as they say. She's been going to school for nearly a month now and she still hasn't made any friends as far as I can tell. It reminds me of when I was little. When

91

I think back, I know that's exactly the way I was. It's not scary so much as heartbreaking."

Sayoko thought of Akari bursting into tears as they were about to leave for school, screaming that she didn't want to go. She bawled even harder when she was handed over to the staff. None of the other kids in the schoolyard were ever crying when Sayoko was there. Just two days ago, she'd overheard an older staff member remarking that it wasn't often they got such a determined crier. But what Akari's distress reminded her of most was not herself as a child; it was herself as a mother, wandering fretfully from park to park.

Aoi had been fiddling with her toenails as she listened. "Yep," she said, rising to her feet and starting for the kitchen. "I know just how you feel—though I don't have any kids myself. When it comes right down to it, I think our whole generation suffers from a morbid fear of being alone."

She raised her voice to make herself heard from the kitchen. Sayoko peered through the opening in the buffet as Aoi reached on tiptoe for something on a high shelf.

"A morbid fear of being alone?" Sayoko said, her voice a question.

"Uh-huh. It's like, if we don't have friends, it's the end of the world, you know what I mean? Somewhere along the line, we had it drummed into us that kids who have lots of friends are bright and happy, and kids who don't have any are dark and gloomy, and dark and gloomy is bad. That's how it was for me anyway. That's what I always thought. Though maybe it's not just our generation. Maybe its universal."

She was preparing bowls of snacks as she spoke. For the last part she seemed to be talking mostly to herself.

Sayoko looked toward Aoi again in surprise. Had she said something to Aoi about the parks? Had she told her about all those months she'd spent moving from one park to the next, irritated with Akari for her inability to blend in with kids her own age even as she faulted herself for not being able to make friends with those children's mothers?

Aoi emerged from the kitchen with a bowl in each hand—one holding potato chips, the other mixed nuts. She set them down on the coffee table.

"Sorry," she said. "I don't cook, so this is all I can offer."

Sayoko looked at the bowls without really seeing them. "You may be right, but...," she started to say in answer to Aoi's previous remark, then stopped, not sure how to go on. She reached for a potato chip and put it in her mouth.

"I remember, when I was a kid, I believed it was bad not to have friends," Aoi said. "And you know, it was pretty painful—to think that. If I had a kid, I'd worry that it was so ingrained in me, I'd pass it on to my child. That's what's scary. Though maybe I should stop this babbling until I actually have one." She burst into a laugh.

"But it really *is* better to have lots of friends, don't you think?" Sayoko said. She almost blushed at how desperate her words sounded. But she simply had to know. To know what kind of person Akari would become? To know whether her own choice was right or wrong? To know where Aoi's remarks would ultimately lead? It wasn't clear to Sayoko exactly what it was she wanted to know, but she felt a powerful desire to understand.

"I'm not around children, so I don't have much of an idea what kind of things can affect how they grow up. But to me, it's a whole lot more important to find something that makes you unafraid of being alone, rather than to have so many friends that you wind up being terrified of solitude. At least that's what I think now."

Sayoko gazed at Aoi sitting on the floor across the coffee table from her. She felt like she'd put her hand out and had it slapped. Right. Maybe what she needed to teach Akari was exactly what Aoi had just said. Maybe it was a mistake to fret over her daughter's lack of friends as she handed her in tears to the nursery school staff each morning, or to feel disappointed that she still hadn't named any new playmates when she picked her up at the end of the day. Sayoko's eyes remained fixed on Aoi as all this went through her mind.

"I wonder...," she began, but again found her thoughts in too much of a jumble to go on and fell silent.

"But I suppose feeling okay even when you can't get a man is carrying things a little too far." Aoi tossed a nut into her mouth, then threw her head back and laughed.

Sayoko's cell phone rang. She didn't need to look at the display to know it was Shuji calling. A quick glance at her watch told her it was almost ten. She picked up the phone and rose to her feet as it rang again.

"I'd better go. Thanks for the wine and snacks. Maybe we can have you over sometime, too. I'll cook up a feast."

"As far as I'm concerned, you could spend the night...but I guess that doesn't work for you. Here," Aoi said, hastily opening her wallet to pull out two ¥10,000 bills and thrust them into Sayoko's hands. "Take this for taxi fare. Just ask for a receipt and bring it to me at the office. Tell the driver to take the toll road. It'll be quicker."

Sayoko started to push the bills away, but then realized she wasn't sure she could even make it to the nearest station without getting lost. She accepted the money with a grateful bow. Aoi offered to walk her out to the main street, but she insisted that wasn't necessary and said good-bye at the door with a casual wave.

Closing the door behind her, she rode down in the elevator and hurried outside, racing headlong down the street. She turned a corner and the main road with a constant flow of headlights in both directions came into view fifty or sixty meters away. Breathing hard, she ran the rest of the way and searched among the endless stream of cars for a cab with its VACANT sign lit up.

In a taxi smelling strongly of its vinyl seat covers, Sayoko closed her eyes and pictured the apartment she had left behind only moments before. She saw Aoi in the living room, not bothering to clear away the glasses and bowls on the coffee table, throwing herself down on the sofa and switching on the TV, sipping at the rest of the wine as she laughed at some comedy routine all by herself. *To find something that makes you unafraid of being alone, rather than to have so many friends that you wind up being terrified of solitude.* She thought she was probably feeling about the same way Noriko had felt when Aoi so lightly laughed off her worries about thumb-sucking.

In the darkness of the back seat, Sayoko turned to look for the building that stood tall above the surrounding neighborhood, trying to pick out the light from Aoi's window shining bright into the night.

6

They had agreed to meet three stations down the line. Aoi said it wasn't necessary, but Nanako insisted it would be better that way.

"You're the one who'll regret it if somebody we know sees you with me," she pointed out.

Not until a family conference late the night before had Aoi finally won permission from her mother to spend summer vacation working at an inn in Izu with Nanako. Aoi didn't understand how her mother could possibly object. It wasn't as if she was asking to go all by herself, nor was she going just to lie around on the beach; she was going with a classmate for an honest-to-goodness job.

During the discussion, Aoi could barely contain her fury. She was more disillusioned with her mother than she'd ever been before.

"It only worries me more to have you going off with a girl from *that* place," her mother had declared.

Under the table, Aoi's hands shook with rage. What did she know about Nanako anyway? Just because nothing was ever good enough for her in this town, she had no right to insult a friend of Aoi's she knew nothing about. The way she said "*that* place," as if the housing complex where Nanako lived was a slum—did she think their own run-down house was some kind of palace?

But Aoi knew that talking back would nix any hope she had of going to Izu. So she held her rage tightly in check. And as she desperately held it in, tears began to spill down her face. They were tears of anger, but her father thought they came from disappointment at having her summer plans dashed, and this moved him to speak up for her.

"She's a junior now. She's practically grown up," he said. "It's time she started getting some experience, and working at an inn is a great opportunity." His cheeks glowed red with drink, but he managed to bring Aoi's mother around. She agreed Aoi could go on condition that she phoned home every night.

But getting permission to go failed to pacify Aoi. She should have lain awake that night bursting with excitement, but instead she lay in bed with tears spilling from her eyes. What had Nanako done to deserve her mother's scorn? The scorn of a woman who herself clung to cheap delusions about her past as if her very life depended on it.

Mrs. Narahashi had remained in a peevish mood ever since their move, finding new jobs and then quitting them one after another, and in recent months she'd been taking her frustrations out on Aoi. When something unpleasant happened at work, it would remind her that her daughter was the reason they'd had to move in the first place, and she'd drop some catty remark on her when she got home. Once while talking about plans for after high school Aoi mentioned applying to colleges in Tokyo, and her mother snapped back in a tone so cold it sent a chill down her spine: Did she really intend to move back to the big city all by herself after making the whole family move away just for her? Another time she as much as accused Aoi of bringing the bullying on herself. With each nasty crack, Aoi's disillusionment with her mother climbed to new heights. But it was the way she'd sneered at Nanako that was truly unforgivable.

In the morning, Mrs. Narahashi offered Aoi a mollifying smile and handed her an envelope filled with cash. "Put this away somewhere in case you get into a jam sometime," she said. "And if you wind up never needing it, you can pay me back double from your earnings." Her smile broadened. It was a rare effort at humor on her part.

Aoi had half a mind to refuse even this peace offering, but she suppressed the urge. Although her employer would be providing room and board, she had little of her own money to take along, and there was no telling when having a little extra cash on hand might save the day.

"All right, double your money back," she said with a smile.

Her mother saw Aoi to the door and sent her on her way with the same wildly flapping wave she remembered from her first day of high school. "Have a nice trip, dear."

When Aoi stepped off the train at the third station, Nanako was waiting only a few meters down the platform and spied her right away. They practically tumbled back onto the train together and collapsed onto facing seats in the nearly empty car, clasping hands and squealing with excitement.

"Yippee, we're on our way!"

"I was seriously worried they might not let you come, Aokins!"

"Did you bring your swimsuit?"

"Are you kidding? What else are we going to do with our free time? I took care of my unwanted hair, too."

"I brought some nail polish and makeup."

"Seriously? This'll be great! We can try stuff out on each other after work every night."

"Except we have to save time for schoolwork, too. I hope you brought your workbooks."

They chattered rapidly back and forth. Nanako was wearing a denim miniskirt with two tank tops layered one on top of the other and, like Aoi, had packed her things in a jumbo-sized nylon bag. It crossed Aoi's mind that they could be mistaken for runaways.

Outside the window, lush green rice fields stretched as far as the eye could see under a cloudless sky. The landscape changed so little, you could almost start to believe that the train was standing still. *Today we finally escape this place,* Aoi told herself over and over.

There were only a few other passengers in their car: an old lady carrying a shopping basket with a light towel wrapped over her head and tied under her chin; a small child and her grossly overweight young mother; and a pimply-faced junior high boy who looked like he was headed for a summer study course somewhere. These were people who would probably spend their entire lives in this place, never able to get away. Wherever they were off to now, they would be going back home later in the day. They might complain of boredom, but they would forever go on fearing everything outside that boredom. As Aoi studied them, she sensed a kind of grim acquiescence flowing out of their bodies into the air around them. *But we're not like them*, she told herself. *We're going somewhere much farther away. We're not afraid of what goes on outside this little place.* The thrill it gave her made her want to shout it out to the entire world.

After about ten minutes of jostling on the bus from Imaihama Station on the Izukyu Line, the girls arrived at "Mickey and Minnie's Place," a family-run inn they had found listed in a recruitment magazine. It was a small, three-story guesthouse located a five- or six-minute walk from the beach. They went around back as instructed and were greeted by a large-boned woman with a dark tan who cut them off midbow before they even had a chance to introduce themselves.

"Hi, girls, just drop your things over there, and I need one of you in the kitchen right away to take care of the dishes. If *you* can do that," she nodded to Nanako, then turned to Aoi, "I'd like *you* to hang out the wash. You'll find some of our private things mixed in, too—sorry about that. I hope you don't mind. Oh, this is the kitchen here, and the laundry room is right on through there. Just empty everything in the washing machines and hang it all up."

The woman kept up a nonstop torrent of words as she showed Nanako to the kitchen and directed Aoi to the laundry room.

This was the first time Aoi had ever seen someone else's laundry room or piles of laundry. She transferred the spin-dried wash to a basket she found by the machines and headed for the backyard.

On her way outside, she passed the kitchen again and caught a glimpse of Nanako standing at the sink, her back to the door, washing the dishes stacked on the counter beside her.

The front of the inn where guests came and went was obviously of recent construction, with a crisp, contemporary look, but the backyard had been allowed to go to weeds. Toys were strewn about on the ground and a plastic wading pool was collecting rain. Standing on tiptoe and squinting into the hot sun, Aoi began hanging up the wash. Buried among the mountain of towels from the guest rooms were children's briefs and undershirts, men's socks, a woman's bra and panties, and the like. The large, suntanned woman who'd greeted them at the door apparently was not one to be embarrassed, Aoi noted, as she continued shaking the wrinkles out of towels and shirts and putting them up to dry.

She and Nanako had traveled no more than five hours from home on the train, and yet the air and the sun felt completely different. It seemed like such a short time ago that she'd been pulling a sulky face at her mother, she could hardly believe she was now in Izu, hanging out a stranger's bra to dry. Sweat trickled down her face. Was it because they were by the sea that the sun felt so much hotter? Maybe in a place like this she'd finally be able to forgive her mother for everything, she thought, as her head started to swim from the heat.

"Keep it moving, dear." Hearing the woman's gravelly voice behind her, Aoi turned. "I've got gobs of stuff for you to do, so I intend to keep your noses to the grindstone." The woman was watching Aoi from the edge of the veranda. She reached into the pocket of her apron for a cigarette and lit up, exhaling her first puff with an audible *Haaaah.*

"I'm Ryoko Mano," she said. "Sounds like an actress's name, doesn't it?" She burst into a hearty laugh. "But sorry, I'm just a pushy old woman. Not that I'm actually all that old yet, but I figure from your perspective even someone in their twenties or thirties is an old woman." She laughed again.

Aoi caught a whiff of the smoke as it wafted by.

"I'll show you around later," Ryoko went on, "but basically, we built the inn as an addition onto the front of our house. We're giving you and your friend our son's room to use while you're here. Hope you don't mind sharing. Speaking of which, you two aren't twins, are you?"

Aoi turned in surprise. "Do you think we look alike?" She wasn't sure why, but she was pleased with the suggestion.

"I don't know. I guess kids your age all look alike to me."

"I'm Aoi Narahashi and she's Nanako Noguchi. We'd like you to know how much we appreciate this opportunity, and we're determined not to let you down."

Aoi bowed deeply, still holding something from the laundry basket in her hand. In a fluster, she realized it was a pair of boxer shorts and quickly pinned it up.

"And I appreciate your coming. You'll meet the rest of my family at dinner. We don't eat until after the guests are all done, so dinner will be around eight-thirty or nine, just so you know. Okay, then. Come find me when you're done with the laundry. I'll need you to get to the baths next."

She threw her cigarette on the ground as she got up and disappeared into the house, gently thumping on the small of her back with her fists.

Aoi could hardly believe all the tasks she and Nanako had to complete before they got their dinner. By the time they finally sat down with the Mano family a little after nine, she was so tired she wasn't sure she had any strength left to eat.

The Mano home was connected to the back of the inn by way of the kitchen. Compared to the newly built appearance of the inn itself, the family quarters behind showed their age, and there was clutter everywhere. In the dining room, cardboard boxes, toy cars, stuffed animals, piles of old newspapers, jars of plum wine, crates of beer, and other odds and ends had been tucked into every nook and cranny.

Aoi sat across from Nanako at the table, joining Ryoko, her five-year-old son Shinnosuke, her husband Futoshi, who was built like a pro wrestler, and his mother Misa as they noisily dug into their food. After everybody had been introduced, Futoshi tried to engage Aoi and Nanako in conversation, but each time they started to respond to his questions, Shinnosuke would interrupt with a loud remark. Soon Ryoko was on her feet telling him to behave himself. A moment later, Misa ladled more miso soup into the girls' bowls without waiting for them to ask. When he got bored with the grown-up conversation, Shinnosuke fooled with the TV remote for a while, then stood on his chair and started dancing. After a time, Futoshi went back to his newspaper, sipping at his beer and nibbling at his meal as he read, while Misa and Ryoko began arguing about different brands of rice.

Never quite sure what to expect next, Aoi and Nanako worked on their fried mackerel and potato salad, catching each other's eye from time to time amidst all the goings-on. Aoi was accustomed to quiet meals with just her mother, and she couldn't remember ever being at a table with all this commotion. She imagined it was much the same for Nanako.

After dinner they washed up the guest dishes, then the family's, gave the guest dining room a once-over, and when the guests were done in the baths mopped the changing rooms and washing areas. It was eleven-thirty by the time the two girls had had their turn in the bath and retreated to Shinnosuke's room for the night.

They found the tatami floor of the boy's room littered with toys and picture books and Legos and discarded clothing. Moving all these things out of the way, they spread futons side by side in the middle of the room, lay down under terrycloth blankets, and switched off the light. A planetarium of glow-in-the-dark stars appeared overhead, plastered across the ceiling. The girls lay staring blankly at the stars for a time, too exhausted to speak. Finally, Aoi broke the silence.

"You suppose Mr. Mano put those up?" she wondered softly.

"Guess he's the doting father type."

"Mrs. Mano sure cracks the whip, but she seems nice."

"I've never worked so hard in my whole life."

"Me neither. I just might die tomorrow."

"But it was kinda fun, too, don't you think?"

Yeah, it was fun, Aoi agreed, but she could no longer find the strength to open her mouth. *It feels weird sleeping in a strange house, doesn't it? You know what, Nanako, we'll probably have to bust our tails again tomorrow, but I don't mind a bit because I'm with you. Let's really show Mrs. Mano what we can do. Let's really wow her.*

Aoi's eyes drooped shut before the things she wanted to say could leave her lips. She tumbled almost instantly into a deep sleep, without even a chance to feel herself drifting off.

It took about five days for the girls to grow used to the rhythms of the inn. Out of bed at seven, ready the kitchen for serving breakfast, clean the dining room and lobby, sweep the front stoop, then get their own breakfast out of the way before guests start appearing in the dining room at around eight. Between serving guests, help with breakfast and cleanup for the Mano family. Once all the guests have eaten and gone out, usually by around ten, clean guest rooms with Mrs. Mano and her mother-in-law. Next come the common areas, including the baths, toilets, hallways, and dining room. Before stopping for lunch, get the two washing machines going on dirty sheets and towels from the guest rooms plus any items the family and they themselves need doing. Eat the lunch prepared by Mrs. Mano and help clean up afterwards, then hang the wash out to dry. When this is done, typically by around two, they can take it easy until four; if they finish later, it means their afternoon break is that much shorter. At four there is ironing to do and beds to make, and after that, dinner preparations. If any last-minute shopping needs to be done, whoever happens to be free at the moment goes. The guests all finish dinner by around eight-thirty, at which point the family and the girls eat supper. Cleaning up the kitchen and both dining rooms brings the day to a close. On quick days they sometimes got through by nine-thirty, but ten was more the rule.

The sooner they completed all their tasks, the more time they had to themselves, so Nanako and Aoi worked intently, avoiding idle chatter and never goofing off. When they were free, they went back to their room to try on makeup and do each other's hair, or they studied together at the family dining table. At night they would sometimes go down to the beach to walk along the water or watch inn guests launching fireworks.

The streets were filled with young men and women from out of town who'd come to vacation by the sea. A buoyant, holiday mood hung in the air everywhere. Café bars open only for the season vied loudly with each other for business each night. When Aoi and Nanako went swimming on their afternoon breaks, young men with gleaming dark tans flirted with them on the beach. About town, a musky smell seemed to catch their noses everywhere they went— even when passing in front of shops selling dried fish or pickles. They saw young men and women not much older than themselves cuddling or cavorting on the beach, hanging out of car windows and whooping it up as they cruised Main Street, or shopping at the supermarket with seawater dripping from their bathing suits. But to Aoi, all these people seemed to belong to another world. Squatting on the tiled floor of the bath and spraying away the sand these people had washed from their bodies held a much greater sense of reality. She enjoyed working. Keeping her arms and legs in constant motion gave her a marvelous feeling of liberation.

"You know, Aokins, I keep wishing I'd been born in a place like this," Nanako said out of the blue one evening as they sat at the dining table with their English workbooks spread before them. The stark white light of the fluorescent fixture overhead seemed to wash the color out of everything in the room. Down the hall they could hear the sounds of the samurai drama old Mrs. Mano was watching on TV.

"I've been thinking the same thing," Aoi said with a gentle smile. She took a sip of lukewarm iced tea.

"Yeah? You too? There's something nice about being by the sea, isn't there?"

"Uh-huh. You feel real easy, like you can do anything you want."

"Exactly," Nanako said. "I can sort of see why so many people like to come here in the summer. It's not just to swim. There's more to it than that."

Breaking off, she leaned back and looked up at the ceiling light. Tiny insects were circling about.

"When I think about it, I've never had to deal with anything all that tough in my life," Aoi said. "In fact, maybe I've actually had it pretty good compared with most people. That's probably why I'm such a softie. But there are times when I get so totally fed up with everything, I just want to blame it all on somebody else and scream curses at the whole world and run away somewhere. Since coming here, though, I've been thinking. If I lived someplace like this and that happened, it seems like I could simply go down to the beach and look at the ocean, you know, and all those messed-up feelings would just melt away. And besides that, I think throwing myself totally into work in a place like this would give me such a great feeling I probably wouldn't even want to blame anybody for anything in the first place."

Aoi wasn't sure exactly what she was trying to say, but as she heard the words come out, part of her felt as if this was something she'd wanted to say to Nanako for a very long time.

"What's it tonight, girls?" boomed Ryoko's gravelly voice as she came into the dining room. "Talking about boys? Confessing summer loves?"

"As if," Nanako said. "Actually, we were both saying we wished we could stay and work here forever."

"You mean it? That's fine by me. Though you do realize permanent staff have to work twice as hard." Ryoko roared with laughter.

"Seriously, Mrs. Mano," Aoi said. "I'd love to live and work in a place like this."

"Don't be silly. The only reason you say that is because you know you'll be leaving soon. If I visited your town, I'd probably go starry-eyed and say I wanted to stay there forever, too."

Ryoko poured two fresh glasses of iced tea from the refrigerator and set them down in front of the girls. For herself she got out a tall can of beer and chugged several thirsty gulps standing right there in front of the refrigerator.

"If you really believe that, then I suggest you try coming sometime. You'll be sick of the place in a day, guaranteed. Won't she?"

"Absolutely. All we've got is a river, and a bunch of schools. Lots of schools. But they're all for smart kids, so everybody sticks their noses in the air and makes fun of us. Plus there aren't any cute boys."

Squatting in front of a cardboard box, Ryoko opened the flaps and pulled out a crinkly bag of rice crackers, then lowered herself the rest of the way onto the floor beside it. She stuck her hand into the bag and began crunching on a cracker.

"Yeah, yeah, and all we've got here is the ocean. Seems kinda funny now, but when I was your age, I hated this place and couldn't wait to get out. Got me a summer job the first chance I had. A big, fancy inn, way better than here."

"Seriously? Where? Someplace else in Izu?" Nanako asked, leaning forward in her seat.

"Are you kidding? The last place I wanted to go was anywhere close. I headed for the mountains. The mountains of Nagano. Ever heard of Togakushi? The first time was my tenth-grade summer, and they treated me so nice, the people there, I went back for winter break that same year, and again the next summer, and so on. I worked up there in the mountains all the way through high school."

Ryoko fell silent and sat studying the can of beer in her hand.

The glass doors facing the veranda and yard were open, and tiny insects clung to the other side of the screens. The brightness of the overhead light spilled out into the darkness, dimly illuminating the clotheslines and abandoned toy cars. *Chirrr chirrr chirrr.* An insect song unlike any Aoi had ever heard droned endlessly on.

"You know, something just hit me," Ryoko said, raising her eyes and looking from one girl to the other, her face completely straight. "You two wouldn't happen to be runaways, would you?"

"No way."

"Hardly."

They both answered at the same time.

"Right. I didn't think so. Kids these days aren't that stupid," she said, rounding her back and laughing. "The summer of my senior year, I went to work at the same place as before, but then suddenly I couldn't stand the thought of going home. I mean, if I went home, the whole college thing was going to be staring me in the face, you know. This was the day when all of a sudden the school you went to mattered more than anything else, and the entrance exams got a whole lot more competitive practically overnight, yet at the same time the number one career choice for girls our age remained stay-at-home mom—which is to say, basically, things weren't so simple anymore. Mind you, this isn't all that long ago I'm talking about. It was practically just the other day, you know, just the other day."

"So did you run away or something?" Nanako said jokingly with a little laugh.

"You got it. I ran away," she replied without smiling. "I went to

Tokyo with a guy who worked at the same inn. A college student. I wasn't in love with him or anything, I just couldn't bear the thought of going home."

Aoi studied the woman sitting on the floor with a beer in her hand. Looking from her dry, brown hair, to her makeup-free face, to her T-shirt with overstretched neck, she tried to imagine this woman as a teenager in high school. A vague picture of a chunky-looking schoolgirl in a sailor suit formed in her mind.

"I went with him thinking we were going to Tokyo, but where he lived turned out to be in the boonies, way out on the outskirts. That's where his school was, too. His apartment was this dingy place with rice paddies all around. Yeah, yeah, I know exactly what you're thinking. I slept with him. He was my first. I mean, what else was I gonna do?"

"This wasn't Mr. Mano by any chance?" Nanako broke in.

Ryoko's eyes doubled in size as she stared at Nanako for a moment, then she fell over backward laughing.

"Give me a break! I wasn't a complete babe in the woods." She lay there laughing and looking up at the ceiling a while longer before sitting up again. "Eventually the landlord of the dingy dump complained about him having a girl there all the time, so I decided to go home—especially since I was out of money anyway."

"What happened to the guy?"

"We wrote back and forth a couple of times, but basically that was the end of it. He didn't come to Togakushi the next year. Anyway, that's why it suddenly hit me a minute ago that you two might've run away from home, too. But I figure kids today are smarter than that."

Rising to her feet, she crushed the now empty beer can in her hands and put the bag of rice crackers on the table between the two girls.

"I've been meaning to mention," she said, changing the subject.

"I have a whole box full of old cosmetics stuff I never use anymore. Would you like it? I noticed you two've been trying things out on each other."

"No way! *You* have *makeup?*" Both girls reacted in disbelief.

Ryoko flashed them a glare. "I'll go get what I have and you can take whatever you want. Oh, it's time for that show you like about those teen rebels. Why don't you go turn it on while I get the stuff? I'll bring everything to the living room."

Her footsteps thumped away down the hall. Aoi and Nanako looked at each other and laughed. Out of the darkness in the yard came the incessant chorus of summer insects, *chirr chirr chirr.*

The kind of personal harassment that made the rounds during their first year in high school had stopped this year, but a new, even more troubling dynamic took its place, spreading beyond the single classroom to the entire class.

"Maybe this is what a caste system is like," Aoi had quipped to Nanako when she first noticed the change, not taking it very seriously.

Homerooms had been reassigned at the beginning of the school year, which of course meant all the social groupings changed as well. The two close friends were now in separate classrooms. Aoi fell in once again with a collection of undemonstrative girls who didn't fit into any other group, while Nanako continued to flit about without attaching herself to any of the different crowds.

In the new order of things, girls from the more popular and attention-getting groups, which is to say those who'd taken the lead in the bullying the year before, in effect formed the top caste, and they considered it their rightful place in life to order those in the bottom caste to do their bidding, or to pick on them or ignore them at will—though they no longer got in any particular person's face the way they had the year before. Once someone became identified with the lowest caste, it was almost impossible for her to rise above that status. Fortunately, the girls in Aoi's group never drew enough attention to themselves to receive bottom-caste treatment, and Nanako's avoidance of any specific affiliation essentially left her outside the caste system to do as she pleased.

As before, Aoi and Nanako hung out together after school, meeting up to go to the river, buying something to eat along the way, talking and laughing endlessly about the new caste system. It came from everything being so dull all the time, Nanako asserted. So totally ho-hum. Day in and day out, their world, their lives, their grades, everything always the same. And because of that, people got antsy and looked for ways to stir things up. Ranking everybody in an arbitrary caste system let them feel important. It was how they kept from going out of their minds.

Something Aoi had observed, too, was that the students at this school had no true choices presented to them, and all they could really do was mark time. For one thing, it wasn't a college prep institution. It continued to tout its founding mission of turning out good wives and wise mothers—even in this day when its students no longer dreamed of marriage as the be-all and end-all of feminine happiness. But the rising aspirations of the students hadn't led to a corresponding improvement in the school's academic ranking, and that seemed unlikely to change as long as its curriculum remained so utterly undemanding compared to other places. Aoi had barely made it through junior high at the bottom of her class, but here her test scores were always well above average. Even if she were to rise to the very top of her class, she knew she'd have a tough time getting into any four-year university.

Most students here graduated without knowing what they wanted to do, except that they didn't want to work, so they enrolled in vocational schools or the local community college, where they hung out with the same old friends, perfecting their bitching skills but otherwise acquiring no useful knowledge before graduating from those schools as well and marrying local boys they'd met at campus mixers or around town. After living here barely more than a year, Aoi could already see the pattern plain as day. Her classmates all knew they would soon be treading the same predictable path the vast majority of prior graduates had traveled. With this fait accompli staring them in the face, an air of resignation settled heavily over the class early in the year. They had outgrown the childish bullying of the year before, but there was a kind of festering rage inside them that made them want to stand atop the heap and lord it over someone. Aoi could feel the pent-up frustrations building all around her.

Sitting on the riverbank and tossing stones into the flow, Aoi and Nanako talked endlessly about the corrosive air that had settled over their classmates as if the frustrations and the pecking order and the limited horizons they faced had nothing to do with themselves.

Then about the time midterms were over, Aoi's worst fears from the year before came true. All of a sudden, for no obvious reason, the entire junior class started giving Nanako the silent treatment, making fun of her and pouring scorn on her behind her back. The slurs couldn't help but reach Aoi's ears as well: She was a people-pleaser and a phony. Her father was a drunk in rehab, her mother was a bar hostess who turned tricks on the side, and her little sister was a JD repeatedly hauled in for shoplifting. The family of four lived in a two-room apartment in a housing complex built by the prefecture, and all they got for dinner was the wild greens Nanako picked along the roadside on her way home. That sort of thing. The utter childishness and the poverty of imagination displayed in these attacks astounded Aoi, but she couldn't deny feeling a surge of relief that she'd never shown herself to be friendly with Nanako at school. Although this was swiftly followed by pangs of guilt, she assuaged those pangs by reminding herself that she honestly knew nothing about Nanako's home life. She stood smugly by while her classmates heaped abuse on her closest friend, but what else could she do, really, when she lacked any knowledge to contradict what they were saying? She had no idea if Nanako had a sister, nor did she know anything about whether her father was in rehab or what her apartment was like, so how could she be expected to defend her?

Soon people were calling Nanako "DP," for dirt poor, but so far as Aoi could tell she remained completely unfazed by this or any of the other insults that came her way. On sunny days at the river and on rainy days under the bridge, in the evening over the straining phone cord and in the notes they surreptitiously passed back and forth, Nanako never seemed anything but her usual happy-go-lucky self. In fact, it was almost as if becoming the class pariah had set her free to rove around more than ever. At lunchtime, she disappeared somewhere off campus, and during other class breaks she would slip into the art room by herself and sit gazing out the window with her Walkman earbuds on.

When Aoi passed by and saw Nanako sitting like that, the words she had once spoken echoed in her head: *None of that stuff scares me. None of that stuff matters to me.* By all appearances, she had meant every word of it, and this aroused in Aoi a deep admiration for how comfortable Nanako was with herself—though she felt an inexplicable burst of annoyance as well.

Perhaps it was this annoyance that prompted her to demand a few days before summer vacation, "When're you going to let me come to your house?"

"You don't want to come to my place," Nanako replied with a snort. "There's nothing there you could possibly want to see."

But Aoi insisted. "You've been to my house lots of times. Once you even just followed me home. Why shouldn't I get to go to your place, too?" she argued

Giving her a weary look, Nanako finally relented. "All right. Fine," she said.

Whether from embarrassment or trepidation or resignation or anger, this was the first time Aoi could remember ever seeing a shadow flit across her friend's customary smile.

Aoi recalled the events of a month ago as she trudged up the street skirting the beach with grocery bags dangling from both hands. The sun had dipped about a third of the way behind a ridge to her right, and it cast an orange glow everywhere. Her beach sandals flip-flopped against the pavement as she hurried on, the cry of cicadas ringing through the air and the smell of barbecue wafting up from the beach. She gazed out across the surf. It was after hours, so no one was swimming, but she could see the sails of several windsurfers bouncing on the water farther out.

"Hey, babe, which guesthouse you working at?" a young man shouted up at her from the beach. Aoi glanced his way but pressed on without offering a response. "Wanna come watch our fireworks tonight?" the voice persisted behind her, but she kept right on going.

The day Aoi went to Nanako's house, refusing to take no for an answer, she had made a decision. No matter what her mother said, no matter even if she had to pay her way entirely by herself, she was going to go to college in Tokyo with Nanako, and she would do whatever it took to get there. They would study like crazy for the exams, starting as soon as they got back from summer vacation. Nanako's grades were poor even at their underachieving school, so she'd have to work double or triple hard for them to have any chance of getting into the same university. But if they had to, they would pour all their summer earnings into exam prep courses together. If worst came to worst, they might have to settle for different schools, but one way or another they were going to get away from home and rent an apartment together in Tokyo.

As she reaffirmed to herself this resolve from the beginning of summer, she recalled the story Ryoko had told them. Ryoko had

113

been their exact same age when she'd made her decision to leave home. She'd gone away all by herself, but Aoi and Nanako would have each other. They wouldn't have to depend on a guy like Ryoko did. Together they could make it work, just the two of them. She was sure of it. They had a whole year and a half to prepare.

"Aoi-i-ins!"

Aoi looked up. Nanako was standing in front of the inn holding Shinnosuke's hand and waving her arm over her head. Their bronzed faces and arms and legs as well as everything they had on glowed with the orange color of the setting sun.

"Welcome back!" Nanako called, jumping up and down. "Mr. Mano says he's taking us out for sushi tonight!" A multipart chorus of cicadas rose all around them.

Ryoko drove the girls to Imaihama Station in the car. Shinnosuke had grown quite attached to the girls in the course of the summer and burst into tears when they got out of the car. It made Aoi's eyes moisten, too.

"I hope you'll come again next year," Ryoko said, then briskly rolled up her window and drove off.

"That was abrupt," Aoi said as she gazed after the car.

They bought cans of juice at the station kiosk, got their tickets from the machine, and walked through the unattended gate onto the platform. The timetable revealed they had twenty minutes until the next train. Finding a bench, they sat quietly sipping their juice as they waited. A densely wooded hillside rose behind the opposite platform, and from it welled a cacophony of cicada voices charging the air with sound. The crowds of vacationers had dropped off sharply after the Bon festival in mid-August, and business at the inn had been very slow for the past week. Now the station was deserted except for the two of them, and when they turned toward the ocean they could see that the beach so recently jammed with people was quiet as well. The seasonal beach huts that offered food and changing rooms were being dismantled.

"Next week is school again already. I can hardly believe it," Aoi said, stretching her suntanned legs out in front of her.

Nanako sipped at her juice and said nothing.

Aoi peered at her. "We should come back next year for sure, don't you think?"

"Uh-huh," replied Nanako in a mere squeak of a voice, smiling weakly.

Wow, thought Aoi, *I guess she's feeling pretty emotional. Maybe she was hurt by the way Mrs. Mano drove off.*

To try to cheer her up, Aoi dug into her nylon bag for the pay envelope Ryoko had given them.

"I think I'm gonna sneak a peek right here," she said impishly. With an exaggerated flourish, she tore off one end of the envelope, blew a puff of air into it, and brought it up to her eye. "Hey, there's a letter of some kind."

On top of the small stack of bills lay a neatly folded piece of paper. She pulled it out and spread it open to find Mickey Mouse eyeing her from the corner of a page filled with writing that looked like the clumsy effort of a child. It was from Ryoko.

"Yikes, her writing's really messy! Well, let's see what I can make out. *Dear Aoi Narahashi and Nanako Noguchi.* I guess she couldn't remember our kanji—she spelled our names out. *It was only a short few weeks, but thank you for all your help. We really enjoyed having you with us this summer.* That's nice. *As you know, this is only the second year since we opened the inn. What you don't know is that the help we hired last summer ran off with the receipts.* No way! Is she serious? *Basically we were naive, and we did some pretty dumb things. It being our first year, we really didn't know what we were doing. Anyway, there was this big to-do, and the whole thing got straightened out in the end, but it was a pretty upsetting experience. I lost my confidence and didn't know if I could go on with the inn or ever trust strangers again. My husband and his mother weren't big on the idea to begin with, so I got to feeling pretty unsure of myself. That's why this year I decided to find some simple country girls.* She adds 'Sorry!' in parentheses and then says, *Even so, I'm ashamed to say I didn't trust you two at first.*"

Aoi glanced sideways at Nanako. She sat with her head bent and seemed to be listening, so Aoi read on.

"*But now I'm just so grateful I found you two girls. You did a wonderful job. You were a hundred times, a thousand times more wonderful than you can ever imagine. I can't tell you how big a help you were to me. I can't tell you how much you helped me get my confidence back. I'm writing this letter because I wanted you to know that. Thank you so, so much. Please come back next summer. Or even this winter. Even if only for a visit and not to work. We'll all be looking forward to seeing you again. Ryoko.*"

That was the end, but Aoi continued staring at the page filled with awkward, schoolboyish writing for several more moments. She was replaying in her mind how Ryoko had said *I hope you'll come again next year* and driven abruptly away, her eyes averted. And how Shinnosuke had been bawling his head off in the seat next to her.

Quickly, she slipped Ryoko's letter back into the envelope and stuffed it deep inside her nylon bag. "The train should be coming any minute now," she said, standing up. Nanako remained seated with bent head. "Are you done with your juice? I'll go throw the cans away."

Deep within the sound of the insects Aoi recognized the clear, piercing pulse of the green cicada. The trees on the hillside were still just as vibrantly green as when she and Nanako had first arrived at the beginning of summer, but that particular voice seemed to announce the approach of autumn.

A faint rumble rose in the distance and gradually grew nearer. Soon a string of white railway cars came into view at the end of the tracks that stretched straight from the station. Standing at the edge of the platform, Aoi turned to her friend still sitting on the bench.

"Come on, Nanako. The train's here."

Nanako didn't move. The train clattered to a stop and its doors slid open. Aoi stepped inside. The passengers getting off were all obviously local people, not tourists. A middle-aged woman with a shopping basket. A grade schooler with a summer academy bag slung across his chest. Ordinary folks from nearby—like those they'd seen on the train when they left home on the day they first came.

"Come on, Nanako! The next train's not for a whole hour! Hurry up and get on!"

Aoi leaned through the open doorway and shouted, but Nanako remained as she was, not even looking up.

The conductor's whistle pierced the air, and Aoi hastily hopped back onto the narrow platform. The doors slid shut and the train slowly pulled out, leaving the two of them behind. The people who'd alighted dropped their tickets in the box at the gate and scattered in their various directions.

"What's wrong, Nanako?" Aoi stepped toward the bench in growing alarm at her friend's unusual behavior. "Are you feeling sick? Did you forget something? Was there something you wanted to tell Mrs. Mano?"

Squatting in front of her like a mother before a small child, Aoi asked as gently as she could. Nanako just stared into her lap.

"Aokins?" she finally said as if it had taken every ounce of her willpower to squeeze it out.

"Yeah? What is it? You can tell me," Aoi urged, putting her hands on Nanako's knees.

Nanako raised her head and their eyes met. "I don't want to go home," she said.

"Well, duhhh, I don't want to go home either," Aoi retorted, starting to laugh, but Nanako cut her short.

"No, I don't mean it that way. I *really* don't want to go home. I don't. I don't. I don't." A huge tear fell from her big, round eyes. She took Aoi's hands and squeezed them hard. "I don't want to go home. I don't. I don't. I really, really don't want to go home," she repeated.

Aoi sat on her haunches in bewilderment, her hands still in Nanako's grip. She no longer recognized the girl sitting on the bench in front of her. *Who is this person? Why am I here? Why is she clinging to my hands like this?* Baffling questions chased each other through her mind. She couldn't help thinking that her real self must actually be sitting on the train right now with the real Nanako, counting out the bills in their pay envelope.

The tears overflowing Nanako's eyes came rapidly now, creating damp stains on her knee-length shorts. Aoi watched as lopsided circles appeared one after another on the beige fabric. Her own hands were turning white in Nanako's fierce grip. Lifting her eyes, she peered under her friend's bowed head. The heavy shadow across Nanako's stricken face gave Aoi the sensation of peering into a deep, dark void. Into a black emptiness that offered no clue as to what might be hidden in its depths.

With a kind of shock, Aoi realized that she didn't know the first thing about Nanako. Ever since visiting her apartment that day, she'd had it in her head that she knew her friend through and through. Or at least she'd been telling herself that the Nanako she saw in front of her was one and the same as the real Nanako.

Always smiling. Gregarious as a middle-aged woman. Accentuating the positive. Talking about what she liked rather than what she hated. Claiming to be unbothered if people snubbed her. Forgiving Aoi for keeping away from her at school. Thoughtfully suggesting they meet three stations down the line. Hanging out with her day after day, talking about everything under the sun. This was the Nanako Aoi knew. But perhaps none of these represented the real

Nanako. Perhaps the real Nanako was somewhere deep inside that mysterious void she had just now glimpsed.

The shrill of the cicadas fell back for a moment as a breath of salty air brushed Aoi's face. Behind Nanako, the sea stretched out to the horizon, glinting like a sheet of glass in the sunlight.

Aoi dropped her eyes to the tearstains on Nanako's shorts. "All right, let's not go home," she said.

Somewhere in the distance she could hear green cicadas adding their voices to the chorus.

7

Lime scale and mold clung tenaciously to the plastic bath stool and refused to come clean no matter how hard Sayoko scrubbed. She wished she could try the mold and mildew cleaner she'd found under the sink, but that was forbidden; she was to use only the supplies included in her own cleaning kit.

The kitchen had looked no less horrendous when she'd poked her head in earlier. The grease-caked range top was thick with dust and hair. Dealing with the mess in there was Misao's job, and she was getting a helping hand from Noriko.

Sayoko decided to let the stool and its matching plastic washbowl soak a while longer in the warm water in the tub while she cleaned out the drain in the floor of the splash area. When she lifted the drain cover she found the opening below almost completely clogged with a mass of hair and slime. She set to scraping the gunk out with a chopstick.

Noriko's training for Sayoko and the Platinum Planet staff was slated to end in only a few more days. Shortly after the beginning of August, they'd graduated from vacant apartments to occupied units. Noriko determined in advance how many cleaners were needed, and sometimes Sayoko went alone, other times Misao or Mao or both went along with her. Either Noriko herself or someone else from her company supervised.

Today's client was an ordinary housewife who lived in a relatively new condominium. An affable, mild-mannered woman who looked about Sayoko's age, she was the sort of person Sayoko might run into in the hallways of her own building. She'd asked them to clean her kitchen and bathroom.

When as usual they had followed Noriko into the apartment, Sayoko and Misao were stunned by the contrast between the impeccable appearance of the woman herself and the abominable state of the rooms she had hired them to clean. Wearing a crisply starched blouse over a flower pattern skirt, she was the very picture of careful grooming, but her kitchen was a hellhole of garbage, grease, and food scraps, the washing area next to the bathtub was overrun by mold and mildew, and the toilet bowl was surrounded by thick layers of dust on the floor and practically black inside. Sayoko cast a surreptitious glance at Misao, who almost imperceptibly raised an eyebrow in return.

After going over with Sayoko what needed to be done in the bathroom, Noriko went to tackle the kitchen with Misao. As they set to work, the client warmly thanked them for coming and settled down in the living room with her little girl to watch a video. The child could not be far from Akari's age. They'd been parked in front of the TV ever since.

Sayoko wondered if the woman didn't ever worry. She and her daughter apparently spent their days cooped up inside watching videos, but wasn't she concerned about the effect an endless diet of such fare might have on her daughter's emotional growth? And how, exactly, had she managed to let things get this bad around the house without it bothering her? Didn't she know molds could be toxic? Had she ever considered that her precious little girl might touch something moldy while being given a bath and promptly put her fingers in her mouth?

Sayoko drew a thick, stringy clump of hairs from deep inside the drain. She flinched at the foul stench and quickly disposed of the glob in her waste bag before sprinkling their special cleanser over the opening. Lathering up her scouring pad, she got on hands and knees and attacked the pink mold growing on the floor tiles. A bead of sweat rolled from her forehead to her temple and on down to the tip of her chin, where it paused for a second or two before falling to the floor.

Noriko turned to glare sternly at Sayoko the moment she and Misao settled into the back seat of the van. "Now listen, Mrs. Tamura," she said, "I know you're a homemaker, too, and I can understand how disgusted you were by what you saw today. You might well wonder why a woman who spends the whole day at home can't pick up a cleaning rag now and then. But you can't let that show on your face. And another thing. Both of you. I don't ever want to catch you swapping looks like that again. You may think no one could possibly notice, but people can sense that kind of thing."

Only moments before, she'd been taking leave of their client with the warmest of smiles, but now her tongue was prickly with irritation.

She started the engine and put the van in gear.

Sitting beside Sayoko with bowed head, Misao peeked at her from the corner of her eye and stuck out the tip of her tongue as if to say *Oops*.

"But I—" Sayoko started to reply, only to be cut off.

"And don't try to tell me otherwise. Our clients are sensitive to things like that—especially the women. They're letting strangers come into their homes to handle their personal stuff, which isn't something you can do without a sense of trust, but no matter how hard you've worked to earn that trust, you show a condescending attitude just one time and it's all over. We're hired help, in case you didn't know. We're in no position to be judgmental about how our employers measure up as housewives or women. Got that? What do you say?"

"Yes, ma'am," Sayoko said sullenly, her voice barely audible. Misao echoed her in a somber tone.

The van made its way out of the underground parking garage,

circling the spiral ramp toward street level. The bright midafternoon sky gradually came into view.

"I have no complaints about your work, Mrs. Tamura. You learn quickly, and you're very conscientious. I can turn you loose on any task and know you'll do an excellent job. But you have to understand that there's a big difference between a vacant home and one with an occupant. How many times do I have to say that before it sinks in? If you two had been there alone today, my company would have lost a client for good, no question about it. And maybe not just one client either, in the end. What do you think happens when she spreads the word to everybody she knows? Word of mouth is everything in this business. You've been asking me about other add-on services, but what's the point of offering extras if you can't even handle basic client relations properly? Do you see what I'm saying?"

Sayoko listened to this prolonged lecture without lifting her head, trying to rub the wrinkles from her fingertips as she fidgeted with her hands.

Noriko dropped Sayoko and Misao off at the nearest station, and they took the train back to the office.

"Is that woman psychic or something?" Misao said. "I mean, we barely looked at each other. How could she have seen us? I say just shrug it off, Chief." To judge from her breezy tone, that's what she'd already done herself.

In recent weeks, Sayoko's colleagues had taken to calling her "Chief." Aoi had apparently told everybody that Sayoko was in charge of the housekeeping venture and they were expected to follow her orders.

The sun beat down on the sea of roofs stretching out beneath the elevated train. Sayoko let out a long sigh as she leaned against the door and watched the houses flowing by.

Mao Hasegawa and Yuki Yamaguchi looked up from the dining table when Sayoko and Misao came in.

"Boy, am I pooped. Today rates a sweet-tooth five for sure," Misao declared loudly. "That kitchen—you really had to see it to believe it."

"Welcome back," Mao said. "If it was a sweet-toother, we've got just what you need. Mr. Sayama from Lucky Productions was here a little bit ago, and he brought us a box of cakes. Let me quick make some tea."

"Cakes? Oh, goody! That's exactly what I need!"

"And you're not going to believe it, Misao! They're from à tes souhaits! Mr. Sayama's such a sweetheart."

"No! For real? I've been wanting to try their cakes ever since they opened!"

Misao took the first empty chair at the table. Sayoko sat in the next and promptly got out her notebook.

"Save that for later, Chief. Let's give our aching bones a rest first. Though I suppose for you today was more like a hot-and-spicy five than a sweet-toother." Misao looked at the others. "Mrs. Nakazato was in a really foul mood today. She practically bit her head off." She turned back to Sayoko. "Right?"

Sayoko smiled vaguely. She had learned over the past few weeks that "sweet-tooth something" and "hot-and-spicy something" were a kind of lighthearted code the girls here used to rate what kind of day they'd had. The basic idea seemed to be that when you got saddled with unreasonable demands or something made you mad, you wanted to burn the bad taste away by eating something good and spicy, while if you were dog tired from a particularly grueling day, you just wanted to collapse and pig out on something sweet. The scale went from one to five in each category.

Pushing her notebook aside, Sayoko took a bite from the cake Mao placed in front of her. Misao leaned forward in her chair and began offering Mao and Yuki a laundry list of the dirt she'd done battle with that day.

After a minute or two, Aoi emerged from the "President's Office" and pulled up a chair to join them at the table.

"Why the long face, Chief?" Even Aoi had taken to addressing Sayoko that way.

"I kind of got chewed out," she said, her shoulders drooping.

"Chewed out? For what?"

"I guess I'm an open book."

"Actually," Misao broke in, her mouth full of cake, "I think Mrs. Nakazato was just in one of her moods today. She really cut loose on Chief."

"It's not so much I was disgusted, like she said, but amazed. I mean, here was a woman my own age with a child close to my daughter's living in a condo almost exactly like mine, and I couldn't help asking myself what it took, what she had to do, for everything to get so incredibly cruddy. Plus I figured no matter how well we cleaned the place up, things were probably gonna be right back where they were in a matter of days."

"But when it comes down to it, without people like that, we'll never get our new business off the ground," Aoi said. "I don't know what Noriko actually said, but if, for instance, you made some wise-crack about how nasty the place was the minute the door closed behind you, I'd be worried something like that might get back to the customer."

"But it would've been the absolute truth," Misao insisted.

Aoi tilted her head and looked off into space. "'There's only one way to win the hearts of your audience,'" she intoned, deepening her voice for effect. "'Always face them with sincerity and humility.'"

Mao burst out laughing. "What in the world is that?"

"Haven't you ever heard it? It's a quote from Frank Sinatra. 'There's only one way to win the hearts of your audience. Always face them with sincerity and humility.' Something like that, anyway."

"I think that'll come naturally once the training's over and we're doing jobs on our own," Yuki said lightly. "I mean, after all, that's what we'll be getting paid for."

"I'm more worried about whether anybody'll want to hire us at all," said Misao. "I mean, like, our training's almost over, but we don't even have a car, and we might as well be completely unknown. If it were me, I wouldn't hire us."

"That seems a bit harsh," Aoi frowned.

"What's to worry?" Mao said. "All we have to do is keep doing what we've always done and be patient, and eventually—"

"In my building," Sayoko interrupted, shifting forward in her seat, "we often get fliers for handyman services and maid services and stuff, so I asked some of the other moms at my daughter's school if they'd save the fliers they got and bring them to me—to see what I could find out. Well, you mention a car, but actually, it turns out some people don't want their neighbors to know they've hired a housekeeping service to come in, so I'm thinking we can actually offer it as a selling point that we don't drive up in a vehicle with our logo plastered all over the side, and that our smaller crews let us come and go discreetly. We can also tout how the same person will be in charge from the initial estimate to completion of the job itself, making sure everything is done to their satisfaction."

Asking the mothers she met at Akari's school to bring her the fliers they got for housekeeping services had demanded courage, but several women quickly took an interest and returned several days later with whole sheaves of papers. The exercise had had the side benefit of putting her on easy speaking terms with quite a few more women than before, she reflected.

"Wow! You've really been thinking about this," Misao said, gazing at her with admiration.

"Along those same lines," Aoi nodded, "for a while now I've been playing with ideas for a web ad, and the question that keeps popping up is product differentiation—how do we distinguish ourselves from everybody else? Like maybe at first we could have a limited-time offer to clean air conditioners or window screens for free."

"Actually, a lot of places offer those services," Sayoko said. "Of course, they're usually optional extras rather than freebies, but the prices are low and they're pretty common. So another angle might be to take care of certain other odd jobs for free. Obviously there're things we can and cannot do, so we'd have to be clear about exactly what, but for example, washing the dishes, or taking laundry to the cleaner's, or picking it up, and maybe cleaning inside the refrigerator or bundling newspapers and magazines for recycling, that sort of thing."

"I wish someone would clean the refrigerator here," Mao quipped, and everybody laughed.

"I'd forgotten about this, but a friend of mine once told me about when she tried a housekeeping service," Yuki put in softly. "She said the person who took her order on the phone and the person who came for the estimate and the person who was actually in charge of the job were all different people, so it was kind of a hassle having to explain what she wanted all over again every time. Having the same person in charge from start to finish like Chief said might be a big plus."

"Maybe our sales pitch should include that real housewives will handle the cleaning," Misao suggested.

"Except only two of us actually fit that bill—Sayoko and Yuki."

"And I may technically qualify because I'm married," the latter noted, "but I don't have any kids, and I don't take care of my house, so . . ."

"I'm not so sure 'real housewives' makes much of a selling point," Aoi said, wrinkling her brow. She lit up a cigarette and exhaled. "Going back kind of to what we were saying before, wouldn't a lot of women be afraid of what another housewife might think about the way they take care of their homes?"

"But there are certain kinds of things only an experienced home-maker is likely to notice," Sayoko countered. "I was thinking about it today. Whether it's the mold on the tiles in the bath, or the air from a dirty air conditioner filter, or tatami and upholstery that get dank from never seeing the sun, there're lots of things around the house that can be harmful to small children. Pointing out the dangers and urging a thorough cleaning would carry more weight if it came from a mother who's dealt with those same concerns in her own home."

"Basically, we first have to figure out exactly how we want to target ourselves," Aoi said. "Noriko's idea is that we should go after singles and sole proprietorships and position ourselves as the low-cost service. And my focus all along has been young people who travel a lot, not the average family with kids. Of course, narrowing it down too much right from the start probably isn't such a good idea, either."

"Then let me ask you this," Sayoko said. "What would *you* look for in a housekeeping service if you decided to use one? What would be most important to you?"

Aoi looked off into space again as she pondered for a moment. "I suppose maybe that they won't be shocked," she replied with a lit-tle snicker. "I mean, when my place gets bad, it's really pretty gross, so, ironically, no matter how much I might want to ask someone to come in, I can't bring myself to do it, because I can't stand the thought of anyone seeing just how far I've let things go. So maybe if someone promised, 'Nothing can shock us! We'll clean up any mess!'—maybe then I'd pick up the phone. But I don't suppose I'm very typical. How about you, Chief? As a mother with a small child at home, what would you look for in a housekeeping service?"

"Well, affordability would be at the top of my list. And after that, I really do think I'd prefer someone who's been in my shoes. I've never hired anyone—we could never afford it—but there were times, back when Akari was smaller, I really would have appreciated some help. Even now, I'd love it if someone could come in just to give the kitchen or the bathroom a quick once-over in the time I'm picking my daughter up at school or taking her in for a checkup. Also, when Akari was really little, there wasn't a day went by that I didn't fret over whether I was doing the right thing with her, so, for example, if I'd had a housekeeper with experience raising kids who could lend me her ear between tasks, I think it might have taken a huge load off my mind. And not necessarily for someone to talk to, even. Just to know this helper was raising kids of her own—that in itself would have been reassuring. Because I really thought the crying in the middle of the night would never end when Akari was a baby. Just like I thought her terrible twos would never end." She paused for a moment, then added, "Though maybe this is just me. I'm not sure I can be considered typical, either."

Sayoko noticed that she had everybody's complete attention, and a gentle wave of exhilaration ran through her as she spoke. She wished she could go on forever. All these years, a vague sense of guilt had been weighing her down—for quitting her job, for turning herself into a homebody, for thinking it such a bother to take Akari to the park, for rejoicing when it rained, for putting her daughter in school in spite of all the voices saying it was cruel—and she'd been in a mild state of depression. But now she could feel that it hadn't been for nothing. It had all been leading somewhere.

Yuki looked up at the clock on the wall. "Uh-oh, Chief. It's after four."

It was easy for Sayoko to lose track of time when their conversations turned to what came next after the training period was over, but everyone knew her circumstances well and she could always count on someone to remind her. Each time it happened, it made her feel like she truly belonged.

"Sorry to have to rush off," she said, getting to her feet.

"See you tomorrow," the women smiled.

Stepping into her shoes, Sayoko glanced back toward the table as she put her hand on the doorknob. The others were carrying on their cheerful chatter amidst swirling clouds of smoke. Closing the door behind her, Sayoko raced down the stairs and emerged under a pale blue sky.

Coming out of the station, Sayoko retrieved her bicycle from the bike lot and pushed it across the intersection before hopping on. Taking the main roads, Akari's school was a seven- or eight-minute ride away, but she could shave about two minutes off her time by pedaling up the avenue of ginkgo trees, turning left at the tofu shop, and cutting through some residential back streets. It was after five now, but the sun still beat down as if it were the middle of the afternoon, and by the time she reached the tofu shop Sayoko felt her blouse sticking to her back. With each turn of the pedals she repeated mentally, *Damn it all! Damn it all!* She wasn't actually angry at anything, nor trying to curse anybody, but she'd lately been chanting this phrase to herself whenever she rode her bike. Somehow even the short seven- or eight-minute trip always felt like it took forever, like barely crawling along in stop-and-go traffic on the expressway. Saying *Damn it all!* helped her push harder on the pedals and let her think she was getting through the exasperating slowness of it at least a moment or two sooner.

Other mothers who'd come for their kids stood outside the gate in twos and threes waiting for it to be opened. A group of women she often ran into at pickup time waved to Sayoko and greeted her as she got off her bike.

"How're things coming with the housekeeping business?"

"I feel like hiring you myself. Maybe I'll dip into the secret stash I've got squirreled away."

"You have a secret stash?"

"Couldn't get by without it."

Chiemi's mother was in home health, Ren's mother worked for

a life insurance company, and Takuya's mother was a freelance translator. Sayoko returned the greetings with a smile, wondering if these women, too, spurred themselves on with quiet shouts of *Damn it all!* as they pedaled their way here.

When the gate was opened, Sayoko made straight for Akari's classroom. She peered through the window from the hallway and found her daughter sitting by herself again, playing with two stuffed toys. Every so often she would raise her head to look around the room. When she finally caught sight of Sayoko at the door, she dropped the toys and came running to meet her.

"Guess what, Mommy," she said softly after throwing herself into her mother's arms. "Today I watched you all day, too. So I didn't cry." Then suddenly she sounded on the brink of tears as she repeated, "I really didn't cry, Mommy."

It occurred to Sayoko as she hugged her daughter tight that she herself had been the one crying hardest on their way to nursery school each morning—not Akari. Maybe Grandma Tamura was right: maybe it really was cruel to put a child Akari's age in school; maybe it really was a mistake for her to go back to work. She'd still been tearing herself to pieces over the decision she'd made. Inside, she'd been the one crying the hardest.

"I'm so proud of you, honey. Thinking about you kept Mommy strong all day long, too."

"Owww! You're hurting me!" Akari wriggled free of Sayoko's embrace with a giggle. Her bright voice filled the hallway.

"See you tomorrow, Akari's Mom!"

Several departing mothers shouted good-byes as they went out the door with their kids. Sayoko offered a hearty wave in return.

It gave Sayoko a decidedly odd sensation to see Aoi working on her laptop at her own dining table. With her eyes pinned to the screen, Aoi pulled a pack of cigarettes from the pocket of her jeans and put one in her mouth, then realized what she was doing and started putting it back.

"That's okay. I don't mind," Sayoko said from the floor by the coffee table, where she was roughing out some ideas for a flier.

With an embarrassed look, Aoi got to her feet and went to stand under the vent in the kitchen. Beyond the buffet divider, Sayoko heard the fan start up. In the tatami room, Akari looked up uncertainly from a picture book spread on the floor, and Sayoko gave her a reassuring smile.

"Mommy, come see," she said, beckoning to her, and immediately began pointing at pictures in the book. "This is a chimpanzee. And here's a giraffe."

Besides putting an ad on the web, Sayoko had suggested they make up a flier to pass out like the ones she'd collected from other operators. The jobs weren't suddenly going to start rolling in the minute they finished training, so in the meantime she could make the rounds of neighborhoods and apartment buildings stuffing mailboxes. Everybody agreed it had to be good for something.

Aoi had arrived at Sayoko's apartment a few minutes past ten, computer case in hand. Not accustomed to strange visitors, Akari fussed and cried for much of the morning, and even after she settled down she continued to interrupt their work by coming up to see what Aoi was doing and then running away, or by wanting Sayoko's attention for something. After lunch she finally started keeping quietly to herself, playing with her dolls or flipping through picture books—though she still eyed Aoi curiously from time to time.

Aoi emerged from the kitchen, and Sayoko handed her the drafts she'd sketched out in pencil. They spent some time going over them together, referring now and then to what other companies had done in the fliers scattered on the floor and making a number of adjustments in the wording and the placement of graphics. When they were satisfied, Aoi began laying out the actual flier on her computer.

Sayoko looked up at the clock on the wall. At his mother's house, Shuji would no doubt be taking a little snooze right about now. Or maybe the two of them were busy trashing Sayoko for refusing to celebrate Grandma's birthday with them. *Well, what do I care?* she shrugged to herself, and suddenly realized how good that felt.

To tell the truth, there'd been no real need for Sayoko to work today. It was Aoi who had come up with the pretext for her, suggesting that the two of them could put together the flier they'd talked about. She'd even offered to come to Sayoko's home to do it, so she wouldn't have to take Akari all the way to the office with her, and Sayoko had gratefully accepted.

It had all started the previous morning when Shuji said out of the blue, "Be sure to get something for tomorrow on your way home."

Sayoko had no idea what he was talking about. "What's tomorrow?"

"My mom's birthday. We do it every year. Why's it so hard for you to remember?" he said as if he regarded it as a serious failing on her part.

True enough, they had observed his mother's birthday each year by visiting her in Iogi on the nearest Saturday, and each year Sayoko had dutifully shopped for a present to take when her husband prompted. She never questioned it. But now she wondered why she had simply done as she was told all those years. Her own parents lived not all that far away in Chiba, and yet never once had Shuji gone to celebrate their birthdays with her, let alone bought them a gift.

Sayoko thought back to Grandma Tamura's previous birthdays. Shuji did nothing but loll about on the sofa all day, while his mother left the shopping and cooking and cleanup to Sayoko without lifting a finger to help. Then if Akari pestered Sayoko for attention when she had her hands full in the kitchen, Grandma blamed her for spoiling the girl and neglecting to teach her manners. "I brought up my two boys under strict discipline, I'll have you know," she would declare, with an endless string of self-serving boasts and admonitions and gibes to follow. Last year Sayoko had picked out a summer scarf made of silk, and her mother-in-law barely glanced at it, declaring she didn't even realize they sold scarves during the heat of summer and setting it aside without so much as taking it out of the box. Noticing Sayoko's sullen silence on their way home, Shuji tried to cheer her up. It was just his mother's way, she shouldn't take it personally, he told her; she wasn't very good at showing her gratitude or joy. Recalling it all now, it was a profound mystery to Sayoko how she could have thought at the time that she was lucky to have such an understanding husband.

Sayoko had related all this to Aoi as she sat writing up her work report at the end of the day on Friday.

"In that case," Aoi had responded with a mischievous smile, "maybe I should tell you you have to work tomorrow. I can insist I need you to help me with that flier you said we should make."

Late that night when Shuji came home, it gave her a positive thrill to be able to say that Aoi had asked her to work tomorrow and she couldn't turn her down.

"Like there's some kind of cleaning that only you can do?" he'd retorted.

She ignored his sarcasm. "It's your own fault for scheduling the party without asking me. And besides, it's *your* mother's birthday, not mine."

As she heard herself saying this, she had to stop herself from chortling aloud. She remembered what she'd learned the night of her welcome party: keep something bottled up inside you and you just feel worse and worse, but put it into words and it turns into something you can laugh about.

Akari had become bored with her picture books and was getting cranky again; digesting her lunch had apparently made her ready for a nap. Sayoko went into the tatami room to pick her up and began gently patting her on the back. The low click of Aoi's computer keys was the only sound in the room. Beyond the sliding glass doors to the balcony, the sky rose high and clear. When Akari's breathing settled into a regular rhythm, Sayoko laid her gently down on the tatami and got a terrycloth blanket from the closet to cover her with.

"Could you come take a look, Chief?" Aoi whispered so as not to waken Akari. "Tell me what you think."

Sayoko tiptoed to the table and looked over Aoi's shoulder at the page she had on screen. "Housekeeping Service" it read in large bold letters, and Aoi had inserted their own marketing phrases into a design based on elements from some of the other fliers they'd looked at.

"This one's for housewives," she said, then scrolled down and added, "and this one's targeted at singles."

"Yeah, they look great," Sayoko said. "You're amazing. How did you learn to draw like that on the computer?"

"This is just clip art that I pasted in. If they look okay to you, I think you said you had a printer, right?"

"Yep. Just a sec." Stepping carefully over her sleeping daughter, Sayoko got the printer from where they kept it in the far corner of the tatami room and carried it to the table. Aoi connected the cable to her computer, plugged in the power cord, and switched the printer on, then clicked the "Print" button on screen. The machine clattered noisily to life. They both stiffened and looked toward Akari. She didn't stir, and they exchanged relieved smiles.

Sitting side by side at the table, they went over the printouts and discussed ways to improve them. After experimenting with different fonts and colors and editing a phrase here or there, they printed out fresh copies to examine again, going through this process several times.

"I wanted to thank you," Sayoko said as she watched the printer puffing away, pushing out the latest version of the fliers. "For rescuing me from what I know would've been a very dreary Saturday."

"No, no, I should be thanking you. If we finalize these today, I can take them to the printer's first thing Monday. And I even got lunch out of the deal. If you find yourself in a similar predicament again, just let me know. I'll be happy to call you in on the weekend. There's always piles of little stuff needing to be done."

Sayoko went into the kitchen and opened the refrigerator. She'd come for iced tea, but some beer she had on hand for Shuji caught her eye, and she thought that might be more to Aoi's liking.

"Woo-hoo! Tea with a head!" Aoi clapped when Sayoko brought a tall can of beer and two small glasses to the table.

Taking a sip from the glass Sayoko poured for her, Aoi tilted her head to one side and surveyed the room.

"You're really quite the supermom, aren't you, Chief?"

"What do you mean by that?"

"Laundry fluttering on the balcony, chilled glasses for beer, getting Akari to go down just like that. It's hard to believe you and I are the same age."

"Oh please. Anybody can do those things. There's no way I could do what you do—calling halfway around the world to charter buses and putting together big fancy tour packages."

"But you're holding down a job, too. You work outside the home and still manage to keep a neat house. My hat's off to you as a woman. Not a dirty dish in the sink, no empty noodle cups on the counter."

"Well, I may have a job, but I never have to do overtime, and it's not brain work. I don't have to push hard all the time the way you do."

"Oh, stop it," said Aoi, slapping her on the back. "We sound like old ladies in a mutual admiration society."

Sayoko poured some beer into her own glass and took a sip. It was cool and refreshing.

A question popped into her head that she'd never thought to ask

Aoi before. "Can I ask you something?" she said. "Are you one of those people who don't believe in marriage?"

"I wouldn't say that. I just don't happen to have anybody at the moment is all. Actually, I was dating a guy last year, but he dumped me when we went on a trip together." Aoi topped off her glass and took another sip before continuing. "You know what he said when he dumped me? He said I was too cheap, everywhere we went. He'd been acting like the last of the big spenders, going around dropping exorbitant tips on everybody we ran into. He claimed his guidebook said that's what you're supposed to do. We eat at a tiny hole-in-the-wall that's not much more than a street stall and he leaves a huge tip. At the hotel he tips people who never even touch our bags, just for answering a question. It was when he started to tip a cabbie even after he'd blatantly overcharged us that I finally said something. I mean, for heaven's sake, we weren't asking the concierge to find tickets to the sold-out opera at the Met or anything. And what do I get for opening my big fat mouth? I get called a skinflint."

Aoi burst out laughing. Not quite sure whether she should join in, Sayoko sat moving her head up and down in tiny nods.

"Some people and their guidebooks. Sheesh!" she went on, her tone taking on a new edge. "Have you ever been on a group tour? They give you these little pamphlets filled with lists of dos and don'ts—how much tip to leave in this or that place, what kind of shops to avoid, that sort of thing. I heard about a tour to Southeast Asia recently where they handed out pamphlets saying don't eat at street stalls, don't drink iced drinks, don't eat uncooked vegetables, and so on—down to the tiniest detail. Well, come free time, some of the people decided to try the fare at a street stall anyway, and they all got sick, every one of them. Of course, you're going to figure the place had a sanitation problem. But I actually think it was the power of suggestion. Seems like people take off their thinking caps when you give them a manual to follow. And when they stop thinking, they stop seeing things, and stop experiencing things in any sort of way that's going to stick in their minds. I mean, something like tips, you're not even gonna remember who you gave them to, let alone how much. But the experiences that make you want to say 'Thank you, thank you, thank you' from the bottom of your heart—those you're not going to forget."

Aoi was in full rant mode now. Sayoko gazed out the glass doors at the laundry fluttering in the breeze on the balcony as she listened.

"The way I see it, you can divide travel basically into two kinds depending on whether your objective is *seeing* or *doing*. Are you touring to visit ruins and museums and such in the area, or to take part in something going on there, like a festival? But the basic premise in either case has to be that you're looking for fresh encounters. Without that, what's the point of going anywhere? Every country's different. All that happy talk you hear about understanding one another and people everywhere being basically the same, it's all a bunch of crap. Everybody's different. And if you don't realize that, you're never going to experience anything truly new. Pamphlets and guidebooks can tell you 'Do this' or 'Do that,' and they can explain local customs for you, but beyond that, I think they actually get in the way of letting you connect with something different from yourself."

Aoi fell silent. She blinked her eyes as if she was surprised at herself and looked at Sayoko.

"Sorry, I didn't mean to go spouting off like that," she said sheepishly. "I guess I do it a lot. Takeshi and the others are always teasing me about it." She reached for the newest printouts of the fliers, which had long since finished printing.

To Sayoko, listening to Aoi hold forth was a bit like listening to a salesman going on at length about the features of some newfangled washing machine. About all she really understood was how different the two of them were. What they saw when they looked at the world around them, what they yearned for, even what they ultimately sought in life—everything about them was different. But to take what Aoi had just said, it was precisely those differences that made it so satisfying to be sitting here talking like this.

She noticed Aoi's glass was empty and was about to see if there was another can she could open, when she heard a key turning in the front door. Startled, she hurried into the hall instead and found Shuji coming inside.

"What're you doing here?" she blurted out.

"What about you?" he said, no less surprised. "I thought you had to work."

"We're working here."

"Here? Doing what?" Shuji said, then added, "Who's 'we'?" He slipped by Sayoko and opened the door to the living-dining room. Sayoko shuffled quickly after him.

"This is Miss Narahashi, my boss. Sorry about the mess. I didn't expect you home so soon."

"It's good to finally meet you," Aoi said warmly. "I want you to know what a tremendous asset your wife has been to us at Platinum Planet. This is what we've been working on today—fliers for the new venture that she's heading up for us. We'll be launching it in earnest the first of the month." She was meeting this man for the first time, yet spoke with poise and an easy familiarity, turning their latest printouts around for him to see.

"Ahh, yes, my pleasure." Shuji was the one who seemed more flustered as he gave only a curt response, then abruptly pushed past Sayoko in the doorway and turned down the hall toward their bedroom. A whimper came from the tatami room: the commotion had apparently awakened Akari.

"Since your husband's home, I suppose I'd better be going." Aoi got to her feet. "I'll just straighten things up a little." She gathered their numerous printouts into a single pile and shut down her computer.

"I have no idea why he's home so early," Sayoko said, "but there's really no need for you to rush off. Please feel free to stay."

"We were basically finished anyway. I'll take this final version to the printer's first thing Monday morning." Akari was crying harder. "There you go, Chief. Sounds like somebody needs you."

As the pitch of Akari's cries rose higher and higher, Sayoko went to pick her up. When she came back, she again urged her boss to stay, but Aoi quickly packed her computer up and took the empty beer can and glasses to the kitchen sink.

Carrying Akari in her arms, Sayoko rode the elevator down with Aoi and saw her to the steps in front of the building.

"We really should do that hot springs thing sometime, don't you think?" Aoi said after the automatic door had closed behind them.

"Yes, we should," Sayoko nodded, sounding wistful.

Aoi hurried off at a trot under the beating sun. After going a short distance she turned to wave her arm over her head. Akari was still crying in fits and starts, but Sayoko lifted the girl's hand and waved it for her, telling her to say "Bye-bye."

"Thank you!" she yelled.

Trees flanked the entrance to the building and continued on down the street, casting deep shadows on the glaring pavement. Aoi's white blouse moved in and out of the shadows as she hurried into the distance. Sayoko stood gazing after her until she could no longer see the flicker of sunlight on the fabric.

Back upstairs, Sayoko found Shuji on the sofa flipping through a magazine.

"What was that?" he snorted. "Your student activity group?"

Sayoko walked past him without a word and set Akari down in the tatami room. The child was still sniffling, having missed several chances to let her tears dry.

"It's not like you're making posters for the campus festival," he added.

"I wasn't expecting you back so early. How's your mother?"

Akari clung to Sayoko's back as she knelt to gather up the picture books scattered on the floor.

"What's the point of going by myself?"

Sayoko was taken aback. "You didn't go? Where've you been all this time?"

"Nowhere in particular. Just wandering around the shops down by the station."

"But wasn't your mother expecting you?"

Still flipping through his magazine, Shuji did not answer. Instead he said, "There's no beer in the fridge."

Sayoko sighed and lifted the clingy Akari into her arms.

"How would you like to go shopping with Mommy, sweetie? Daddy's in a bad mood because we're out of beer."

"What's that supposed to mean?"

"I need to shop for dinner anyway, so I might as well go now."

She turned down the hall toward the front door.

"Want me to come along?" Shuji called halfheartedly after her, but she pretended not to hear.

"Are we going out, Mommy?" Akari asked several times as Sayoko helped her into her shoes.

Sayoko pedaled her bike wondering if she might overtake Aoi on her way to the station. She watched the shadows of the trees ahead for any sign of her, but all she saw were other mothers with small children in tow and some older kids coming back from the swimming pool.

8

Aoi and Nanako traveled from Izu to Ito, from Ito to Atami, and from Atami to Odawara, getting off the train wherever the spirit moved them as they gradually made their way toward Yokohama. They saw no vacationers anywhere, and a yawning end-of-summer stillness hung over every place they went. As they hopped from town to town, finding cheap hotels where they could stay for around ¥3,000 each without meals, Aoi's thoughts drifted repeatedly to the day she visited Nanako's home just before the start of summer vacation.

People were saying Nanako and her family lived in a two-room apartment in a prefectural housing project, but it turned out to be an old complex put up by the Japan Housing Corporation. Boxy, four-story buildings stood in orderly rows, separated by decaying play parks that obviously hadn't seen a child in quite some time. Small sandboxes were littered with empty chip bags and soda cans. Wooden swings with rotting seats hung on rust-covered chains. Brown tonic-drink bottles and cigarette butts were scattered here and there on the ground.

Walking a half step behind Nanako, Aoi thought of the picture she'd had in her mind when talking to her on the phone. With the handset from the hall pressed to her ear, listening to the rhythms of Nanako's breathing at the far end of the line, she had imagined a spacious and immaculately kept home. But the housing complex they were now making their way through seemed a closer match to the description going around at school.

Nanako led the way into a building with a large E painted on its side. Aoi trudged up the dark, narrow stairs with her eyes fixed on her friend's back. The apartment was on the third floor.

The door Nanako inserted her key into had peeling blue paint and no nameplate. "Come on in," she said unceremoniously as she opened it and went inside without looking at Aoi.

Aoi would never forget her first impression on stepping into Nanako's apartment. It was unlike any other apartment she had ever seen. Not that the rooms were particularly cluttered or badly in need of cleaning. They simply did not look like a place anyone made their home. Immediately inside the door was the kitchen with enough room for a small dining table, beyond which were two four-and-a-half-mat tatami rooms, side by side. It was the sort of floor plan you might see almost anywhere, and was no doubt repeated in every other unit in the building, yet the space within its four walls lacked the feeling of a home. It felt more like the waiting room in a train station somewhere, or like the deserted play parks she and Nanako had walked by on their way through the complex. Aoi was startled, even frightened a little, by what she saw.

Instead of the lived-in coziness of a home, it had a stark, institutional air. Both the sink and drainboard were piled high with instant noodle cups, box-lunch containers, and juice and beer cans—not one dish in sight. A swarm of little flies circled three black trash bags heaped in the corner. Except for a refrigerator, the kitchen had none of the usual appliances or furnishings: no table, no dish cabinet, no sideboard, no microwave, no rice cooker. From the middle of the low ceiling hung a single naked light bulb.

Nanako strode across the open space where the dining table would normally stand and went into the tatami room on the left. Aoi followed. This room, too, was nearly bare. On the far wall was a window that let in little sunlight, thanks to the proximity of the next building. Beneath the window sat a low tatami desk, the only furnishing of any size in the room. A cassette player, some women's magazines, a black telephone, a pair of shoes in an open box, a 14″ TV, and an athletic bag were scattered haphazardly about the worn and faded tatami.

"Can I get you something to drink?" Nanako said, still not meeting Aoi's eyes as she dropped her yellow shoulder bag on the desk. When Aoi said nothing, she returned to the kitchen and opened the refrigerator to see what she could find.

Aoi took the opportunity to peek into the second tatami room. A pillow and terrycloth blanket lay in disarray on the floor, and a rainbow of gaudy outfits adorned an entire wall. A half-eaten bag of chips and several crushed aluminum cans were strewn on the floor.

Nanako came back from the refrigerator with two cans of orange juice.

"One more room than everybody thinks," she said. She looked at Aoi for the first time since entering the apartment and smiled, then continued in what was for her an unusually belligerent tone. "So, now you've seen the much-talked-about poorhouse. Are you happy?"

But Aoi didn't think poverty had anything to do with the unsettling, even eerie, feeling she got from the apartment. It was a bewildering puzzle to her what life had been like for Nanako growing up in these rooms—or for that matter, what life was like for her living in them now. How exactly did she spend her days here, and with whom—in these rooms that seemed so utterly out of keeping with family meals and togetherness.

Aoi recalled her earlier impression of Nanako, of someone growing up among nothing but pretty things, protected by loving parents taking the utmost care not to expose her to the seamy, ugly side of life. That's what she'd thought. But what a laugh. This was the exact opposite. Nanako had grown up in this place effectively on her own, protected by no one and almost certainly exposed to countless things she should never have had to see. Aoi stood dumbfounded.

"I know people are whispering all kinds of stuff about me, but it doesn't bother me," Nanako said, sitting on the tatami and taking a sip of her juice.

"Because stuff at school isn't what matters to you?" Aoi asked, remembering what Nanako had said before.

"There's that, too, but more than that, what people are saying about me right now, it's not really about me, it's about them. It's not my baggage to carry. Why should I want to shoulder everybody else's burdens and beat myself up over their problems? I'm not that big-hearted."

These words were lost on Aoi. As when her friend had declared that nothing scared her, she assumed they were mere bravado.

They both fell silent as they sat and sipped at their juice. Suddenly a key rattled in the front door, and several high school girls came in. They wore a style of uniform Aoi had never seen before, with skirts that went nearly to their ankles, like kimono, and they had makeup caked on as thick as an actress on stage.

Ignoring Aoi and Nanako, the gaggle of girls trooped noisily into the adjoining tatami room, then reemerged several minutes later dressed in gaudy street clothes and went out the door again. Breathing the powerful perfume they left in their wake, Aoi watched them go with her mouth agape. She half wondered if Nanako was letting strangers use her apartment as a changing room.

"My little sister and her pals," Nanako explained with a little chuckle, her eyes averted. "You saw the dogface with the heaviest makeup and the tightest perm? That's my sister."

Aoi started home about the time the cracked cement wall opposite the window turned orange in the evening light. Her friend came along to the bus stop and stood with her until the bus arrived. While they waited, they joked and laughed and talked about one thing and another exactly the way they always did. As if Aoi had never set foot in Nanako's house. As if Aoi had seen nothing, and nothing had been revealed. And ever since that day, Aoi had stopped trying to learn anything more about Nanako's private life. Whether the things her classmates said about Nanako were true or not, she, at least, was determined to hold her gaze on the Nanako she could see with her own two eyes.

As the weeks went by, Aoi remained unable to resolve the disparity between the smiling girl in front of her and the home she had visited that day. Only after leaving Izu did the image of Nanako growing up in that hollow ruin of an apartment begin to make sense to her. She realized she really hadn't known anything about the real Nanako.

Aoi had told her parents she'd be home on August 24, but both that day and the day school was scheduled to start went by without the slightest sign of concern from Nanako. It apparently never occurred to her that they could be picked up as truants, or that somebody might see their pictures in a missing-persons bulletin and report them to the police. Far from being weighed down by such worries, she seemed to gain new vitality with each passing day.

Nanako was the one who suggested they try staying at love hotels. Since most inns and B&Bs charged per person, even the cheapest places were always going to set them back six to seven thousand yen a night, she said, but love hotels charged by the room, so they should be able to stay for well under six thousand, especially if they took advantage of bargain time. Plus they provided things in the rooms that other places didn't. When Aoi asked what bargain time was, Nanako explained matter-of-factly that after a certain time at night, usually around ten o'clock, you could stay until nine or ten the next morning for virtually the same price you'd pay for a two-hour "rest."

When they got off the train at Oiso, they had to walk quite a distance before finally coming to a cluster of love hotels along Highway 1, skirting the coastline. An aura of illicitness hovered over the entire area, and Aoi's steps faltered as she fought off a sudden attack of the jitters unlike any she'd ever experienced before. But Nanako picked a hotel and marched right in without the slightest hesitation. Affecting a practiced air, she studied the panel that showed the available rooms, pushed a button, and took the key from the slot. Aoi stood and stared, as if watching a stranger from some unknown land.

In the less than two weeks since they left Mickey and Minnie's Place, Aoi had noted with growing alarm how quickly their money disappeared on just food and shelter, so both the lower cost and the extras that came with the room were a welcome change. The cheap hotels they'd used before this hadn't even provided shampoo, but the love hotels typically supplied not only shampoo and rinse but facial wash and lotion, sanitary napkins, cotton swabs, and even potato chips and coffee.

Aoi admired Nanako's street smarts and pluck, and was grateful for them, but at the same time she felt more strongly than ever the presence of the impenetrable void she'd first sensed at the station in Imaihama. The boldness Nanako demonstrated contained a reckless, self-abandoned element that somehow reminded Aoi of the apartment she had seen, with its all but forsaken air.

The void she had glimpsed in Nanako stirred faint feelings of dread in Aoi, but it also held a strong attraction for her. Its deep, dark emptiness was like a black hole whose powerful gravitational field could vacuum up all fear and anxiety and misfortune and hesitation and boredom and hatred—and every other brand of negative energy that swirled about in this world—and let her feel at ease.

"You know what, Nanako?"

In the bathroom of a love hotel named Extracurricular Lessons in Chigasaki several days later, Aoi raised her voice to be heard over the sound of the shower. Nanako was rinsing peroxide from her hair in the glass-enclosed splash area next to the bathtub, her body wrapped in a towel.

A scare they'd had two days before this, when a woman who acted like she might be a truant officer came up to them at a supermarket in town, had led them to make some adjustments. Since the large nylon bags they both carried attracted too much attention, they cut their luggage to a minimum by dumping all their extra clothing, towels, swimsuits, sunscreen, and anything else they didn't absolutely need in a trash bin at the station. One thing they hung onto was the makeup Ryoko had given them, which they plastered on to make themselves look older. And a little while ago they'd bought a bottle of peroxide at the drugstore to bleach their hair.

"What?" Nanako's answer was muffled by the spray of the shower.

"When I'm with you, I feel like I can do anything," Aoi said, leaning against the wall of the dressing area.

Nanako twisted the handle and the shower fell silent.

"Of course we can do anything," came her utterly self-assured reply.

Aoi no longer felt nervous or hesitated as they approached the heavy upholstered door. She knew all the discos were basically the same.

On the edge of the commercial district east of Yokohama Station flowed a small river whose banks were lined with food stalls. Aoi vaguely recalled her father warning her in junior high to stay away from that part of town because it wasn't safe. She didn't realize this was the place her father meant until she and Nanako had already made several trips to the discos in the area.

They pushed through the door and were enveloped in a darkness filled with deafening sound and continually flashing colored lights. The floor in the middle of the room was jammed with dancers like a commuter train at rush hour. Not even glancing at the dance floor, Aoi and Nanako found a table in the corner. They took turns watching their things while the other went to fill up a plate at the buffet. The menu remained mostly the same from one day to the next: greasy macaroni gratin, dried out pasta, soggy fried chicken, oversalted fries. Today they also found steamed dumplings, pizza slices, and toasted rice balls. The girls sat across from each other with their plates piled high, tucking away their main meal of the day without a word. Aoi glanced at their reflections in the wall of mirrors. There sat Nanako, her hair a shocking blond; across from her was Aoi, who'd learned from Nanako's mistake and achieved a good shade of brown. They both looked like strangers to her. On the floor the dancers were now gyrating to the sounds of Kajagoogoo.

"This sure beats the other day."

"You mean the Love Queen? Gag. That place was bad."

"Shall I go get some sodas?"

"Let's wait. We still might get somebody to buy us whiskey sours or something."

This was the third week of September. For a week now, the two of them had been wandering around Yokohama, staying at love hotels near stations like Hiranumabashi and Shin-Yokohama and Higashi-Kanagawa. They looked for work during the day, going without lunch, and in the evening they found a disco having a ladies' night or handing out discount coupons and filled their stomachs at the all-you-can-eat buffets. When they were lucky, college students or young workers would come over to chat them up and buy them drinks, and in one case they made a date to meet again several days later and the guys had paid their admission.

As they were eating, a man in a business suit approached with beads of sweat standing out on his forehead.

"Aren't you girls gonna dance? You keep eating like that, you'll wind up like pigs."

Aoi sneaked a peek at Nanako, who shot her a look. Getting the message, she ignored the man and went on twirling her fork in her pasta.

"Snooty bitches," he spat out as he walked away.

The music changed to Earth, Wind & Fire and a cheer erupted from the dance floor.

Aoi herself couldn't tell the difference between this man and the twenty-year-old office worker who'd treated them to bowls of ramen the night before, but Nanako seemed to have a sixth sense that told her whether a guy was safe or not. Aoi had no way of verifying how often her friend actually got it right, but at least so far, following her instincts had not gotten them in trouble.

It was just about eighteen months since Aoi had left Yokohama, but she felt nothing on her return: neither nostalgia nor loathing. It was as if she had come to a town she'd never seen before, and she was surprised to find it such a lively place. No doubt she would have the same reaction if she went to Isogo Ward, where they had actually lived. After all, she'd done nothing but watch her step all those years; she'd never had a chance to look up at the sky overhead or buildings and signboards around her. If she'd never really gotten to know the town she lived in then, why should she have any feelings for it now?

They'd come to Yokohama hoping to find work. When they left Mickey and Minnie's Place, they had the money they each started out with and the rainy day funds Aoi's mother gave her, plus the pay they'd received from Ryoko—altogether about ¥450,000. But despite staying at love hotels, washing their clothes by hand, walking if it wasn't too far, and going without breakfast and lunch as well as in-between snacks, their money was melting away at an alarming rate, leaving them with barely ¥200,000 after less than a month. Aoi started keeping accounts in the notebook she'd been using for English, hoping to turn up some nonessential expenses they could eliminate, but found they were only spending on necessities. Their biggest splurge was when they bought themselves one long-sleeve outfit each after arriving in Yokohama.

They needed to get serious about looking for work, so one night at a hotel in Tanmachi they filled out résumé forms, entering fake information for everything but their names, and the next day they began making the rounds of the job boards tucked down passage-ways in underground malls and retail towers like Porta and Joinus and More's and Lumine, applying for every opening they could find. When necessary, they split up, one of them looking for new listings while the other went on interviews. But whether because their résumés looked suspect or their bleached hair sent the wrong message, they kept getting turned down day after day. For the time being, going to discos gave them the best return on their money. The buffet tables were all-you-can-eat, and they had a good chance of getting someone to buy them drinks or treat them to a late-night snack.

Several others came up to their table that night, but Nanako blew them all off. When it was after ten, they got up and headed for the door. A slow number was playing, and pink spotlights swept back and forth across the couples swaying in each other's arms on the dance floor.

Bare bulbs lit up the food stalls lining the riverbank, their reflec-tions flickering on the water. An endless stream of cars could be heard speeding by on the expressway overhead, and the lights from buildings all around brightened the nighttime sky. Two middle-aged drunks staggered past shoulder to shoulder, slurring the words of an off-key song as they barely managed to hold each other upright. A pair of lovebirds came along arm in arm, lost in their private rap-ture. The voice of Madonna spilled from the open door of a coffee shop. A ridiculously low-slung car crawled by with its windows rolled down and techno music blaring from speakers.

Until coming here with Nanako, Aoi had never actually seen any of Yokohama's nightlife. She found it dazzling and loud and gay, without the slightest hint of a shadow anywhere. Or maybe, she thought, the exuberance she felt came not from the attractions of Yokohama itself but just from being with Nanako.

As she took in the color and clamor of nighttime Yokohama, Aoi thought of her mother. She felt truly and deeply sorry for her—for the woman who deluded herself about the glorious life she used to live in this town, and who couldn't stop looking down her nose at everything since their move. Her mother had to be absolutely furious with her right now. She'd implied more than once that Aoi had only herself to blame for the bullying. After bringing it all on herself and forcing the entire family to move away to the country just for her, Aoi had run merrily off without a care—there could be little doubt that this was how her mother viewed her disappearance. She'd never be able to forgive her for it, the poor woman. She would probably pass the rest of her days in that town she so detested, complaining without end, regarding everything around her with all the contempt she could muster, and flitting unhappily from one dreary job to another.

"I was hoping we could get someone to take us to Penguin's Bar again," Nanako said. "But we didn't meet any deep pockets today."

"You liked the place that much?"

"Sort of, I guess. I mean, we had such a good time when that guy took us there the other day."

"Well, some days are bound to be washouts. You have the key to our coin locker, right?"

"Yeah, I've got it. Where do you wanna go tonight? That hotel over toward Mitsuzawa? I liked that place, didn't you?"

"You mean the Blue Moon? Yeah, let's go there. I just wish these love hotels would let us stay more than one night at a time."

Finding their locker, they retrieved the bag that contained their combined possessions and started toward the west side of the station. Several girls about their own age walked by in the other direction, sizing them up with their eyes as they slipped past. Paying them no

attention, Nanako began singing the chorus to the song she and Aoi
had heard spilling from the open coffee shop door near the disco.

Like a virgin, oooh, oooh . . .

At the hotel, Aoi flopped across the double bed on her stomach
and opened her notebook. Subtracting today's expenses from yesterday's balance put them under the ¥200,000 threshold for the first
time.

"Crap. We're seriously running out of money."

"How much do we have left?" Nanako asked from the sofa, where
she was watching a singing show on TV.

"¥192,175."

"Sounds like a lot to me." She turned back to the TV and started
humming along with Seiko Matsuda.

"Actually, it's really not that much, if you think about it," Aoi said,
sitting up. "We're averaging about ¥10,000 a day, which means we've
only got nineteen more days like this. If something comes up that
costs more, we won't even have that long. In way less than a month,
we'll be flat broke."

Nanako stopped humming and turned to look at Aoi on the bed.
Their eyes met, and neither of them moved as Nanako seemed to be
considering something for a moment.

"I'll go make some money tomorrow," Nanako said evenly.

Several seconds passed as Aoi wondered what her friend might
have in mind. "What do you mean? How?" she finally asked.

"The easiest way there is. I never told you, but I know where to
go. That day we split up and I was looking for shops that were hiring, I found this place where girls go to be picked up by guys. A guy
tried to pick me up, too. It's no big deal, far as I'm concerned, so if
we need the money—"

"But aren't you a virgin?" Aoi interrupted. *What a stupid thing to
say*, she thought the moment the words left her lips, feeling very silly.

"Look, it's like I said before about all that garbage at school. I couldn't care less about stuff that doesn't matter. There's only one or two things that really matter to me, and nothing else is worth wasting my worries on. Can't scare me. Can't hurt me."

She held Aoi's gaze as she said it, her voice utterly calm.

That's bull and you know it, Aoi wanted to say, but she stared back at Nanako, unable to open her mouth. She's actually serious, she realized. She'd really do it. She'd stand on a corner without the slightest fear or misgiving and go off with any old guy who propositioned her. And no doubt she'd come back completely unscathed, too. Because anything that might hurt her would be sucked into that deep, dark void.

Why had Nanako wanted so desperately not to go home that day in Imaihama, Aoi asked herself as she continued to hold her friend's gaze. She had imagined it was because Nanako couldn't bear the thought of being picked on again. And because she hated that empty shell of an apartment she lived in. And because she felt like she would suffocate for the lack of any future, any real choices. But Aoi couldn't help thinking now that her friend truly didn't care about any of those things. In that case, why in the world had she broken down and sobbed that she didn't want to go home? What had made going home such a distressing prospect to her?

A chill gripped Aoi's spine. She suddenly felt like she was standing on a clifftop with a sheer drop below. Her sense of reality—her awareness of where she actually was, in a hotel room—was rapidly deserting her.

"No, Nanako," she said. The sound of her voice seemed to come from somewhere far away. Nanako's eyes remained on her, unblinking. "I've got a better idea," she continued, speaking very deliberately. "We can shake down my old classmates for money. If they don't have enough on them, we can make them get more. I know where they live." Her voice still sounded very far away, and her sense of reality

154

remained attenuated. Despite that, or perhaps because of it, the fear that had gripped her moments before began to ebb. "We just have to get a knife. If we catch them alone and wave a knife in their face, they'll be so scared, they'll be practically throwing their money at us. Especially when they see your blond hair. They'll be jumping out of their skins." She felt calmer now. Nanako was staring at her, her face still a blank. In the middle of that blankness a mouth gaped open. No doubt this was also how her own face looked, Aoi thought as she held her gaze. She kept her eyes fixed on Nanako as if looking into a mirror. Somewhere very far away the sugary tones of a song by the Checkers poured from the TV.

They were on the roof of the four-story Domile Isogo looking out over the city. It was the building where Aoi used to live. The sun had begun to dip beyond the urban skyline, casting an orange glow on everything in sight. Here and there the tall gray silhouettes of high-rises thrust up from the cityscape like blades piercing the sky. Among them also rose the slender, soot-covered smokestack of a public bathhouse, spewing white smoke into the same orange sky. Only days before, the breeze had still felt warm against their skin, but now it brought a chill. A long-sleeve shirt was barely enough to stave off the cold.

"What do you suppose 'domile' means?" Nanako wondered out loud.

"I have no idea," Aoi replied, thinking, *What kind of question is that at a time like this?* "Though I could tell you what 'amigo' means," she added before realizing her answer was just as stupid as the question.

"What're you talking about? 'Amigo' isn't anything like 'domile,'" Nanako said, and broke into a cackling laugh.

A few hours ago, they had carried out their first shakedown. Their victim really could have been anyone, but as it happened, Aoi had spotted Kumiko Takahashi working at the McDonald's on the west side of the station several days before.

She and Kumiko had gone to grade school together. In fifth and sixth grade they'd been in the same class, and Kumiko told Aoi she stank. She knocked Aoi's lunch on the floor. She hit her on the head with a blackboard eraser. She yanked Aoi's skirt up and laughed like crazy right along with the guys. They were in the same class again in eighth grade. The older Kumiko had given up such antics, but she went out of her way to avoid speaking with Aoi. She avoided even meeting her eyes, apparently not wanting to acknowledge Aoi's existence in any way. But this wasn't to say that Kumiko was especially mean to her. Everybody in Aoi's class treated her more or less the same way, so she bore no special grudge against Kumiko in particular. She would have been just as inclined to lie in wait for Chitose Hara or Hidemi Matsukawa if she had seen one of them working at McDonald's.

After buying a folding knife at Mitsukoshi Department Store, they waited at the back door of McDonald's for Kumiko to get off. She emerged still in uniform once to put out some trash. Aoi and Nanako watched from around the corner of the building.

A few minutes after four, she came out again with a coworker. Nanako and Aoi tailed them at a distance, taking care not to be noticed and waiting for them to split up. When they reached the bus plaza on the west side of the station, her companion waved good-bye and went her own way. Kumiko proceeded down the steps to the underground mall. Aoi shot Nanako a look and they made their move. Catching up with Kumiko at the bottom of the steps, they grabbed her by the arms from both sides and pulled her into the service area behind the staircase. "Hand over your money," Nanako demanded. Kumiko promptly opened her purse and took out her wallet, relieving Aoi of the need to brandish the knife she'd slipped into the pocket of her jeans. With trembling fingers, she pulled out several bills and thrust them into Nanako's hand as Aoi looked on. Seven thousand yen. "More," said Nanako. "I'm sorry, that's all I have," squeaked Aoi's former classmate in a barely audible voice, her face tense with fright and her eyes averted. She had put on some weight since junior high. Her ears were pierced. She had pimples on her cheeks and chin. Nanako stuffed the money in her pocket and released her hold on Kumiko's arm. Kumiko staggered back to the mall concourse and fled.

For a split second as she turned to go, Kumiko looked Aoi square in the face, but she gave no sign of recognition that she was looking at someone she knew. Aoi gazed blankly after her as she disappeared into the passing crowd. None of it had seemed real to her. And thanks to that, she had experienced no fear, no jitters. She just kept hearing a ringing in her ears that she wished would go away.

Scoring ¥7,000 brought Aoi no joy; instead, a strange, dull pain arose in the pit of her stomach. She felt like she'd forced down something bitter and hard to digest. She noticed no bounce in Nanako's step, either, as they drifted aimlessly along the underground mall. "You know what, Aokins?" Nanako said in a woolly voice as they neared the entrance to the station. "I'd like to see where you used to live." And so they had come to Domile Isogo.

"Kumiko didn't even recognize me," Aoi said, grasping the fence that encircled the roof of the building with both hands. The concrete roof felt cold beneath the seat of her pants.

"The brown hair and makeup might have something to do with it," Nanako pointed out.

Clouds in many different shades of pink moved slowly across the sky. A red-on-white neon sign declaring *If it's saké, it's Ozeki* flickered to life in the distance.

Someone new was living in the third-floor apartment where Aoi had once lived. As when they'd first arrived in downtown Yokohama, she felt no particular emotion when they got off the train at Isogo

Station, nor when they came out onto the bustling street of shops she used to walk up and down every day, nor when they reached the apartment building that had been her home from the time she was in kindergarten. She felt neither nostalgia nor loathing. It was like approaching a building she'd never seen before in a town she'd never visited.

"Want a caramel?" Nanako asked, fishing a small box of the candies from the pocket of her jeans. The folded bills she'd stuffed in the same pocket fell out and a gentle gust of wind started to carry them away. Aoi jumped to her feet to chase after them. As she picked up the money, a deep pang of guilt sliced through her, unlike any she had ever felt before. Keeping her face averted, she wedged the wad of bills into her own pocket and sat back down on the concrete where she'd been before.

"I've been meaning to ask you something," she said.

"Yeah? What?"

"How come you write your name 'fish child'?" she asked, watching the orange sky slowly yielding to indigo. "I've never heard of the kanji for 'fish' being read *nana*." She tossed a caramel into her mouth.

"It's from a kind of weaving. You know how our town is pretty big in textiles, right? Apparently there's this really pricey fabric they call '*nanako* weave,' and they write it that way. My grandma chose the name for me."

"You have a grandma?"

"Not anymore. She died when I was in grade school." Nanako carefully peeled the wrapper from a caramel and placed it on her tongue. "Believe it or not, there were five of us in that same tiny apartment. Then Grandma got cancer and had to go into the hospital, but the weird part was, nobody seemed the tiniest bit sad. They happily went about divvying up the space. Like my little sister would have the right-hand room, me and Mom would share the left, and Dad would get the space in the kitchen. It was so stupid. And they started throwing out Grandma's things right and left—her chest of drawers, the plum wine and pickles she loved to make, lots of other stuff."

The hallway lights flickered on in an apartment building diagonally to one side. The blast of a car horn echoed through the dusk. The caramel in Aoi's mouth was rapidly shrinking as she chewed.

"But I'm in no position to criticize," Nanako went on. "Grandma was wasting away really fast, and I couldn't bear to see it, you know, so I never went to visit her in the hospital. Then one day they told me she'd died, and it was like this great big sense of relief. I thought, shit, what kind of coldhearted jerk am I? I'm so cold and mean, I must have no heart at all."

Chewing on her caramel as she spoke, Nanako paused and looked hard at Aoi sitting next to her.

"Tell me honestly, Aokins," she said. "Do you want to go home? Are you tired? Are you maybe wishing you could just go on home?"

Aoi returned her gaze. She noticed for the first time how dark it had become. Nanako's face floated dimly in the gloom.

"No, I'm not wishing I could go home," she said.

When they left Izu, she'd been convinced that a glorious future lay ahead of them, somewhere far away. She was sure that all the pieces were going to fall perfectly into place, and that she and Nanako would reach that future together. In fact, she still believed this. If they could just find jobs, the wheels of fortune would begin turning their way. But ever since arriving in Yokohama, she'd begun to wonder if maybe there was no such thing to be found, no matter where they went. Just as the good life her mother remembered living in Yokohama never really existed, maybe the place where she and Nanako could be together, and the wonderful future where everything would go the way they wanted, didn't exist anywhere either.

"I'm not wishing I could go home," she repeated, "but I'm definitely feeling tired." The moment she'd put it into words, her weariness seemed to grow. She ticked off in her mind all the things they had to do: Get something to eat with the money they stole. Find another love hotel where they could spend the night. Lie on the bed and enter today's expenses in her account book. Think about how they were going to make some money. Keep on chasing that elusive rainbow. Her head spun to think about it all. She felt so utterly drained, she could scarcely imagine even getting to her feet right now.

All of a sudden an image rose up in her mind. On a country road stretching straight into the distance, several classmates hurry by, turn to wave, then race on ahead with their skirts flouncing about their knees. It felt to her like something she had seen long, long ago, in the distant past.

"I'm tired, too," Nanako said quietly.

Aoi turned to look out over the city again. Night had fallen. Thousands of lights large and small dotted the deep, indigo darkness enfolding the city. As she stared at the nighttime sky spreading before her, she recalled the bright lights that had dazzled her eyes in downtown Yokohama. The relentless flicker of neon rose up against a darkness without bound. Now, as yesterday, she felt as though she were gazing not out across a resplendent city, but down into a pit so wide and vast its edges could not be seen.

"You know what, Aokins?" Nanako said, slurring her words like someone trying desperately to stay awake.

"What?" Aoi asked back, thinking she probably sounded much the same.

"It seems like we're always going but we never get anywhere."

It was exactly what Aoi had been thinking without being able to put it into words.

"Yeah," Aoi nodded. "I wish we could go somewhere much farther away."

"Somewhere much farther away," Nanako repeated in a flat monotone. Then grabbing the fence with both hands and leaning her face against it, she said, "Maybe we should just hold hands and jump, on the count of three."

Then maybe we'd finally make it someplace, thought Aoi before the full implication of Nanako's words could sink in. Someplace where they wouldn't feel so tired. Someplace where they wouldn't have to find another hotel for the night, or worry about how they were going to get the cash they needed. Someplace where everything would go the way they wanted.

With a childlike innocence, Aoi still felt like she could do anything at all when she was with Nanako.

If...it's...saké...it's...Ozeki. The words lit up in sequence on the massive neon sign. Aoi stared at the words until they blurred and she could no longer make out what they said. After a while she realized that the persistent ringing in her ears had finally gone away.

9

"Settle down, Akari! That's enough!"

The force of her own voice startled Sayoko. Not long ago, one stern look and Akari would have burst into tears, but now she remained unfazed no matter how sharp her mother was with her. Not only that, she raised her voice right back, determined to have her way.

"But I wanna play! I wanna play!"

"If I stop to play with you, I can't make your dinner."

"I'm not hungry."

It still made Sayoko proud each time she realized her daughter was carrying on an actual conversation with her. But the moment she heard the pot boiling over on the stove, the conversation became a source of exasperation instead.

"What am I going to do with you?" she exclaimed, racing for the kitchen and switching off the burner. She tried to go back to shaping the meatballs she was halfway through when interrupted, but Akari came squealing and giggling up behind her, pulling on her leg and straining upwards.

"Up! Up!" she pleaded.

"Don't you remember, sweetie? You said you wanted meatballs."

"I don't want meatballs!"

"This'll only take a minute, so please go watch TV until I'm done, okay?"

"I don't wanna watch TV!"

The child reached over the edge of the counter dangerously close to the cutting board, which had a large kitchen knife resting on it. Sayoko quickly pushed the board out of reach, but in the process knocked the bowl of ground meat sitting next to it onto the floor. Akari let out a shriek. Sayoko looked down at the meatball mixture splattered across the linoleum, feeling thoroughly fed up with making meals and washing dishes and everything else.

"For goodness sake, Akari, I'm just about out of patience with you!"

She grabbed her daughter by the arms and was half carrying, half dragging her from the kitchen when Shuji walked in.

"Don't you think you should take it a little easy?"

He dropped his briefcase and a magazine onto the table and looked at his wife as if he couldn't quite believe what he was seeing.

"You don't understand, dear. She was grabbing for things. She could have hurt herself. I had to get her out of the kitchen."

Akari threw her head back and burst into tears, holding her arms out toward her father. Instead of picking her up to comfort her, he merely loosened his tie and switched on the TV.

"Mommy seems to be pretty cross," he said.

Back in the kitchen, Sayoko squatted on the floor to scrape up the mess. Quickly taking stock, she decided simply to give the meatballs she had ready to Akari and Shuji and make do for herself with rice, miso soup, and pickles. Sigh.

"I didn't get home till nearly seven either, I'll have you know," she said. "Akari wanted meatballs, she insisted she wouldn't eat anything else, so when the supermarket was all out of their beef and pork mixture, I had to go all the way to the butcher shop on the other side of the station. Then the minute I get home and start dinner, your mother calls and won't let me go for nearly an hour, wanting to know when we're going to have another baby, browbeating me to quit my job and think about more important things. I finally got back to the kitchen a little bit ago, but now Akari refuses to let me cook."

And that's not the half of it, she went on inside her head. *I'm so hungry I could drop. I worked straight through without any lunch, and then had to run all the way to the station, fight the rush-hour crowds on the train, and pedal like crazy to pick Akari up in time, so I haven't had a bite to eat all day.*

Suddenly aware that the living room was strangely quiet, she looked up. The TV was on, but Shuji was nowhere in sight, and a dry-eyed Akari sat enthralled by a Mickey Mouse commercial.

"Dinner will be ready in fifteen minutes!" she yelled, loud enough for Shuji to hear her in the bedroom where she assumed he'd gone to change.

Just then her husband reappeared in a T-shirt. "I already ate today," he said. He came into the kitchen and pushed past Sayoko to get to the refrigerator.

"Why can't you call when you decide to eat out?" Sayoko snapped, on the verge of hysteria. "What good is your cell phone if you won't use it?"

Taking a beer from the refrigerator, Shuji glanced at her but held his tongue and went back to the living room. He plopped down on the sofa and spread open the evening paper.

Sayoko began dropping meatballs into the pan of bubbling tomato sauce. Doing her best to control her voice, she said, "Honey, if you're not doing anything, could you give Akari a quick bath?"

Shuji got to his feet and lifted Akari into his arms. "Look out, kiddo, I think we want to stay out of Mommy's way tonight. Let's go take a bath," he said, and went out the door. The low but unmistakable click of the tongue Sayoko caught as he stood up clung to her ears like the glue from a messy sticker.

"You know, if you're in over your head, you can quit anytime you want," Shuji said when Sayoko came back to their bedroom after putting Akari to bed.

Sitting at her dresser, she looked at Shuji in the mirror. He lay in bed flipping through a magazine.

"In what over my head? Quit what?"

"This housekeeping job," he promptly replied. "Seems like things have been a little bit off kilter around the house lately. You're on edge a lot, and sometimes I think you come down too hard on Akari. I don't think it's a bad thing for you to be working, but it doesn't make sense if it's too much for you."

"It's not."

"That woman the other day, she owns the company, right? She's got some nerve barging in here on the weekend like that. You'd think she'd have more consideration. I bet she's one of those bosses who'll push you right over the edge if you let them. If you ask me, I don't think she's a good fit for you."

"That's not how . . .," Sayoko started to say, but then pursed her lips. She couldn't very well tell him that she'd asked Aoi to come so she could get out of going to his mother's.

"Don't they say personality development depends a lot on how much time you spend with your mother before the age of three? I mean, Akari just turned three this year, and up to now she spent all her time at home with you, so maybe it's not such a good idea to suddenly shove her out of the nest. Why not wait to go back to work till she's a little older? Cleaning other people's houses is fine, but it seems counterproductive if it means you have to neglect more important things at home."

Sayoko opened her mouth to respond, but the rejoinders she wanted to offer piled up so fast they made her head spin. Not knowing where to start, she simply said, "You think just like your mother."

"My mom always stayed at home, so naturally she thinks that's best."

"Are you even aware that Akari has changed? Have you been

paying attention? She's learned to make friends, and she's talking a whole lot more than she used to."

And that goes for me, too—not just Akari. Why can't you see that? she added to herself, annoyed at how obtuse he could be.

"I'm not saying you shouldn't work," he said. "In fact, if you remember, for a long time I was actually urging you to work, back before Akari was born. But you chose to stay at home. Now suddenly you decide to go back to work, and things start to feel kind of out of whack for Akari and me, and even for you. That's all I'm saying. Besides, what you're doing now isn't like your other job, where you had real responsibility and put together projects on your own. I mean, nothing's going to grind to a halt if you're not there, right? So I'm just thinking maybe you should quit this job, take some time off, and then when you eventually go back on the market, give yourself all the time you need to find something more worthwhile, like the job you had before."

Sayoko stopped dabbing cream on her face and turned to look at him. "More worthwhile?"

She was trying so hard to keep her voice from shaking that the words came out in a throaty whisper.

Shuji apparently didn't hear. "Just think about it, okay?" He tossed the magazine on the floor and closed his eyes.

Quickly smoothing the dabs of cream into her skin, Sayoko sat and stared at herself in the mirror for a time, then turned to pick up the magazine he'd dropped on the floor and started down the hall. Instead of taking the magazine directly to the rack in the living room as she'd intended, she laid it on the table while she went into the kitchen and poured herself a glass of iced tea.

She retraced her steps and sat down in the semidarkness of the dining table, lit only by the light spilling from the kitchen. After a moment she reached over to draw the magazine closer and began flipping mechanically through the pages one by one without consciously looking at any of them. Soon her eyes began to fill, blur-ring the words and pictures that were flashing by. A tear spilled from her right eye, and she hastily brushed it away. This is silly, she told herself. There's nothing to cry about.

She distinctly remembered telling Shuji that the old wives' tale he'd unquestioningly repeated about kids before the age of three was no longer considered valid today, and it had never in fact had any scientific basis. She'd also spoken to him more than once about how amazingly lucky they were to have a place open up for Akari in the nursery school at such an odd time of year, as well as about the school's educational philosophy and classroom atmosphere. His attitude always seemed to be that it wasn't his problem, and since it was true that everything stemmed from Sayoko deciding to go back to work, she'd resigned herself to this just being the way it was.

She continued slowly turning the pages of the magazine she had no interest in reading.

When she found her job, Sayoko had promised herself several things to make sure there wouldn't be any problems. No matter how busy she got, she would keep up her house. She would not put ready-to-serve food from the deli bin on the dinner table. She would not let dirty dishes pile up in the sink. She would not send clothes that required ironing out to the cleaner's. To her mind, she had kept these promises. But she was beginning to wonder what she gained from them. A tidy house, meals made from scratch, and drawers full of neatly ironed clothes represented what Shuji took for granted—the zero point. Let one thing go awry, however small, and she was immediately in negative territory. No matter how frantically she drove herself, no matter how much loving attention she gave her family, she would never be adding, only multiplying, and no matter how many times you multiply zero, you still have nothing but zero; you never get a positive number.

Sayoko turned another page and stopped. She lifted the magazine a little to catch more light from the kitchen and leaned in for a closer look. The picture seemed familiar. "Bring in the New Year in a Tropical Paradise," it said in large display type emblazoned across the two-page spread. Along the edge of the right-hand page was a description of the Garden Group hotels, and at the very bottom it said, "For further information, call Platinum Planet, Inc." She realized it was a picture she'd seen at the office—a spectacular undersea shot of coral and tropical fish in breathtaking turquoise-blue water. In the darkened dining room, Sayoko stared on and on at the picture as if doing so might allow her to pass through the page into the dazzling sea beyond.

August was nearly over, and the training period with Noriko Nakazato came to a close. To the bitter end, Noriko had continued to nag her about her manner with clients, so part of Sayoko still felt nervous about coming out from under her instructor's wing; but another part of her breathed a sigh of relief. On the final day, Noriko took her to a large home center, where they went over the various tools she'd need for different cleaning tasks, from buckets to scrapers to chopsticks to ice picks and more, and Sayoko purchased all the items she recommended. An agreement was already in place for Noriko to supply Platinum Planet with cleaning agents and vacuum cleaners at wholesale. All that remained was to wait for job orders to start coming in.

She did have three jobs to get her started, from people who had connections of one kind or another with Platinum Planet. The first was a downtown apartment where an elderly couple wanted their bath and toilet cleaned, as well as a study that was turning into a storeroom. The second was a one-room apartment being used as a private office. And the last was the toilet and washstand at a pub located about five minutes' walk from Platinum Planet. None of them were particularly large jobs, so Sayoko handled them by herself.

Perhaps because the clients were acquaintances, she received no complaints, but neither did she get any compliments for a job well done.

Aoi and the rest of the staff had been marketing the new service on the Internet and through direct mail since sometime in August, but no further orders had come in by the time these first three were done. So Sayoko began spending her three days a week passing out fliers. In view of how accommodating Aoi had been with her employment letter and the nursery school schedule, she even stuffed mailboxes on other days when she passed apartments or condominiums on her way to pick up Akari from school.

On this particular day, Sayoko was pounding the pavement mainly in Setagaya Ward. Pocket map in hand, she wandered the tangled streets of residential neighborhoods in search of condominiums and apartment buildings. Each time she came to one, she headed straight for the bank of mailboxes by the entrance and pushed a copy of her flier into every slot. The early-September day was a scorcher, and after several hours of tramping about, her head was in a daze. As she made her way between a tightly packed jumble of single- and multi-family structures on both sides, the cramped lane ahead appeared to sway back and forth in the blazing sun.

What would tomorrow bring? The future wavered before Sayoko like the street in the midday heat. She was distributing these fliers in order to generate more business, but there were limits to what she could do alone. As he had made abundantly clear, Shuji was not going to offer any significant support or encouragement to her as a housekeeper. If jobs began to roll in and things got busy, she could count on Misao and Mao to step in, and if that still wasn't enough Aoi would no doubt be prepared to recruit someone new. But would Sayoko herself ever be able to put any more energy into the job than she was putting into it now?

She turned a corner. Houses that looked like they'd all been cut from the same mold stood like mirror images on either side of the street. They seemed to go on forever, shimmering in the heat.

When Sayoko staggered back to the office feeling ready to drop, she found the staff and Takeshi Kihara all gathered around the dining table with Aoi. She heard none of the usual jocularity and laughter, so she gathered it was a serious meeting of some kind.

Nobody so much as glanced at Sayoko as she entered; their eyes were all fixed on Yuki Yamaguchi, who was reading from a document in her hand. Trying not to make any noise, Sayoko tiptoed past the group to Mao's desk in the staff office and collapsed onto the chair. Lowering her bag to the floor, she pulled out the bottle of iced oolong tea she'd bought at lunch and took a couple of lukewarm swigs.

"Whatever happened to that tourist promotion thing that came up before?"

"It basically fell through."

"You have to understand. That was going to be a ten- or twenty-year venture. You can't hook up with someone you don't even know for that kind of commitment without some real strong motivators."

"Our backs are to the wall and we're quibbling about motivators?"

"Now just a minute. No one said our backs are to the wall."

Sayoko concentrated on writing her daily report, only half listening to the talk flying back and forth across the dining table. But then something on the desk facing Mao's caught her eye. It was made of black fabric and neatly folded up. She reached across to unfold it and discovered it was an apron. The name "Platinum Cleaning Service" was emblazoned on the bib in white letters, with the company's Saturn-like logo printed beneath it.

Why didn't I know about this, she wondered. The dazed feeling that she'd had in the midday sun was back. *Nothing's going to grind to a halt if you're not there, right?* She heard Shuji's voice in her ear as if he were standing over her shoulder, and she instinctively looked up.

"What do you think, Chief? That's the sample for your new uniform."

Aoi's voice from the dining room broke through Sayoko's thoughts almost as if she'd read her mind. Sayoko turned to find the entire staff looking at her through the doorway.

"I think it's rather chic myself," Aoi added with a proud smile.

"Well, yes, it does look pretty sharp, but I don't think I'd have chosen an apron," she said candidly.

"Oh? Why not?" Aoi asked, her smile dissolving.

"You spend a lot of time on your hands and knees when you're cleaning, so an apron like this tends to get in the way. Something like a T-shirt would be more practical, or I suppose maybe a really short apron. And it may seem illogical, but black actually makes the dirt stand out more. Dust and grease turn instantly into white or shiny spots."

As she spoke, Sayoko felt her fatigue melting away. She enjoyed being asked for her opinion.

"Oh, shoot, I never thought of that. I guess I should've asked you first."

Getting up from the table, Aoi came into the staff office and took the apron in her hands. Sayoko noticed a subtle change in the air around the dining table; with their prior discussion on hold, everybody looked a little at loose ends. She began to regret having spoken up, but Aoi seemed determined to press on with the matter as she quickly tied the apron around her neck.

"So could we maybe have them cut off about here?" she said. "Or would it be better to just start all over? What do you think, Chief?"

"Never mind that now, Miss Narahashi," Misao broke in. "We need to stay focused on what we were talking about before."

"Right," Junko said. "Since housekeeping isn't our main line of business and we don't even know what the prospects are, we should be going easy on the expenses anyway." It was clear from her tone that she was losing patience with Aoi.

"But you never know," Takeshi countered. "Housekeeping could wind up saving our neck, so we need to take it seriously and pay attention to what Chief has to say."

"Listen, everybody." Aoi turned toward them as she untied the apron. "It's almost five, and I know Mao, at least, never got any lunch. How about we take the rest of our discussion to another venue?"

"There you go again," Takeshi said jokingly. "Add beer and stir. A recipe for meetings guaranteed to mess things up."

"But sitting here looking grim at each other obviously isn't going to get us anywhere. So why not thrash it out over some dinner? It'll give everybody a boost, and we won't have to feel rushed. What exactly did we have left to talk about anyway, Yuki?"

"The red flags in our year-to-date figures."

"Right, right, the red flags. Who wants to face stuff like that stone sober? Let's go, let's go. It's on me."

Glancing at one another with strained smiles, the others rose from the table. Sayoko watched absentmindedly as they made their way out the door with considerable clamor.

"So Chief, the plan is to continue our meeting somewhere else. It'll probably drag on late, but you could excuse yourself at some point if you want. Why don't you come along?"

Sayoko wished she could. Even if it meant waiting until after they'd dealt with whatever the red flags were, she would welcome the chance to talk more about their uniform, as well as to discuss the general outlook for the housekeeping venture. She'd come to enjoy expressing her views and hashing things over with Aoi and the others. But she checked her watch.

"I'm afraid I don't have time," she said, forcing a smile.

"Right, sorry, I keep forgetting how strict they are about pickup at the nursery school. Don't worry about it. The meeting's not that important. I'll make sure we talk about the apron, too. If it looks like we can swing it, I'll plan to have them redesigned—in which case I'll give you a call. Shorten it, and change the color to . . . um, what would you say?"

"I guess gray, or maybe blue."

"Got it. All right then, please put the key in the mailbox when you lock up, and just leave the AC running." She added a sing-songy "Bye!" and started for the front door.

Sayoko listened for the click of the latch. The apron lay like a shadow where Aoi had let it fall at her feet.

When she opened the door to leave a short while later, she nearly bumped into Takeshi.

"Oh, hi," she said, looking up at him in surprise. "Did you forget something?"

"Yeah, my cell phone. Are you on your way home? Can I give you a lift?" He slipped off his shoes and went to rummage among the clutter on the table for his phone.

"A lift?"

"If we take the expressway, it'll be faster by car than by train."

Takeshi found the phone and slipped it into his pocket. Sayoko watched him uncomprehendingly as he turned around and came back to the door.

"What about the meeting?"

"It's basically just going to be a drinking party. And besides, I'm not an employee and my opinions don't carry much weight. So, how about it? I'm headed that direction anyway today, so it's no trouble. We should make it in about thirty minutes, is my guess."

Sayoko glanced at her watch. Anything that got her to Akari's school even five minutes sooner was welcome.

"If you're sure it's all right," she said.

"Absolutely." With a grin, he took the key from her to lock the door.

Takeshi maneuvered the car deftly down the narrow residential lanes of their neighborhood onto the main street. The foliage over both sidewalks shone lush and green in the light of the sun. The city remained very much in the grip of summer on this September day.

"This is nice," Sayoko said from the passenger seat. "You're sure I'm not imposing?"

"No, really, it's right on my way, so I don't mind at all. But tell me, how's it going with the fliers? It must be pretty tough-going in this heat."

"You do what you have to do. If we don't start getting some orders soon, my hiring will turn out to have been a complete waste."

"That's the trouble with Aoi. She jumps into things without any clear plan."

Traffic on the expressway was light. Sayoko checked her watch again to see how they were doing. As he drove, Takeshi reached down to pick up some CDs that were scattered underfoot.

"Did you ever think about working on the main side of the business? The travel side?"

"If Miss Narahashi asks, I'd be happy to. But she hired me for the housekeeping service, so . . ."

"Well, what with one step leading to another, the housekeeping operation is now officially under way, but to be honest, I still have my doubts. At that drinking party or meeting a while ago, whichever you want to call it, I got the sense that people aren't entirely on board with it yet. What's your take on it, Chief? How do you feel about the way Aoi's handled it? Basically, right now, you're no different from an hourly temp hired to pass out fliers. Don't you find that kind of worrisome?"

The CD cases lay forgotten in his lap as Takeshi rattled on. Sayoko couldn't quite figure out what he was asking or what his point was, and he was beginning to get on her nerves. But he plowed ahead without waiting for an answer, taking apparent pleasure in picking apart Aoi's management style. The woman wasn't cut out for running a business, she was far too haphazard and impulsive, he said, ridiculing various things she'd done and cracking jokes at her expense. There was little actual bite to his criticisms and they seemed to presume a certain chumminess between them, so Sayoko felt obliged to laugh along from time to time. But the truth was that she didn't really find his remarks very funny.

"And this whole housekeeping thing, the way I see it, the light bulb probably went on when she was talking with Mrs. Nakazato sometime or other, and she gaily decided to take the idea for a spin. But it's hard to see it coming to Platinum Planet's rescue anytime soon."

"Still," Sayoko cut in, "it's a going venture now, and I, for one, am not approaching it 'gaily,' as you put it."

Takeshi glanced across at her. "Of course you aren't," he said, furrowing his brow. "But that's the problem right there. It's pretty damned rude to you, don't you think, for Aoi herself to be approaching it so casually?"

"I'm sorry, I'm afraid you've lost me." She forced a smile to hide her growing irritation.

"I'm just saying, Aoi has this way of taking on one thing after another at the drop of a hat, and a lot of times it's the staff who pay the price down the road. At this point the housekeeping operation looks like it could be more of the same, since you're basically handling it all by yourself, and I just wondered how you felt about that."

"What are you—the complaints department?" She'd tried to make it sound like a joke, but she could hear barbs in her voice.

Takeshi threw his head back and laughed. "I suppose that's not too far off the mark," he said ambiguously.

Sayoko still didn't really know who Takeshi Kihara was, or why he was always hanging around the office or what exactly he was trying to get out of her at this moment. It left a sour taste in her mouth.

"The truth is, I'm Aoi's biggest fan," he declared. "She may be all over the map, but she's also got some very interesting things going on, and I think I can learn a lot from her."

At the wheel, Takeshi launched into another long-winded speech, but Sayoko merely offered a vague word from time to time as she kept an eye on her watch. She didn't know why, but no matter how hard he tried to clarify things, he only seemed to make them murkier. Barely listening, she began repeating a single thought to herself: *Soon I'll be with Akari.*

Takeshi eventually seemed to notice that she had tuned out. He stopped talking and slipped a CD into the player.

Soon I'll be with Akari. Picturing in her mind the route she usually pedaled from the station to the nursery school, Sayoko looked for the sign announcing the Musashino exit to appear overhead. The billboard atop a tall building in the distance was taking forever to draw near, and the sun-beaten scene outside the window seemed to be at a complete standstill.

10

With an ear cocked toward her mother's movements downstairs, Aoi crept on tiptoe to the phone in the hallway, lifted the handset, and swiftly punched in the number. She listened impatiently for the ring, but as before, all she got was a high-pitched woman's voice announcing, *The number you have dialed is no longer in service.*

"Would you like a little snack, Aoi? I made some cream puffs."

At the sound of her mother's voice, Aoi hastily returned the handset to its cradle. Her mother had no doubt been watching the phone downstairs: a green light lit up on it when the upstairs extension was in use. It seemed to Aoi that her mother spent every minute she was home monitoring the phone in the living room.

"No thanks," Aoi replied, returning to her room. She sat on the bed and looked out the window. The rice had been harvested, transforming the paddies into a vast expanse of black and brown. Beyond them, the mulberry fields had turned yellow. A dull gray sky stretched endlessly overhead.

Aoi had never been alone in the house since coming home. Although Mrs. Narahashi would have liked to quit her job and stay home full-time, the economic realities didn't permit it, so Grandma came to keep an eye on Aoi the four days each week her mother was at the bakery. The constant guard hardly seemed necessary. Why would Aoi want to leave the house when there wasn't anywhere for her to go?

She had never consciously decided that she wanted to die. She'd merely longed to go someplace other than where she was. Someplace where she and Nanako had no need to shake anybody down, no need to find another hotel every night, and no need to worry about truant officers' eyes.

When she first came to and opened her eyes, Aoi saw only white, and for a moment she actually believed she had arrived in that new place. There'd be no more muggings, no more hotel rooms, no more disco buffets, no more keeping track of every last yen they spent. But where was Nanako? Slowly turning her head to look for her friend, she found herself peering instead into her mother's weeping face. Behind her was her father, his face drawn tight. They were calling out her name, their voices far away at first, then gradually nearer, and Aoi realized that she had gone nowhere at all. "Where's Nanako?" she asked, but her parents gave no indication that they had even heard; they simply went on calling out her name over and over.

She was in a private room, but there was no TV or radio. Her mother changed the flowers in the vase on the nightstand every day. Aoi later learned that when she and Nanako made their leap, they'd landed not on the pavement in front of the main entrance but on the roof of the bicycle shelter standing to one side. The tin roof had cushioned their fall and bounced them off onto a soft patch of lawn, allowing them to escape with only some very nasty bruises, no broken bones. But during the time she was in the hospital, she could get no sense of what was going on, why she was being kept there, where Nanako had gone.

Her parents asked no questions. "This is the hospital where you were born, dear," Mrs. Narahashi kept repeating, her face like a wooden mask. "I was actually planning to go home to Grandpa and Grandma's to have you, but you decided you wanted to come out almost two months early. I remember it was one of the hottest days of the summer. I went into labor way before I expected to, so we rushed down here to the closest hospital, and the next thing we knew you were born. Your dad and I knew right away we wanted to name you after a summer flower, but it took us a long time to settle on which one. Since you were premature, they had to keep you in an incubator, and I cried myself to sleep every night because they wouldn't let me hold you. Then when they finally did, I was so happy the tears poured out even harder. I swore to myself, no matter what happens, I'm going to protect this child. You were so amazingly tiny, and so unbelievably precious, even the nurses were lining up for a chance to hold you." Aoi's mother recounted the same events all over again every time she remembered another detail.

Mr. Narahashi stopped by each evening but, as always, remained a man of few words. He sat on a folding chair and asked her with a diffident smile whether there was anything he could bring her—something in particular she wanted to eat, perhaps, or some manga she'd like to read. Neither he nor her mother responded to Aoi's questions about Nanako's whereabouts.

Besides the almost daily checkups and tests, she was scheduled to talk with a therapist as well. The sessions took place in a gleaming white room, where a woman who spoke in exceedingly soothing tones asked her if she had a favorite teen idol, what subject she liked best at school, which of her teachers she didn't get along with, and all sorts of other things Aoi could hardly have cared less about, trying to make it seem like they were just having a friendly chat. This person wouldn't answer Aoi's queries about what had happened to Nanako, either. Like the doctors and the nurses, all she said was that she hadn't heard anything and didn't know.

Aoi's mother accompanied her everywhere she went, whether to tests or to the therapist or to the toilet. One time when Aoi emerged from her therapy session, her mother was not on the nearby bench where she always waited. Aoi thought she had probably stepped into the ladies' room, so she walked down the hall to the hospital store to buy some juice. As she got in line for the cashier, she noticed the magazine rack across the aisle and idly began scanning the covers of the news-and-gossip weeklies. A headline on one of them jumped at her as if it had been cut out and placed in relief: *High-School Girls Leap from Roof After Fugitive Love Affair.*

Aoi slipped out of line and pulled the magazine from the rack. The story was about her and Nanako. Her parents had reported her missing in early September. A major search was mounted, focusing mainly on Izu and Tokyo. Her mother had apparently told the police that Aoi felt too embittered about Yokohama to ever go near the place again. But those weren't the kind of details Aoi cared about. She frantically scanned ahead, searching for any clue to Nanako's condition and whereabouts. Unfortunately, before she could learn anything, her mother rushed up and tore the magazine from her hands in an absolute frenzy. "Your grandma's here," she stormed. "She brought you those cakes from Hasegawa's you like. Come back to your room and we can all have a snack together." Her shrill tone and the hell-bent look on her face were completely incongruous with what she was actually saying. All eyes in the store were on her.

Later that day when her father offered to bring her something, Aoi asked him to pick up one of the weekly magazines for her. Such a pained look came into his eyes that for a brief moment she actually thought he might burst into tears, but when he appeared the next day he brought a manga weekly with him. Hoping even a magazine like that might say something about her and Nanako, Aoi pored over it from cover to cover, reading the letters to the editor and feature articles and everything. But she found no mention of them or the incident.

She remained in the hospital for about two weeks. When she was finally discharged and her father drove them all home to Gunma in his taxicab, she still hadn't been able to find out anything about Nanako. Her mother told her on the way that she could stay home from school until after winter vacation. Not that her mother's say really mattered, since Aoi had no intention of going anyway. She knew school was more than she could handle right now. The first thing she did when she got home was to dial Nanako's number. An emotionless female voice announced, *The number you have dialed is no longer in service.*

Either her parents or her grandmother had been on watch twenty-four hours a day ever since. They continued to ask no questions and to remain silent on the subject of Nanako. Aoi spent the days in her room upstairs, gazing out the window and watching the autumn landscape slowly give way to winter.

But even in her seclusion, Aoi was able to begin putting some pieces together. She quickly realized that the men and women she saw hanging around outside at all hours were reporters from the media. And she learned that Nanako had survived the fall without serious injury, like herself, but was taken to a different hospital. She'd stealthily searched the entire upstairs, sneaking into her parents' room and rifling through their drawers until she came across several tell-all magazines hidden in her mother's seldom-opened kimono chest. Back in her own room, she'd read them cover to cover.

She learned a number of other facts from the magazines as well. The journal in which she'd detailed their daily expenditures was found after their leap, and when it revealed that the two girls in question had been staying at love hotels, the media jumped to the simplistic conclusion that they were lovers. Or they deliberately chose to play it that way for its sensational value. And so the tawdry tale took shape: the two girls had found a summer job together in Izu intending from the start to run away afterwards; they'd consummated their passion in a succession of love hotels and haunted Yokohama's discotheques night after night; but despairing of ever gaining acceptance for their forbidden love, they'd resolved to die together.

As far as Aoi was concerned, none of this tale had anything to do with her. It lacked a single shred of truth. And this meant, too, that everything the magazines said about Nanako must also be false. For example, one magazine claimed that her father was in drug rehab and her mother worked as a hostess at a cabaret, while another said her father was in jail on a misdemeanor conviction and her mother was a hooker in Takasaki who only came home on weekends. Others claimed her father had run away with a younger woman, or that her mother was the mistress of a CEO somewhere. The only background for Nanako that Aoi could trust was the apartment she'd seen with her own two eyes—the black hole of a place that bore no clues to its occupants' identities or their lives.

Presumably because they'd failed to find any such sordid details with which to embellish Aoi's story, the scandal writers portrayed her only as an earnest and attentive student.

Taken collectively, even without any basis in fact, the articles presented a neat little story line of Nanako as seducer leading Aoi around by the nose. Even readers smart enough not to fall for every hackneyed detail were likely to pick up this much. That was what hurt Aoi most.

What a bunch of retards! They've turned us into a couple of lesbos. Isn't it a scream? People are such dimwits. Say, maybe we should always show up at school arm-in-arm from now on.

Aoi thought she heard Nanako's scoffing voice and looked up, her heart skipping a beat. But all she saw was her own summer uniform hanging against the yellowing wall panel.

Before this, Aoi's father had rarely made it home for dinner, but now he seemed determined to join them at that hour every night. Aoi's favorite foods appeared on the menu day after day. Hamburger steaks and omelets, gyoza and savory custard, tuna sashimi and macaroni gratin, and so on—often several dishes at a time with no regard for how well they complemented one another. The TV that had always been on now sat silent. In its place her parents kept up a constant flow of pointless banter as if they belonged to some kind of improv comedy act—taking care always to stay on happy topics. Aoi had no appetite, but she knew the dinner show would go on and on, escalating in inanity until she finished, so she forced herself to keep her chopsticks moving.

One day Grandma was on duty while Mrs. Narahashi was away. She was in the living room watching *Mito Komon*, the samurai drama she was hooked on, with the TV turned up so loud Aoi could hear the dialogue all the way upstairs. Tuning in and out as she sat gazing from the window, Aoi suddenly straightened up, bounced to her feet, and pulled on a pair of jeans over her pajama bottoms. She hadn't gotten dressed in days. Slipping just a sweater on over her pajama top, no coat, she grabbed her coin purse and started tiptoeing down the stairs. The show stopped for a commercial break, and Aoi froze against the wall near the bottom, waiting for the action to resume. When the commercials ended, she took a deep breath and stole down the hall to the front door. Taking care not to make a sound, she slid her feet into a pair of sneakers and very slowly rotated the lock. She looked over her shoulder but saw no sign that her grandmother had heard. *Mito Komon* blared on.

Opening the door, Aoi slipped outside into the cold. Once she was beyond the gate, she broke into a run and raced as fast as she could for the bus stop. It was a quiet weekday afternoon, and there were no other pedestrians in sight. The reporters and media crews long camped out in front of the house had recently pulled up stakes and gone elsewhere. She waited forever for a bus to come, stamping her feet impatiently. Her breath was white. Numbness crept into her fingertips. She realized how long it had been since she was last out of the house.

Relying on her memory from the one time she'd made the trip

183

before, Aoi transferred to a second bus and rode to the stop nearest Nanako's apartment complex. She ran through the rows of identical buildings looking for the one marked E, then charged helter-skelter up the stairs to the familiar door and punched the button on the intercom again and again. There was no answer. Her shoulders still heaving, she reached for the knob.

It turned. She yanked the door open. Three bare rooms stood before her.

The piles of empty food containers and the bags of trash in the corner were gone from the kitchen, as was the refrigerator, and the other two rooms had been stripped even of the tatami mats on the floor. The only thing left from before was the view of the building next door, visible through the windows of the now tatami-less rooms. Aoi stood frozen with her hand still on the doorknob, gazing in shock at the emptiness before her.

But what had changed really, she asked herself. When she was here before, the rooms already had no air of human habitation, offered no smells of daily life. They'd felt no different than they did now. Was it possible, perhaps, that Nanako still lived in these utterly empty rooms?

Aoi removed her sneakers and stepped inside. It was a clear, sunny day outside, but the apartment was dim and gloomy. The linoleum floor, decorated here and there with food stains and cigarette burns, creaked under her feet. She wandered about the rooms taking deep breaths, hoping she might capture some faint whiff of Nanako's presence. But she could make out no smells at all. Nor could she pick up the slightest hint of that mysterious void she had found within her friend. The frigid floor felt like blades cutting into the bottom of her feet as she walked, reminding her that she'd rushed away without putting on any socks. When she stood still on the painfully cold floor, all she could hear was her own labored breathing.

She decided to try going to the place Nanako called her secret hideout. Even if Nanako wasn't there either, it seemed possible that she might have left some kind of message in the spot where they used to spend endless hours together after school.

To her disappointment, she found nothing of the sort either on the riverbank or under the bridge—only colorless clumps of withered grass drooping limply in the winter air. She searched in the grass for quite some time to see if she could at least find an ice cream wrapper or something that one of them had discarded before they went to Izu. All she turned up was an empty liquor bottle and a yellowed newspaper, neither of which she'd ever laid eyes on before.

Mrs. Narahashi stood blocking the hallway when Aoi arrived home. She hadn't been scheduled to return until much later, so obviously Grandma had noticed that Aoi was missing and called. Aoi mutely pushed past her and started up the stairs.

"What in heaven's name is your problem?" her mother screeched from behind. Aoi slowly turned around. She saw tears streaming down her face. "I've had it up to here with you! What is your problem? Can't you see how hard we're all trying? For you! Thinking only of you! We're doing the best we can! What else are we supposed to do? What more do you want from us? Just tell me!"

Grandma came scurrying out of the living room and threw her arms around her daughter. "I'm sorry, dear. It was my fault," she said in a quiet voice. "I was too wrapped up in my show." She turned to fix Aoi with a stern look. "You need to apologize, young lady," she huffed. "Don't you know your mother was worried sick?"

"It's too much!" Aoi's mother shrieked, unassuaged by Grandma taking the blame. Her streaming tears and running nose formed large drops at her chin and dripped onto her blouse. Aoi stared blankly. "It's just too much! What have I done to make you hate me so? Can't you see how hard I'm trying? What more do you expect me to do? What more do you want from me? Tell me! Don't just stand there! Say something!"

Aoi slowly parted her lips. A burning lump had formed at the back of her throat. She moved her mouth to form a question, but no sound came.

"What? I can't hear you! Speak up!" her mother screamed.

After several more attempts, a dry, husky sound finally issued from deep in Aoi's throat. "Where did Nanako disappear to, Mom?"

With a lump still lodged in the back of her throat, Aoi was sure she must be crying, but her eyes remained as dry as her voice.

11

The four-year-olds from the Peach Room were jumping rope to a bouncy tune. Some of them managed to skip on and on without tripping once, while others got their legs so tangled they gave up and plopped down on the ground. A cloudless sky stretched high overhead.

Kneeling on her plastic picnic blanket, Sayoko turned from the camcorder she'd been fiddling with to the program flier at her knee. She'd looked over the schedule countless times already, but she reviewed the order of events once more. After the four-year-olds finished jumping rope, next would come the parent-child event for the under-twos, followed by the parent-child dance for Akari's class, the five-year-olds' dash around the track, and then Akari's other dance.

It was Field Day at the nursery school, with colorful banners and flags and paper decorations adorning the front gate and playground, lively music blaring from specially erected loudspeakers, and the entire student body turned out in one place. Overwhelmed by all the unusual hoopla, Akari clung to Sayoko's blouse with one hand, refusing to let go. Even when a girl from her own class came by to say hi, she ducked uncertainly behind her mother.

The four-year-olds completed their rope jumping, and the loudspeakers announced the start of the next event. Mothers carrying toddlers in their arms began to gather in the middle of the field looking distinctly self-conscious. It being Saturday, quite a few fathers had turned out as well, making it a family affair. Some were dressed in suits. Perhaps they had to go straight from here to the office afterwards, Sayoko speculated as she squinted through the blinding sunlight at the unfamiliar faces assembling on the field.

Shuji, too, had been looking forward to Akari's first Field Day. He dug out their long-neglected digital camcorder and shot some footage to make sure it was still working, and he even horsed around practicing the parent-child dance with Akari. But then he'd come home late last night saying he had to work today after all.

"Oh, what a shame!" Sayoko had said, and she'd meant it sincerely. It truly was a shame that his work had to intrude on this particular Saturday; it truly was a shame that he had to miss the Field Day he'd been looking forward to with such anticipation.

But Shuji thought she was being sarcastic and responded with the hurt look of a child who's been given a tongue-lashing.

"My work isn't like yours, you know," he said. "I can't just ask someone else to fill in for me like you can. If I don't go, everything grinds to a halt."

Sayoko reminded herself that she'd heard this line from Shuji before, so she ought to be used to it by now. But somehow the sting of his words refused to go away.

Platinum Cleaning Service had finally received its first request for a quote the week before. In fact, they'd gotten two requests, one after the other. They were from addresses where Sayoko had made the rounds stuffing mailboxes, and she went out herself to write up the estimates. Both clients lived in condominiums and had small children under school age. The first woman, in Kyodo, had a boy about Akari's age and mentioned that she left for work at ten. In Sasazuka, a woman quite a bit younger than Sayoko greeted her at the door with an infant strapped to her back. She said she worked as a freelance illustrator.

In each case, as Sayoko went over the estimate with her prospective client, explaining the time and cost factors and answering any questions, she found herself drifting into the illusion that she and the woman sitting across from her were old friends. Friends who'd dumped on their husbands, shared insecurities about child rearing, and laughed over in-law troubles together. Friends who'd made solemn schoolgirl pledges to always be there for each other if they were ever in need.

Surveying these clients' grease-encrusted kitchens, mold-infested baths, and living rooms strewn with toys and laundry and dust bunnies, Sayoko no longer experienced the disgust or bewilderment such sights had provoked in her before. Her only thought was of how desperately she wanted the clients to pick her for the job instead of someone else. And if they did, she wanted to do all the cleaning herself without help from Misao or Mao, polishing the rooms to a fine sheen with her own two hands. She wanted to give someone she felt close to a moment of respite, even if only for the brief time each job would take.

She could not get either of the women to sign on the spot. Both said they'd get back to her after interviewing some other operators. Even so, she made her way back to the office with a deep sense of satisfaction.

She knew perfectly well that she hadn't accomplished anything particularly momentous. But it was something. The woman once stuck in a depressing cycle of park hopping had decided she wanted a change, got off her duff, and, starting from nothing, made herself part of something bigger than herself—jumping right into the fray to thrash things out with the other women, learning from her mistakes by trial and error, and slowly but surely giving shape to a new housekeeping business. And to Sayoko, that in itself was far more important than the questions Shuji kept bringing up—of whether her work was worthwhile, or she was easily replaceable.

Ren and Chiemi from Akari's class were nearby, clowning around as they practiced some of their dance moves together. Noticing the sidelong glances Akari was casting their way, Ren's mother invited her to come play, and she finally got to her feet and toddled over to join them.

Chiemi's mother turned to Sayoko. "It was kind of funny. My little missy here wanted to know, 'Do we have practice again today?' I said, 'No, honey, today's the real thing,' and you should have seen how big her eyes got."

"Akari was the first one out of bed this morning at our house," Sayoko said. "I found her standing there dancing all by herself. I could hardly believe it!" she laughed.

The music started up, and the parents on the field began dancing to the beat while holding their toddlers in their arms. Akari and her playmates stopped what they were doing and watched with open mouths.

Sayoko thought she heard someone call "Chief" and instinctively glanced in that direction. She was smiling wryly to herself that no one here would ever think to call her that, when she caught sight of Aoi waving at her from the other side of the closed gate. She leaped to her feet and ran toward the gate.

"What are you doing here?" she cried. "How on earth did you know where to find me?"

It made no sense. Why would her boss show up at Akari's school?

"I tried to call," Aoi said, pausing to catch her breath. Her eyes were a little puffy, as if she hadn't had much sleep. "I couldn't get through to your cell, but I had business in Kichijoji—which is practically next door, right?"

"My cell? I guess I didn't have it turned on."

"Right. Anyway, I was in the neighborhood, and I knew the address, so I decided to just come."

"For my daughter's Field Day?"

"Actually, no. Not that. It's about those jobs you quoted last week." Aoi paused again and took a deep breath. "We got them! They called this morning to say they want to go ahead. They want us to do the job! Both of them!" she exclaimed.

Sayoko's eyes bulged wide. Her mystification over Aoi's appearance at her daughter's nursery school was gone.

"We did it!" she shouted, jumping with excitement.

"Yippee!" Aoi jumped up and down, too.

Sayoko clasped her hands through the bars of the gate. "We did it! Wow! We really did it!" she repeated.

"So anyway, I had some business in Kichijoji this morning, and Kichijoji's almost next door, right? Well, I remembered you saying today was your daughter's Field Day, so I thought maybe I could find you here to tell you the news personally, and I rushed right over!"

Sayoko nodded as she listened, still holding Aoi's hands. A bead of sweat rolled down Aoi's temple.

"I wasn't sure," Sayoko heard herself saying, "that what I'm doing was really worthwhile, you know? But it is, isn't it? I mean, even if I have no experience and my social skills leave a lot to be desired, I still have something to offer, right?"

"Oh, shut up already! You learned the business from scratch and now you've won your first contracts. None of it could have happened without you."

When Aoi hesitated midsentence, then abruptly shifted to a more soothing tone, Sayoko realized she was crying. The music for the under-twos ended, and the crowd applauded. Another up-tempo tune began pouring from the speakers into the clear blue sky. *Silly,* thought Sayoko. *What am I crying for? I may have won two contracts, but it's the results that count. I haven't even started yet.*

"I'm so-o-o happy!" she said. She was crying and sniffling and smiling all at the same time.

"Hey! Could you make up your mind whether it's gonna be tears or smiles?" Aoi joked. "But before you do that, how about you open this gate and let me in?"

"Oh dear, I'm so sorry. Actually, I'm supposed to dance with Akari any minute now. If you have time, I'd love for you to stay and watch."

Wiping her eyes and nose with the back of her hand like a child, Sayoko rolled the gate open.

Aoi stayed to the end of the program. She even offered to operate the camcorder, first shooting Sayoko and Akari in the parent-child dance, then elbowing other moms and dads for the best angles when Akari and her classmates danced by themselves. Despite her last-minute rehearsal this morning, Akari stood frozen like a doll when the music started; only her eyes darted back and forth, following the movements of the other kids around her.

"Dance, Akari! You can do it!"

Sayoko and Aoi tried to cheer her on at first, but she looked so funny standing there, they were soon doubled over with laughter.

"You know what?" Sayoko said as Aoi prepared to shoot again. "When I'm with you, I feel like I can do anything."

Aoi turned and fixed her eyes on Sayoko for a moment. Sayoko's heart skipped a beat as the eyes seemed to drill into her with questions. *You say you feel like you can do anything, but what exactly do you hope to do? What exactly did you have in mind?* The questions flashed through her head, but before she could contemplate any answers, Aoi broke into a broad smile and nudged Sayoko with her elbow.

"Let's not blow this too far out of proportion now," she snorted. "Just because they accepted your bid doesn't mean the job is done."

Raising the camcorder back into position, she shouted "Go, Akari!" at the top of her lungs.

"I've been thinking," Aoi said with the mischievous smile of a child about to do something she knew she shouldn't do. They were passing through the gate as the crowd broke up after the last event on the day's program. "Selling your first job calls for a celebration. What do you say we go on that hot springs trip we talked about?"

"When?" Sayoko asked.

"Right now," Aoi replied coolly.

"Now?" Sayoko raised her eyebrows.

"Uh-huh, right now. The three of us. You and me and little Akari. Tomorrow's Sunday, so it's perfect."

"Now?" she asked again.

Mothers pushing bicycles with their children strapped into kiddie seats milled about outside the gate, talking and laughing loudly, still bubbling with the day's excitement. Several women waved to Sayoko and said good-bye as they headed for home.

"It's not even two o'clock yet, so we could go almost anywhere we want, but I suppose we should keep it fairly close. Enoshima's maybe a little too close, though. How about Atami? I know a great place to stay in Atami. We could gaze at the ocean, enjoy some tasty eats, and soak up the waters."

Aoi spoke in a hushed tone, as if she were unveiling some rare and treasured object. Sayoko stared back with her mouth agape. *There's just no way*, her better judgment told her, but another part of her was urging, *Why not?* It irked her to think of the evening she had in store otherwise: Shuji coming home without the slightest inkling of her triumph, she greeting him as though nothing had happened and watching Aoi's video with him. Her husband kept putting down what she did as the kind of work that anybody could fill in for in her absence, but the fact of the matter was that he couldn't even feed himself a decent meal if she wasn't there, and she felt like teaching him a little lesson.

"You'd like to go, too, wouldn't you, honey?" Aoi squatted down to be at eye level with Akari. The child giggled sweetly as she slid around behind Sayoko's legs. She seemed to have become quite a bit more comfortable with Aoi today.

"Maybe I'll just do it," Sayoko murmured.

"All right! That's the spirit!" Aoi swept Akari into her arms and rubbed cheeks with her.

"Sto-o-op! Let me go-o-o!" Akari giggled again as she tried to wriggle free.

Coming out of the station, they crossed the traffic plaza and headed down a narrow street lined with aging hotels. At the end of the street the view suddenly opened up and the sea spread out before them.

"Wow!" Sayoko exclaimed, stopping in her tracks.

Aoi promptly sat down on her haunches to rest. In a partying mood, she had downed two beers followed by two saké one-cups in rapid succession and fallen into a drooling slumber on the train ride from Tokyo. Now on her feet, the effects of the alcohol were catching up with her.

"Ugghh! I don't feel so good. I guess I got a little carried away."

"Look at that! We're here! It's the ocean!" Ignoring the red light, Sayoko grabbed Akari's hand and scurried across the street, clambered over the guardrail, and came to a halt on the sand. With the sun still high in the sky, the flat face of the sea glittered brightly. The beach was all but deserted. To one side stood a food stall with a huge cob of corn pictured on its sign.

Sayoko started for the water but felt Akari dragging her feet. She looked down.

"What's the matter, sweetie?"

Akari stood with her feet planted firmly in the sand, pulling back on Sayoko's hand with astonishing strength. Her face was drawn and her entire body clenched in fear.

"Oh, that's right," Sayoko realized. "You've never seen the ocean before." Chuckling at the sight of her daughter turning herself into stone, she squatted down beside Akari and tried to reassure her. "It's okay, sweetie. You can relax. It's nothing to be afraid of. You actually went to the beach once when you were a baby, near Grandpa and Grandma's house in Chiba, but I guess you don't remember. I promise, you don't need to be frightened. Isn't it pretty?"

Akari stood glaring at the endless expanse of water, her lips sealed in a firm line. Aoi finally caught up with them, gasping for breath.

"Where do you get the energy to run like that, Chief?"

"Can you believe this child?" Sayoko said, pointing at Akari with a chuckle. "She sees the ocean for the first time and she's petrified."

"Wow! You never saw the ocean before? Then this'll be an experience to remember!"

Apparently forgetting how winded she was, Aoi swept the frightened girl into her arms and dashed for the water. Akari screamed like she'd been set on fire. Sayoko hurried after them, the soft sand grabbing at her feet.

Since she still had her plastic picnic blanket with her from Field Day, Sayoko spread it on the beach, and she and Aoi sat down with the sobbing child between them. Nothing stood in the way of the sun, and it felt to her as if summer had returned.

"I really can't believe this," she said.

"What?" Aoi said, stretching out on her back.

"That I'm here. It hardly seems possible."

Aoi stared up at the sky. "It's not as if we flew to France or Egypt, for goodness sake. We're only a ¥2,000 train ride from Tokyo."

"I know."

Akari wouldn't stop crying, so Sayoko rummaged in her bag for a piece of candy and put it in her daughter's mouth. The girl still whimpered occasionally as she sucked, clinging tightly to her mother, but she also turned now and then to cast a curious eye at the sea. Low waves rolled onto the beach in a spray of white foam, then left

195

their white traces on the sand as they receded. The crash of the waves reached their ears a split second later. A black kite soared high overhead.

"I'm getting hungry. I'll be right back."

Aoi leaped to her feet with her wallet in hand and hurried off toward the food stall. Minutes later she returned with two ears of roasted corn-on-the-cob and two cans of beer. Handing one of each to Sayoko, she sat down cross-legged and bit into her corn. A whiff of burnt soy from the basting sauce filled Sayoko's nostrils, and she dug her teeth into her own toasty warm piece. Akari had finally dried her tears. She reached for Sayoko's corn, wanting a taste.

"This reminds me of when I was in high school," Sayoko said. There'd been a period during her senior year when she and her then best friend spent a lot of time going to the beach a couple of short train rides from where they lived. They sat on the sand and talked for hours on end. She could no longer recall what they talked about, but she remembered how forlorn she always felt when she saw the sun beginning to set.

"I hated going home, so we hung around as long as we could, until the sky was completely dark. Because once we go home, tomorrow's automatically going to follow, right? That was the part I hated, I think, more than anything."

"It reminds me of high school, too," Aoi said. She sat with her legs crossed, gazing off at the horizon.

"You lived near the ocean, too?"

Aoi didn't answer. Instead she said pensively, "There's something refreshing about the beach, isn't there? It's so easy to procrastinate, putting things off day by day, but then the next thing you know you've got a whole pile of stuff bearing down on you, *oof*, demanding immediate attention. Suddenly the pile feels so heavy, you just know you're going to collapse under its weight. But then you come to the beach and look at the ocean, and it's like the whole pile just melts away. Maybe it's only an illusion, but I always feel this tremendous relief somehow."

Sayoko looked at Aoi. She had no way of knowing what might be included in the "whole pile of stuff" that bore down on a woman who ran an entire business. But it was certainly true right now that her own pile of things—the day-to-day irritations, the pent-up rage with nowhere to go, the nagging uncertainty about the future—seemed to be melting away like the foam on the beach.

"Maybe when we get old, we should build houses together by the sea," Sayoko said. "Spend our days sipping tea and watching the waves roll in."

"Now you're talking!" Aoi said. "You can't imagine how many times I've fantasized about something like that. With a whole bunch of kindred spirits living right next door to each other, you know."

When Aoi said it, it no longer seemed like a mere fantasy; it sounded closer to the finished blueprint of a readily attainable dream.

"Mommy!" Akari interrupted loudly, holding her hands up for her mother to see. They were covered with sauce from the corn. "I'm sticky," she said plaintively, sounding nearly ready to cry again.

"I know! Let's go wash them in the ocean!" Aoi exclaimed, putting down her half-eaten cob of corn. She picked Akari up and raced toward the surf. When they reached the water's edge, Akari burst into tears again, screaming at the top of her lungs. Aoi bent over to touch the child's hands to the water, then ran from an approaching wave with whoops of laughter. Squinting her eyes, Sayoko watched them go through the same motions again, and then again. Aoi's red coat lifted in the breeze. Akari's shrieks began to sound as much like laughter as crying. Their gold-bordered silhouette danced at the water's edge against the glittering sea beyond.

The sun tilted lower in the sky as if drawn toward the horizon by some hidden power. A band of orange light stretched up the middle of the sea like a kimono sash unfurled on the waves.

The flurry of crying and fussing and laughing and panicking had worn Akari out, especially after the excitement of her first Field Day, and she grew droopy in Sayoko's arms. She nodded off for a moment, then jerked back awake. "Mommy, guess what?" she said, drowsily trying to reinsert herself into the conversation. A few gentle pats on the back later she drifted off again.

The setting sun reached the horizon and rapidly began to sink, bathing the sea with crimson light. Overhead, the sky had already darkened to a pale indigo.

"Brr, it's getting chilly," Aoi shivered. "Shoot! I just realized I forgot to call for a reservation. The place I was thinking of is on the hill right behind the station. Let's just show up and see what they say." She got to her feet and brushed the sand from her clothes. "And after steeping ourselves in the springs here tonight, we could head to Hamamatsu in the morning for their famous eel, and on to Nagoya by evening for chicken wings and beer. Wouldn't that be perfect? Then another hop, skip, and we can stuff ourselves silly on Osaka cuisine the next night."

Aoi's breezy tone brought a good-humored laugh from Sayoko. *And the day after that, it's look out, Kobe, here we come!* she almost quipped, but instead the smile melted from her face. Suddenly she was asking herself: Where exactly did she think she was going? What if it wasn't just to Hamamatsu or Nagoya or Osaka that she was stepping out, but to somewhere much farther away—somewhere so far away she could never find her way back?

When I'm with you, I feel like I can do anything.

As the remark she'd made earlier that day played back in her ear, Shuji's face rose before her. This was the man who never lifted a finger to help with parenting or household chores and regarded her work with open contempt. It hit her with a chilling jolt that being with Aoi really did make her feel she could do anything. Why go on nursing her grievances? Why not leave her unappreciative husband

and strike out on her own with Akari? Somehow, being with Aoi gave her the illusion that she could do it; they would survive. Just as it had made her decide to come to Atami.

But Sayoko grew uneasy about staying for the night. She'd set out on an overnight jaunt thinking it would serve as a light slap on the wrist for Shuji, but it struck her now that even a single night away from home could easily blow up into something much bigger. Wasn't there something far more vital for her to be doing than staying in Atami tonight? If she had time to soak in some hot springs bath, shouldn't she be sitting down face to face with her husband and getting all her discontents and grievances and doubts out into the open?

"You know what?" Sayoko said as her companion stepped over the guardrail separating the beach from the road. Aoi swung around to look at her. "If we don't have a reservation anyway, how about we just go on home today? Maybe find a nice place to eat first, and then go on home."

"Why do you say that? If you're worried about the cost, it's no sweat. I'm treating," she said easily. Sayoko thought she'd grown accustomed to Aoi's glib ways by now, but the words stuck cloyingly in her ears.

"It's not that," Sayoko said. "I didn't bring a change of clothes for Akari, and sleeping in a strange place, she might wet the bed or wake up crying."

"That's no problem. If she needs clean clothes, we'll go buy some," Aoi said cheerfully. "I'm sure we can find a kiddiewear store in the shopping arcade. And it won't bother me if she wets the bed or cries."

As she listened to this, it suddenly dawned on Sayoko how utterly different their two worlds were. Was Aoi going to take out her wallet and offer to pay again at the kiddiewear shop? Would she really remain so unperturbed as she watched Sayoko frantically changing wet bedding or trying to quiet her sobbing child?

"I'd love to go on to Hamamatsu or Osaka or wherever," Sayoko said, forcing a smile. "But running away isn't going to get me any-where, you know. And besides, the day after tomorrow it's back to work already. Time to wrestle with our responsibilities again. We're not schoolkids who can fritter our days away at the beach anymore."

The smile dissolved from Aoi's face and a hollow blankness spread in its place. "Running away?" she murmured in a barely audible voice.

Taking alarm at the sudden change in her, Sayoko hastened to explain. "I was thinking maybe I could teach my husband a lesson by going away for a night without his consent," she said. "But I real-ized, just running away from my problems like that isn't going to accomplish anything. The thing is, I really do feel like I could go to Osaka with you, or to the ends of the earth, so at this rate I could wind up abandoning my husband for good."

Normally, Sayoko would have expected her just to laugh and make some lighthearted remark about runaway wives. Instead, with her face still a complete blank, she squeezed out in a wisp of a voice, "Did somebody say something to you?"

"Excuse me?" Sayoko said, uncomprehending.

"What are you afraid I'll do to you?" Her lips curled into a smile again. But it was a different kind of smile from before—a cynical, fatalistic smile.

Unable to make any sense of what Aoi was trying to say, Sayoko could only think that she must have hurt her feelings by turning down the invitation. It surprised her to discover that Aoi had such thin skin, but this was the only explanation she could imagine for the abrupt change she had observed.

Then it came to her: Aoi really couldn't comprehend that there were people in this world with circumstances different from her own. This was the woman who'd so eloquently argued that everybody was different, and the differences were what made encounters meaning-ful, yet she seemed incapable of imagining the tiniest part of what it might mean for a homemaker in charge of a household to be gone overnight without notice—or the firestorm it could provoke even if she did call home at this point.

Akari stirred in Sayoko's arms and lifted her head.

"Where are we, Mommy?" she asked sleepily, looking one way and another. "I wanna go home. I want Daddy." She pressed her face back against her mother's chest looking ready to cry. It was as if she'd expressed what was in Sayoko's own mind.

She turned back to Aoi. "I'm sure you'll discover when you have a family of your own, that if you don't plan things ahead, you can get into all kinds of messes. What's a single night, you might say, and that's what I thought, too. But I really do have to think about my little girl."

Akari had started to whimper. Sayoko gently patted her on the back.

"Of course," Aoi said. The fatalistic smile was now gone. "Sorry if I took too much for granted. I'm still footloose and fancy-free, though, without anyone waiting for me at home, so as long as I'm here I think I'll stick around and enjoy myself a bit. The station's right up that way." She reached into her coat pocket for her phone and quickly punched in a number.

"Um, just one thing," Sayoko said, trying to get her attention, but she had her ear to the phone with her head down and ignored her. Akari was crying in earnest now, her voice echoing into the darkness over the light spilling from the gift shops along the street.

The call connected and Aoi's face lit up. "Hi, it's me. I know this is kind of sudden, but do you happen to be free tonight? How'd you like to win a deluxe overnight stay in historic Atami? The friend I was supposed to come with stood me up, but I'm already here, and it seems a shame to just turn around and go back home, you know? Ha ha ha, that's right. If you're busy, I'll think of someone else. Really? Are you sure? Great! I'll just be hanging out, so call me when you get here. And don't you dare grab anything to eat along the way. There's going to be a full-course dinner waiting for you. Uh-huh. See you then."

She punched the END button and turned to Sayoko as if noticing her still standing there for the first time.

"Oh, it's ¥1,950 to Tokyo, isn't it? Are you short? Do you need me to pay?"

"No, I'm fine."

"I figure I'll just kill some time down this way until Takeshi shows up. See ya," she said, promptly turning her back and hurrying off toward the shopping arcade in the opposite direction from the station.

Takeshi? Aoi had called Takeshi? She'd chosen Takeshi Kihara to fill in after Sayoko "stood her up"?

In stunned disbelief, Sayoko gazed after her receding figure.

"Go home, Mommy!" Akari was wailing between sobs. "I wanna go home!"

"Yes, dear. We're on our way." Sayoko noticed there was a quiver in her voice as she tried to comfort her.

She bought two box lunches at a kiosk inside the station before climbing the stairs to the platform. The dimly lit platform was almost empty. Sayoko lowered her daughter onto a bench and sat down beside her, but Akari immediately started fussing to be picked up again.

"Mommy's tired," Sayoko said.

"Up! Up!" the girl clamored, trying to climb onto her mother's lap.

The friend I was supposed to be with stood me up.... Sorry if I took too much for granted.... Aoi's voice lingered in her ears. *Are you short? Do you need me to pay?*

The entire texture of the day she had been through slowly began to change shape in Sayoko's mind. Aoi hadn't actually come to deliver the good news about the jobs; she'd come to horn in on Akari's special day at school. She hadn't invited them to Atami to celebrate; she'd roped them in to help her blow off some steam.

In her effort to climb onto Sayoko's lap, Akari inadvertently kicked their lunches off the bench onto the platform. She instantly froze in anticipation of a scolding, peering warily into her mother's face. Sayoko stared vacantly at the white plastic bag lying on the concrete. A voice on the PA announced that the train for Tokyo was approaching and a few moments later it roared into the station. Rising slowly to her feet, Sayoko stooped to pick up the bag.

"I'm sorry, Mommy," Akari said, still tense with apprehension. "I'm sorry."

The coach was not very crowded, so Sayoko and Akari had a four-seat box all to themselves. They sat side by side and ate their meals. When they were finished, Akari lay down with her head in Sayoko's lap and fell asleep. Sayoko gazed at her own reflection in the window.

In his usual happy-go-lucky fashion, Takeshi was even now on his way to Atami, where he would meet up with Aoi and spend the night with her at a hot springs inn. *How tacky*, Sayoko thought. *How tacky of Aoi to turn to the likes of him.*

But a moment later she realized her own behavior had been no better. Knowing Aoi would cover her if need be, she'd tagged merrily along to Atami—before coming to her senses and heading home, yielding her place to Takeshi. She'd foolishly allowed herself to believe that she could follow Aoi's lead and do whatever she wanted.

The expression on the face floating in the darkness beyond the window reminded her of herself as a child after being scolded yet again for chewing on her nails.

12

Neither of her parents raised any objections when Aoi said she wanted to go to the closing-day ceremonies. Aoi thought her mother might come along, but she waved good-bye at the door.

At school, everything seemed far away. Her classmates gave her a wide berth, keeping their distance as they talked amongst themselves. If she thought she heard somebody calling her name and turned to look, the conversation would come to an instant halt and there'd be awkward smiles all around. Both the large closing-day assembly and the homeroom formalities seemed to be taking place on the other side of an invisible wall that wrapped around her.

Aoi had hoped she might find Nanako attending, too, but when she peeked into her classroom her seat was empty. She asked some of Nanako's classmates if anybody knew where she was. Sorry, but no one's told us anything either, they said, their voices surprisingly warm. This answer, too, sounded as though it came from beyond a thick, invisible barrier.

After the ceremonies, Aoi came out the gate under cloudy winter skies. A familiar taxicab was parked nearby.

"Aoi!"

Catching sight of his daughter, Mr. Narahashi dropped his cigarette at his feet and called to her with a cheerful wave.

"I thought maybe we could go to Isezaki—just you and me," he said with a big grin when Aoi had settled into the passenger seat. "We won't tell Mom. Christmas is coming up, so we can pick out something for your Christmas present. I'll get you anything you want. Within reason, of course—nothing outrageously expensive."

He was more talkative than usual as they drove across the Wata-rase River into a district where small stores lined the street, then took a right onto the highway leading out of town.

"I think back to when we first moved here, and I remember having a pretty tough time for a while, not knowing the roads or where anything was. I often had to ask my passengers for directions, and this one guy really chewed me out once. 'If I'm paying you to get me there,' he says, 'why the hell should I have to navigate?' He was pretty steamed up. That's ancient history now, though—over a year ago. These days people call me the best cabbie in Gunma."

The sun peeked through a break in the thick clouds, casting its weak rays on the earth below. The South Pacific ornaments Aoi was accustomed to seeing in the cab had been removed. Gone was the lei that used to hang over the rearview mirror. Gone were the gaudy flower-pattern cushions on the back seat. Gone were the plastic vines draped over the front seatbacks.

"I see you took down all those weird decorations," Aoi said, feeling a bit sorry for her father having to hold up the conversation all by himself.

"Yeah. Your mother said I should. She thought they were in poor taste. Actually, I had quite a few passengers tell me they liked them. But then people who got in late at night after they'd been drinking could get pretty spooked sometimes. They'd think they were halluci-nating or something."

He burst out laughing. Aoi wondered if getting written up in the magazines had had something to do with the ornaments coming down.

"I'm glad you got rid of them, Dad. They were kinda tacky," she said, trying out a little laugh.

"Yeah? You thought they were kinda tacky, did you?" He laughed again, too.

Fast-food franchises and family restaurants dotted the route. Watching them slip by outside the window, her father asked, "How are you for lunch, Aoi? Does the short day mean you didn't eat at school?"

"I'm not hungry."

"Well, be sure to tell me when you are. I know a great ramen shop."

"I'd expect nothing less from Gunma's best."

They turned to look at each other and laughed.

For a time the view outside the window alternated mostly between low-rise residential and rice paddies. Here and there a larger industrial building rose above the surrounding houses. The sun was breaking through more now, and the ridgeline of the mountain became visible in the distance as the clouds lifted. Dropping her eyes from the passing scenery, Aoi fiddled with the buttons on her overcoat. School regulations allowed students a choice of two styles—single- or double-breasted. Most of her classmates chose singles, but Nanako and Aoi had agreed on getting doubles in the fall of their first year.

"Isezaki has Nichii and lots of other department stores, so you can choose any present you want," her father said. "A stuffed toy. Something to wear. Anything at all."

So Nichii's a department store? Aoi imagined Nanako asking from the back seat in a cheery voice. She glanced over her shoulder, but there was of course no one there—only a freshly laundered seat cover so immaculately white you might wonder if you dared sit on it.

"I can't think of anything, really," Aoi said, lifting her eyes again.

Her father looked at her. He had the same pained expression he'd had when she asked him to bring her a magazine in the hospital.

Hoping to reassure him, she hastily added, "I mean, not for Christmas. But there's something I'd like for my nineteenth birthday."

"Are you kidding? That's not for a long time yet," he said. "But what is it?"

"A silver ring."

"A ring? That's an awfully grown-up thing to want. Sure, absolutely, I'll buy you a ring. No need to wait until you're nineteen. We'll get you one today at Nichii." Her father had raised his voice cheerfully, obviously much relieved. "But why settle for silver? I'll get you platinum."

"Is that stronger than silver?"

"It's a lot more precious. And silver tarnishes. Gold's better than silver, too, but if you start wearing gold rings at your age, people might think you're some gangster's moll or something. I don't suppose you know this, but your mom's wedding ring is platinum."

He started to tell her about when they went to buy the wedding ring, but Aoi cut him off.

"The thing is, it can't be for Christmas. It has to be for my nineteenth birthday."

"Why's that?"

"It's a secret," Aoi smiled enigmatically. "So I don't want anything today, but maybe I can see what they have at Nichii. In platinum."

"Good idea, good idea. Believe it or not, I've got a pretty good eye for this sort of thing. It's amazing what you can pick up by talking to passengers, even about women's finery. I bet I actually know more than your mom does."

He laughed boisterously. It reminded Aoi of the way he laughed at the dinner table during his improv performances with her mother.

"Dad," she said softly when his laughter had died away. "I want you to know how sorry I am."

Her father said nothing; he just stared at the road ahead with his hands on the wheel.

In Isezaki, they looked over the ring selection at Nichii as well as several independent jewelry stores, but they got back into the cab for the return journey without having made any purchases. Since her father seemed deflated at having come away without spending anything on her, Aoi asked him to take her to the ramen shop.

They were most of the way home before he finally pulled off the highway in front of a tiny hole-in-the-wall establishment, none too clean looking, with only a sticky counter to sit at. Aoi and her father sat side by side, slurping from the bowls of noodles the cook placed in front of them, topped with slices of roast pork. The light of the setting sun poured in through the window.

"Aoi?" her father grunted when he was about half finished, staring into his bowl. She looked up. "After this, I have to take a little nap and drive all night, you know." He stopped to slurp up some noodles and take a sip of the broth, then stared into his bowl again. "And I'm supposed to get back around noon tomorrow. But in the morning, when you get up, if…I mean, if it just so happens…"

Aoi kept her eyes fixed on him as he talked into his bowl, fumbling for words.

"In the morning, your mother goes to the bakery at six, and Grandma's supposed to come as usual to be with you while she's gone, but I'm gonna talk to her. 'Cause I could never sway your mother, you know, but Grandma might be more sympathetic."

He stopped again. Taking a bite of pork, he chewed for a moment, then wiped his mouth with the back of his hand and dropped his voice even though no one else was listening.

"So anyway, if it just so happens that Grandma isn't there when you get up, then I want you to come to the Shirahige Shrine."

"What for?" Aoi's heart was thudding.

"I'm gonna bring Nanako Noguchi to see you."

He picked up his bowl with both hands and took a long, noisy swig of broth.

"But why…how come…where is Nanako? How'd you find her?" Aoi's heart was pounding so hard it hurt.

"You'll have to ask her that. I can't tell you anything. I'm already gonna be in big trouble if your mother finds out about this," he said, finally turning to look at her, "but since you won't let me get you anything for Christmas..." He smiled with those same pained eyes he'd shown her before.

Holding a bite of noodles with her chopsticks in midair, Aoi averted her gaze and stared at the back of his glistening, sun-darkened hand.

When she saw Nanako standing by herself on the other side of her father's idling cab, Aoi thought she must be dreaming. She still felt that way after rushing up to her and clutching her arm. She had in fact dreamed of this moment so many times.

"You look great, Aokins!" her friend said with a little laugh.

Standing a head shorter than Aoi, Nanako beamed up at her. Her breath made a white cloud in front of her nose. She was wearing the matching double-breasted overcoat she'd bought with Aoi the year before, and to judge from the pleated skirt protruding below the half-length coat, she was apparently in full uniform. Aoi wished she had done the same, instead of coming in jeans and duffle coat.

There were so many things she'd wanted to ask Nanako when she saw her. About after their jump. About her present situation. Where she'd moved to, and why. How to reach her. She was also sure she would cry when they met. She'd even worried about being so choked with tears she couldn't get her questions out. But her eyes remained dry, and none of the things she'd planned to ask seemed the least bit important anymore. Instead she found herself lapsing immediately into lighthearted platitudes as if they'd seen each other just the day before.

"You look like you've lost weight. You been dieting?"

They hopped into the back seat together. Like yesterday, Mr. Narahashi had posted his OFF DUTY sign in the front window.

"Where to, ladies? Your wish is my command," he said jokingly.

"In that case, how about Izu?" Nanako said.

"Or Yokohama," Aoi added quickly.

"Ai-yi-yi. You ladies don't exactly look like you've got that kind of change."

"How rude!" Nanako said, pointing her nose primly in the air. "Okay, fine! I've got ¥1,000 on me. Take us however far that gets us."

The well-heated cab filled with laughter.

Aoi's father put the car in gear and drove slowly through the misty morning air. Few people were out yet at this hour. They passed a jogger and an elderly man walking his dog.

Nanako glanced at Aoi with a self-conscious smile. "How do you like my two-tone hair?" she said, pointing at her head. "Pretty pathetic, hunh? My little sister keeps finding funny names to call me."

Her hair had grown out black again on top but remained bleached below the ears.

"Well, mine's pretty bad, too. Can you believe this?" Aoi said, pointing at her own jet-black hair. "My mom went and bought some blackener. Makes me look like a granny, don't you think?"

Not sure what to say after that, they both fell silent. They merely looked at each other and smiled every now and then. Feeling increasingly awkward as the silence continued, Aoi racked her brain for something to say but came up empty. She noticed Nanako periodically glancing at her watch and grew uneasy. Did they have a time limit? Or was it perhaps that Nanako didn't really want to talk to her anymore?

A few minutes after seven, Nanako leaned forward in her seat and said, "Mr. Narahashi, can we go to the river?"

The car wound through a series of narrow streets to the edge of town where the houses broke off and the view opened up. The Watarase River spread before them. Aoi caught her breath. Brightly mirroring the morning sky, the water shimmered before them in the purest shade of blue she had ever seen.

"Wow!" she said, pressing her forehead to the window as her father pulled over near a bridge.

"It's only this time of day that the color gets like this," Nanako said softly beside her.

"I never knew."

"That's because you always went to school later. By sometime before eight, it goes back to its normal color."

"I never knew," Aoi repeated. She thought of Nanako leaving home long before the starting bell and stopping by her favorite hiding place to stand breathlessly watching the river—in grade school, in junior high school, and until a few months ago in high school. Crisp images of Nanako rose before her as if she were recalling something she had witnessed with her own eyes. She now understood why Nanako had been paying so much attention to her watch: her friend had wanted to show her the river as it reflected the sky at this precise time of day.

"Is it all right if we get out, Mr. Narahashi? I promise I won't run away."

Without a word, Aoi's father operated the lever to open the rear door. They walked out onto the bridge.

"I'm gonna be changing schools," Nanako said quietly as she and Aoi peered down at the river over the railing.

"Because of what we did?"

"Not really. I'm sure people will draw their own conclusions, considering the timing and all, but actually that has nothing to do with it. I mean, think about it. My parents didn't bother to file a missing persons request even after a whole month went by, so you can't expect a little fuss like that to shake them up. No, it's a bunch of other family stuff. I have to move in with one of my relatives."

A cloud slid slowly across the face of the river. Nanako's white breath melted into the frigid air as she spoke.

"Do they live a long way from here?" Aoi asked.

"Depends what you mean by a long way, but my family are all dyed-in-the-wool Gunma people. So the farthest would be like Minakami or Shimonita. Of course, in another year or so, I can get out on my own. I just can't do that yet now."

211

Aoi had no idea where either of those towns were. "Do you know what your address will be?"

"Not yet. I'll write when I do," she said, her eyes fixed on the river.

Mr. Narahashi was leaning against the car with his back to them, puffing on a cigarette and looking up at the sky.

"Promise?" Aoi said.

"Have I ever broken a promise?"

"We'll see each other again, right?"

"Of course we will," Nanako said. "It's not like I'm moving to outer space." She gazed in silence at the river for a time, then turned to Aoi with a faint smile. "I guess people are built stronger than you might think, hunh?"

Not sure what Nanako was talking about, Aoi said nothing.

"We were really pretty stupid," she added and turned back to the river.

Aoi finally understood what her friend meant. The river flowed quietly beneath them, its wondrous color never changing for a moment. Aoi felt as if she were still on the roof of Domile Isogo, gazing out over the city as it was falling into twilight.

"We never did get anywhere," Nanako sighed.

"What I wonder is where we were trying to go."

Nanako did not reply. Aoi looked for a way to change the subject.

"Guess what, Nanako. Remember that thing we said about rings on our nineteenth birthdays?" Nanako looked up at her. "My dad says platinum's better than silver. So I decided I'm going to give you a platinum ring. That way you'll get to be even happier than with silver." As she said it, she felt tears welling in her eyes, and she hastened to add, teasingly, "Especially since I figure you'll never find a boyfriend."

"Then that's what I'll give you, too." Nanako looked her straight in the eye as she said it but did not crack a smile.

They fell silent again and stood staring at the gently flowing river with their elbows planted on the railing.

"It kind of feels like the river's actually the sky, doesn't it?" Nanako said. "Like the sky's flowing by under our feet. Standing here watching the water, it's as if you're actually standing somewhere way up in the sky, and you can't tell where you are anymore. Does it feel that way to you?"

Wanting to experience the feeling exactly as she had described it, Aoi fixed her gaze fiercely on the water. A swatch of sky as wide as the river slid by beneath her, and a peculiar floating sensation came over her, as if her feet were suspended several centimeters off the ground.

"It really does," she said.

By the time they returned to the car, six flattened cigarette butts littered the ground at Mr. Narahashi's feet. The girls climbed back into the rear seat without a word.

"Shall we go for another spin, then?" he said cheerfully as he got in behind the wheel and started up the engine.

They circled about town repeatedly, driving past the train station that was growing busier by the minute, past the deserted gate of one of the other high schools, down the still-shuttered main shopping street festooned with Christmas decorations, out onto the highway dotted with fast-food outlets, and back along the river that had now returned to its usual color. Aoi gathered that her father intended to stay within the city limits. Soon the view outside the window was repeating itself: the bustling station, the shuttered shopping district, the dusty highway, the river. Rather like herself, thought Aoi—trying to go someplace but never getting anywhere, and ultimately winding up back where she started.

Neither of the girls spoke. Nanako's hand brushed Aoi's on the seat between them. Aoi quietly took it in her own and squeezed, and Nanako squeezed gently back. With hands clasped, they watched the town flow by, each from her own window. For a brief moment, Aoi thought she saw the two of them in their summer uniforms walking past outside the window—two high school girls doubling over with laughter, nudging each other in the ribs, carrying on about something or other with their heads tilted together. Tea and cake at Hasegawa's. The sky on New Year's Day. The savory grillcakes at Fukufuku-tei. Billy Joel. Koike's potato chips. The moment when the wind dies down at three on a summer afternoon.... They were naming at random all their favorite things as if determined to fill the world entirely with things they liked.

A few minutes after nine, the car pulled into the turnaround in front of the station.

"Thank you so much, Mr. Narahashi," Nanako said with her hand on the door. "This would've cost a fortune if the meter was going. I'll pay you back when I've worked my way up in the world a bit, okay?"

"Right," he chuckled, "but I don't think I'll hold my breath."

He got out of the car to open Nanako's door.

"See ya!" Nanako flashed Aoi a smile and slid out of the back seat. She trotted quickly off toward the ticket gate without waiting for Aoi to get out after her, turning when she was partway there to wave her arm high over her head. Aoi waved back from the car as the tiny, double-breasted figure of her friend shone radiant in the winter sunlight.

Her father pulled out into traffic again with Aoi alone in the back seat. Tears gushed from her eyes as if the floodgates had been opened by a switch not linked to her own will or wishes. She tried to hide them from her father, twisting her face awkwardly out of his line of sight in the rearview mirror. The tears refused to stop, chasing each other down her cheeks and falling to the hand that only moments before had been in Nanako's. All she felt in that hand now was a gaping emptiness. She pressed the other hand firmly against her lips to keep herself from crying out loud. As her nose began to run, she instinctively sniffled, and her father turned to look over his shoulder. She doubled over in her seat and let the tears flow. Now that her father knew the state she was in, she wept without restraint. Her own sobs filled her ears.

"Just remember, Aoi, it won't be long before you can see her anytime you want again," he said gently, trying to comfort her. "I understand she'll be moving away, but it's not like she's going overseas or anything. And even if she were, traveling to other countries isn't such a big deal anymore, you know. So maybe you have to wait a while because your mom and your teachers will make a fuss, but you can always write, and if you can just be patient for now, you'll get to see her again real soon. All right?"

Aoi nodded as he repeated his words of comfort, but inwardly she was crying out in anguish. *Why don't we ever get to choose anything for ourselves, Dad? We might think we're choosing, but all we're really doing is grasping at thin air. We don't even get to choose which way to step with our own two feet. Tell me, Dad. What if something happens to Nanako, and she gets hurt, and she's crying and in terrible pain? What could I do for her? I can't rush to her side, I can't even send her messages by flashlight. What do we grow up for anyway? When we grow up, do we finally get to decide something for ourselves? Do we finally get to step whichever way we want without having to lose the people we love?*

Their house came into view ahead.

"When you see Grandma, you be sure to thank her, now, you hear?" her father said sternly.

Aoi's chin dripped like a broken faucet from her overflowing eyes and nose.

"I will," she squeaked, mustering every ounce of strength she had left.

13

"Oof, I really can't believe how wiped out I am," Junko Iwabuchi moaned again, clinging to a hand strap with both hands as the train sped toward Shinjuku. She'd been grumbling nearly nonstop since she and Sayoko started back to the office.

"Doesn't this have to be, like, breach of contract or something? I mean, I thought I was signing up for a desk job. How come all of a sudden I'm a cleaning lady? We at least deserve to have a car, don't you think? Sometimes Takeshi drives you, right? Why does it always have to be the train when it's my turn? It's not fair."

Sayoko nodded vaguely as she listened, glancing up at the luggage rack now and then to make sure the bag containing her cleaning bucket was staying put.

"And what's with the old lady sending us out to do her shopping? Sacks of rice and potting soil and all that other heavy stuff. Since when is that on our list of services? We're not a handyman agency."

In October, almost as if Sayoko's first two successes had primed the pump, cleaning orders started coming in one after the other. The size of the job determined the size of the crew: for studio units, or when only the kitchen and other areas with plumbing needed attention, Sayoko could usually handle the job by herself, but for whole apartments with two or more bedrooms she needed at least one pair of helping hands, and sometimes two. The sudden influx of work meant that things were no longer quite as organized as at first, and they sometimes found themselves scrambling hectically from one job to another, but they'd come through so far without any serious complaints or slipups, and the operation seemed to be getting safely off the ground.

For Sayoko, the worst days were those like today, when she had to team up with Junko. Besides her constant griping, she was an indifferent worker. More than once Sayoko had had to frantically redo an area Junko had supposedly finished. The woman also made no effort to hide her feelings when they found rooms in particularly bad shape. Sayoko now understood all too well why Noriko Nakazato had been such a stickler about client relations.

Transferring in Shinjuku, they got off at Okubo and found Takeshi Kihara waiting for them at the ticket gate. Junko had apparently been expecting him. She waved and swerved off in his direction.

"Hey, Chief!" she said, turning to Sayoko with a bright smile. "Want to stop at Jonathan's? It's been a tough day. Let's treat ourselves to something sweet." She seemed like a totally different person from the woman who couldn't stop grumbling on the train.

Shown to a booth by the window, Takeshi ordered coffee and Junko tea and cake. Sliding in across from them, Sayoko asked for café au lait. As soon as she got settled, Junko began repeating her litany of complaints for Takeshi to hear. Sayoko stole a glance at him periodically as he listened.

"Well, maybe it's because we're shorthanded," he finally observed in a measured tone, "but there's no question that things aren't running very efficiently right now. I guess Miss Narahashi assumed we wouldn't actually get all that much work, but now that it's pouring in, I'd say it's time to draw a clear line between the cleaning crew and the travel business. I mean, if we go on letting the travel side shrink while we're putting out fires on the cleaning side, Platinum Planet's going to wind up as nothing but a housecleaning service."

Junko agreed vocally with each point as he spoke. It was still before five, but the earlier sunset at this time of year already gave an orange cast to the world outside the window.

Sayoko did not know, nor did she care, whether Takeshi had in fact gone down to Atami that day—or what had transpired between him and Aoi if he did. Back at work on Monday, Aoi had treated Sayoko in exactly the same way as usual, as though nothing had changed. If Sayoko finished a job early, she suggested they have tea. She invited Sayoko to the monthly networking parties and showed no particular displeasure when she said she couldn't make it.

Sayoko, for her part, now drew a very conscious line between herself and Aoi. Before Atami, she had wanted to be closer to her, but since that trip, she'd come to believe that what constituted closeness for Aoi was something like high school girlfriends going to the bathroom together—a relationship unlikely to survive if either of them even once declined to tag along because she didn't need to go.

Sayoko glanced at Takeshi from time to time as he continued his smug commentary. After trying to draw her out in the car on the way to Akari's school, had he come here today to do much the same with Junko?

"If you ask me, Miss Narahashi is way too full of easy talk," Junko said between bites of cake. "If we're in a slump, shouldn't we be jumping at opportunities like that tourist promotion thing? But no, the motivators aren't there, she says. Sure beats me how she finds so much motivation in housekeeping but not in domestic tourism— especially considering she's so queasy about cockroaches she won't even deign to visit us on the job."

She paused and started waving her arm at the window. Turning to look in that direction, Sayoko saw Misao Sekine hurrying toward the door of the restaurant at a half-run.

Moments later, Misao slid into the booth beside Sayoko. "Can you believe it?" she moaned, still trying to catch her breath. "First I had to chase down CDs by Morning Musume and Ayu and SMAP and Arashi, and then it was DVDs of *Terminator 3* and *Charlie's Angels*

218

and the NHK morning drama. I mean, good grief! What does any of that have to do with work?"

She flipped quickly through the menu and ordered a soda float.

"For the Japanese staff at Garden Group, right? You got the honors?" Junko said sarcastically. "Really! If she wants to play at being friends, she should buy her own gifts."

Sayoko looked back at Misao, still not quite sure what this was all about.

"She's big on goodwill, and on a little bit of kindness going a long way, but I'm sorry, sometimes she just goes too far. I mean, we're running a business here, not a charity." Misao paused and leaned low over the table before continuing in a hushed voice. "She's at the Cultural Center in Shibuya today."

"Another one of her lectures?" Junko said. "Isn't that just peachy. What can she possibly have to offer anyway? Seriously. Everything she does is a complete mishmash."

It had taken Sayoko a while to realize they were talking about Aoi.

"Actually," Takeshi broke in, "I've always thought she has a certain kind of charisma, so giving lectures and talks is probably right up her alley. And besides that, her speaking fees go straight into company coffers. Without them, the current squeeze would be even worse."

Almost as if he'd flipped a switch, Takeshi's defense of Aoi brought a fresh outpouring of invective from Junko and Misao, both heaping abuse on their boss's leadership style. Sayoko could scarcely believe her ears. She'd long been aware of Junko's disgruntlement, but Misao's low opinion of her came as a complete surprise, especially since she'd always seemed so friendly with Aoi. Even more shocking was the vehemence of their attack, which went well beyond mere grumbling and criticism. Sayoko listened in continual astonishment as the Aoi-bashing flew back and forth across the table, her café au lait getting cold.

Between the lines, she gathered that the sudden launching of the housecleaning operation had served to ignite smoldering dissatisfactions among the staff. The problem was that Aoi had all the business savvy of a bulldozer, plowing ahead without any clear plan, just pushing whatever came up that day from one side to the other. With a bizarre sense of personal virtue, she acted as if moneymaking were a dirty word, like some youthful idealist. She had no appreciation of the responsibility she bore for her employees and tried too hard to be buddy-buddy with them. . . .

Sayoko's eyes drifted toward the greengrocer across the street as the exchange continued. She was aware that Aoi had recently begun accepting engagements to speak about her experiences as a woman entrepreneur. Once upon a time Sayoko would have dismissed her colleagues' venom as nothing but envy for their boss's newfound recognition, and she would have quickly excused herself. But today she remained glued to her seat, nursing along her now completely cold coffee with tiny little sips, wanting to hear more.

Soon she began to notice a pattern in Takeshi's interjections. The two women would disparage Aoi's leadership, and he would come back with something positive to say about her. This invariably prompted the women to slam her even harder, escalating eventually to nasty personal slurs that no one could ever claim were funny. When temperatures rose to that level, Takeshi would step in again with a calming word or two and deftly steer the conversation back to company issues, drawing from the women some entirely new string of complaints about the situation at work. It was hard to tell whether he did this consciously or unconsciously, but one thing seemed clear: this man had a special flair for getting people to put aside any qualms or circumspection and willingly spill their guts.

"You've been awfully quiet, Chief. You must be wondering what kind of disaster-in-progress you've walked into. I mean, Platinum Planet is so different from other places. It's hardly like a real business even."

"But Chief's got it easy. Even if the whole operation implodes, even if the housecleaning runs into trouble and comes to a stand-still, she's got somewhere else to go. She has a home to look after, and a husband to take care of her."

"Run into trouble?" Sayoko said, forcing a smile. "That's what we're working so hard to avoid."

"Actually, that's missing the point," Takeshi broke in, his tone unusually serious. "It's not what you do to avoid running into trouble, it's how you're going to deal with it when it comes. And the problem is, especially for the housecleaning side, there's absolutely no plan. Basically, if you have to ditch at the last minute because of some emergency, then one of the other girls has to drop what she's doing in her usual job and fill in for you. Miss Narahashi says she knows you're in a different category from the rest of us. Nobody else has any children, so until now, if something drastic happened, everybody could stay on at the office however long it took to clear things up. That doesn't work for you 'cause you have to leave at a certain time, plus you never know when your little girl might come down with a fever or something. So the boss knows she needs a backup plan. At least that's what she says. But—"

"I've never once had to 'ditch,' as you put it," Sayoko interrupted. She'd tried to say it with a smile but could feel the tension in her cheeks. *I'm in a different category? A backup plan for when I have to ditch?* Why did she even have to listen to this kind of thing?

"Not so far, no. I'm talking about what could happen down the line. But ultimately, as you know, she'll say something like that and then go dashing off to your daughter's Field Day on a whim. That's the way she is. Of course, that was on a Saturday, but there's no telling when she might take off on a regular weekday, too."

Sayoko's eyes shifted away toward the window. It left a bad taste in her mouth to learn that Aoi had discussed Akari's Field Day with Takeshi when they met in Atami.

"What's this about your daughter's Field Day?"

"I basically think she doesn't have enough faith in us."

The two women spoke at the same time.

"It's not that she doesn't have enough faith. It's that she has too much," Takeshi said, again taking Aoi's side.

Sayoko didn't really want to talk about Akari's Field Day, so she casually changed the subject. "I'd forgotten about this, Junko, but a while back you mentioned Miss Narahashi had been in the papers for something. What was that about?"

There was a palpable change in the air at the table. Misao and Junko exchanged looks with tight little smiles.

"Oh, it wasn't that big a deal, really," Junko said as if trying to brush her off.

"Did you get asked too, Chief?" Misao said. "Did she invite you on a trip, or back to her place maybe?"

"Huh?"

"She has a predilection for that sort of thing."

"Careful now. That's not a very nice word to use," Misao said. "Not that we're knocking her, but basically, she likes to hang out with women."

"You're both blowing things way out of proportion," Takeshi elbowed in. He turned to Sayoko. "She's just got a slightly different sense of boundaries, that's all. She may come across as the eternal optimist, but she actually has a bit of a dark past."

His gaze seemed to say that he knew what he was talking about. Sayoko absently let her eyes drift down to his mouth as she waited for him to continue.

While the others carried on with their conversation, Sayoko excused herself and went back to the office. Yuki Yamaguchi was on the phone with someone in the staff office, and Aoi was going over some documents in the tatami room. Sayoko sat down at the dining table and opened her work diary.

Aoi noticed her starting her report. "Welcome back, Chief," she said cheerfully. "There're some cream puffs in the fridge."

Sayoko nodded in acknowledgment but said nothing and kept at her writing. When she was done, she gathered her things together and got to her feet.

"See you tomorrow."

As she moved toward the door, Aoi came hurrying after her. "Did you notice that new ramen shop on the way to the station?"

"Sorry, but I'm in kind of a rush. Bye." Cutting her short, she made a quick bow and left, scuttling down the stairs as if fleeing from something.

The sun had gone down and half the sky had turned a pale shade of indigo when Sayoko emerged onto the street. She quickened her steps, running all the way to the station building, through the ticket gate, and up the stairs onto the platform. With perfect timing, a train pulled in, so she stepped aboard and stood holding onto a hand strap, heaving hard to catch her breath.

The story Takeshi had launched into with such apparent relish immediately rang a bell with her; in fact, she recalled the details quite clearly. This wasn't to say it had blown up into a huge scandal or triggered widespread cultural repercussions. The Morinaga candy-poisoning incident that took place around the same time created a much greater stir, as did the murder of an Osaka youth by class-mates who decided they'd had enough of his bullying. The attempted double-suicide of two high school girls in Yokohama had filled the pages of the weekly magazines and tell-all tabloids only briefly before being forgotten by most people.

But Sayoko had reason to remember it. That same summer, as a junior in high school herself, she had lost every friend she had in one fell swoop. Although she'd never been a particularly popular girl, she had a group of friends she'd been going to school with since seventh grade. They went to the usual teen hangouts together after school, and they called each other on the phone every night. But now she was summarily dumped by them merely for having different college ambitions.

Everybody else had decided early on not to attempt the entrance exams for four-year schools. They were going to settle for the nearby community colleges and trade schools that would accept them on recommendations alone. Sayoko set her sights higher. She wanted to try for a major university in Tokyo, so she signed up for an intensive exam-prep course lasting all summer. Her friends called from time to time to invite her out for some fun, but she begged off in favor of studying. Then, when school started up again in the fall, they refused to speak to her anymore. They went off somewhere together at lunch, and they slipped out of the classroom without inviting her along at the end of the day. When she rang them at home, they pretended to be out; if she tried to talk to them at school, they gave her the silent treatment.

Sayoko couldn't understand it. She'd said no only a handful of times. Set against five years of friendship, it was next to nothing. Did that mean the real reason for the sudden chill lay somewhere else? Perhaps there was something about her personality, or something she said or did, that had rubbed them the wrong way all along, and the events of the summer merely gave them a convenient excuse to finally cut her off. Once this thought got hold of her, it refused to let go. New fears crept into her mind. What could it be that they so disliked about her? What was wrong with her? Who had she inadvertently offended? Had she really done something so bad she deserved to lose all her friends?

Since her school was a combined junior high and high school, the circles that friends moved in had been in place since seventh grade. There was simply no way for Sayoko to find a new group in eleventh. She was now stuck doing everything on her own, and all of a sudden the school became an eerily quiet place. The clamor of her classmates and the laughter of younger students came to her like the muffled sounds from a television set next door.

Even Sayoko didn't know why a story about two high school girls attempting suicide struck such a chord with her when she first saw it on the morning news. She went to the library and read all the articles she could find about it in the newspapers and magazines.

According to the reports, the two girls had taken a summer job together with the intention of running away afterwards, then spent weeks wandering around entertainment districts here and there before going to the condo where one of them used to live and jumping off the roof. The weeklies claimed they were lesbian lovers, but Sayoko wasn't interested in this type of scandalmongering. She wanted to know what their relationship had been like. They went to an all-girls school, just like her. How had they become friends? What had they talked about? What made them decide to run away? During all those weeks on the run, were there days when they grew tired of each other and stopped being friends?

At school, Sayoko continued to be ostracized during her senior year, but she found a new friend at the exam-prep academy she enrolled in. She and a girl from a coed high school discovered they were planning to take the exam at the same university, and they started meeting up on their way to the academy and going together. On days when they didn't have classes there, they met to go to the library instead—or to the seashore. They would sit on the deserted autumn beach and talk about everything under the sun. When she was with this girl, the former friends who'd given her so much heartache the year before seemed hopelessly immature. They were nothing but a bunch of bores who hung out together for no good reason and got their kicks from blackballing an innocent friend. The quietness at school ceased to bother her, and the fear that she must have something terribly wrong with her began to fade. As she sat and talked with her newfound friend, she recalled her unanswered

225

questions about the relationship of the two girls who'd jumped off the roof, and she thought maybe it was something like their own.

As it turned out, they wound up going to different universities. Sayoko phoned her friend nearly every night, but she was always out. Even when she left a message with the girl's mother, she never called back, and although they had previously made plans to meet, she stood Sayoko up every time. It was summer before Sayoko finally reached her on the phone.

"You never call back," she said accusingly.

"I've been busy," her friend said, sounding peeved at being put on the spot. Then she lowered her voice and asked, "Don't you have any new friends?"

What Sayoko thought of then was not the countless hours that she and this person had spent together, but the girls she'd read about in the gossip columns two years before. What had they done after they survived their plunge, she wondered. Had they gone on to college, and to live in the here and now, putting their hand-in-hand leap completely behind them and resenting anything that brought it to mind again? Or did they perhaps remain hand-in-hand today, without ever knowing the sting of betrayal or mutual loathing?...

It was the kind of wound that time heals, and in fact Sayoko had forgotten all about it. But now, with Akari pulling her toward the candy aisle while she tried to examine the packages in the deli bin for something quick to put on the table, she recalled vividly the feeling of suffocation that had gripped her chest at her friend's words. From her present distance, she had difficulty understanding how something as trivial as that could have driven her into such a petrifying daze, as if the entire world had been turned upside down, but at the same time she thought she could see that every one of the choices she had made since then—the choices that made her who she was today—had in some way been determined by that moment.

"I actually know one of those girls," Sayoko murmured, still not quite sure she believed it. But there could be no mistake. Her memory of the time and the place and their ages matched the details she'd made Takeshi repeat so many times he began giving her strange looks. One of those two girls was this close to her now.

"What, Mommy? What did you say?"

"Nothing, dear. We need to get some milk, and then we're done." Sayoko looked down at Akari and smiled as she maneuvered down the aisle bustling with last-minute shoppers before the store closed.

Sayoko thought of the girls she'd wondered so much about in her late teens. What did it mean to be close to someone? She'd longed to know the answer to that question. But maybe that wasn't how it had been at all. Come to think of it, hadn't she read that one of the girls was leading the other around against her will? Which would mean Aoi hadn't changed one bit since she was in high school, Sayoko suddenly realized, feeling as though she'd discovered a vital new fact about her employer. The girl Aoi had led around by the nose must have been someone very much like Sayoko herself—someone who got caught up in Aoi's gung-ho pace, could never bring herself to say no, and eventually found herself past the point of no return on that rooftop. She might even have phoned Aoi up later, sometime after they'd finished high school, only to hear her say curtly, "I'm busy. What do you want?" Picturing the scene, Sayoko saw herself in a high school uniform standing in the place of Aoi's best friend.

Sayoko went through the checkout, bagged her groceries, and took her daughter's hand as they left the supermarket. Night had fallen outside. As they started up the darkened sidewalk, Akari sang a song she'd learned in school that day. Sayoko was sweating from the crowded, overheated store, and even with the night air chilling her skin it took a long time for the sweat to dry. When her song was finished, Akari began prattling on about her day. Sayoko responded absently. The smiling image of Aoi urging her to spend the night with her in Atami faded in and out in front of her eyes, over and over and over.

There were no cleaning jobs scheduled that day, so Sayoko arrived at her usual time expecting to spend the day stuffing mailboxes. Normally she opened the door to the sound of phones ringing and people talking, but today the office was silent. The sliding doors to Aoi's room were shut, and the staff office was empty. The amber rays of the early winter sun warmed the houseplants on the windowsill.

Sayoko checked the schedule of upcoming jobs posted in the staff office, and quickly began loading bundles of fliers into her tote bag. She heard the clatter of a sliding door opening, and Aoi appeared in the doorway. It was obvious that she had spent the night at the office and just woken up. Her face was puffy with sleep and she was dressed in sweats.

"Perfect. Just the person I wanted to see. Do you have a minute?" she said groggily.

Sayoko took a seat at the dining table while her boss shuffled sluggishly into the kitchen to get the coffeemaker going. Still looking half-asleep, Aoi blankly watched the machine gurgle, not saying anything. When it stopped dripping, she poured a cup for Sayoko and a mug for herself and sat down across the table.

"Okay...here's the deal. I want to turn all of the housecleaning over to Noriko from here on out," she said, staring into her mug, looking pale without her makeup. "And I'd like your help here in the office now—on the travel side of things."

Sayoko sat gazing at her, unable to digest what she was hearing. Aoi took a noisy sip of coffee. She offered no further explanation.

"I don't understand," said Sayoko when Aoi remained silent.

"There's been a revolt. I suppose that's what you'd call it anyway," she said, glancing up at Sayoko with her familiar smile. "Three people gave notice all at once. I know I need to start looking for replacements right away." She paused for a moment, looking into her mug. "I need to start looking for replacements," she repeated in a low voice, "but even if I can find them quickly, there'll be a gap before they actually start. So for a little while, until things get back on track, I need your help here in the office. You can take a break from housecleaning."

"Three?"

"Junko and Misao and Mao. They'll all stay on the books through the end of the month, but they immediately wanted to know about claiming vacation time and how long they'd have insurance coverage and stuff. What do they think this is—some kind of blue-chip corporation? They better not expect any fancy severance package, that's for sure."

"But what about the jobs we've got scheduled?"

"That's why I'm saying, I want to turn the ones already in the pipeline over to Noriko's company, and the same for any new requests that come in. We'll stop advertising right away. The thing is, Yuki Yamaguchi will be moving to Canada with her husband in March. That's not part of the revolt—I already knew we'd be losing her, which is why I was having her teach Misao how to handle the books. I thought it was all under control, but now this. Ouch. If only I'd known, I'd never have put Misao on it in the first place. Anyway, I was hoping maybe you'd be willing to step into the accounting spot."

Takeshi popped into Sayoko's mind as she sat listening. The mass exodus had to have been his doing. He had lent an ear to Junko and the others and encouraged them to air their complaints, at times voicing his own agreement and pretending to be completely sympathetic, even pointing out Aoi's shortcomings himself, at other times singing her praises precisely to elicit their heated denials, and through it all he had been building solidarity among the three disgruntled employees. But why? Wasn't he one of Aoi's cronies?

"What about Takeshi?" Sayoko asked bluntly.

Aoi continued staring into her mug, her lips twisting into a faint, self-mocking smile.

"Ahh, yes, dear Takeshi. He isn't actually an employee, temporary or otherwise, so there's no question of his quitting. But I somehow doubt we'll be seeing him around here anymore."

"But..."

Sayoko was about to blurt out something about Atami and the two of them being on sleeping terms, but she bit back the words.

"He's such a sleazebag. A tiny little company like this, he ought to know he's not gonna find any juicy pickings, but he has to come sniffing around, sticking his nose in where it doesn't belong and stirring things up."

"But what possible good does that do him?"

"Who knows? Maybe he's planning to start up his own company with the people he lured away. In the time he was pretending to help, he had plenty of chances to cozy up to our consultants and our tax accountant. I suppose he figured if someone as disorganized as me could run a company, he could do at least as well. But look at them. They're a bunch of idiots who don't actually care one whit about travel. What they care about is making money, but if that's all they've got driving them, I can tell you right now they'll never last. For that matter, I figure they've all three of them slept with the jerk. When that comes out, it could be the day of reckoning right there, even before anything else."

Aoi rattled on, scarcely pausing for breath, and Sayoko had to look away. It seemed the simultaneous desertion of her workers had hurt Aoi more than Sayoko could imagine. She had never heard her speaking of others with such venom before, and she didn't feel comfortable hearing it now.

Her spirits sagging, Sayoko found herself trying to remember why she'd ever wanted to go back to work, why she'd decided to thrust herself back into that messy world where one had to deal with all sorts of different people. If only she hadn't come through this door that day, she could have remained blissfully ignorant of Aoi and all the squabbles that surrounded her here. She would have been spared her own high school memories, as well as her growing discontent with Shuji.

"But I thought you and Takeshi were close," she put in before Aoi had a chance to go on.

"Yeah, I know," she admitted without the slightest hesitation. She lit a cigarette, exhaled, and smiled. "When something went badly here at work, it felt so good to have someone to talk to, someone who'd lend an ear and tell me he understood. You have a husband, so you probably don't realize, but it's hard to find people you can really talk to about your work."

Sayoko bristled. She had been constantly at odds with Shuji since starting work. She'd even cried herself to sleep some nights, despite telling herself she had nothing to cry about. Why did Aoi always make assumptions like that, when she didn't actually have the first idea what Sayoko had been going through? But she said nothing. She simply stared at the coffee Aoi had placed before her, feeling very awkward.

"Well, we've kind of gotten off track, but what do you say? Will you do it?" Aoi leaned across the table and peered at Sayoko.

Sayoko was remembering the first time she'd met her in this room. *Oh, wow, can you believe it? We went to the same school!* Aoi had exclaimed excitedly, leaning closer over Sayoko's résumé as if to make sure it was true. *We might've bumped into each other under the ginkgo trees, or in one of the dining halls!* she'd beamed. She sounded almost like a student again.

"I...I don't know. It's all so sudden," Sayoko mumbled almost inaudibly.

I thought you knew, she wanted to say. *Even when my own husband sneered at what I was doing, I thought you, at least, knew how*

231

seriously I took the work that I helped build up from scratch. But again she said the words only in her heart.

"It's sudden all right. But I promise I won't ask you to stay late, and I think being such a small operation means we can accommodate you more easily. You could even bring Akari here if need be. Which reminds me. Have you heard of this place called the Family Support Center? I thought it might be something you could take advantage of and I looked into it a bit—you know, because you're always worrying about making it to the school at pickup time. Anyway, if you need me to find out more or look for other things like that, I'll help in any way I can."

Sayoko's face burned. She'd known about the center for quite some time. They matched families that were past their child-rearing years with young families nearby to help with tasks such as nursery school drop-off or pickup and babysitting after school. She'd seriously considered signing up a number of times—there was no telling when help like that might come in handy—but she'd always held off because she was leery of having to deal with people she didn't know. What if there was a problem of some kind and things got messy, she worried, and continued to drag her feet. Now she felt as if Aoi was chiding her for that. A retort—that she'd never asked for that sort of help—formed on the tip of her tongue, but she said nothing, and simply sat staring down at her hands folded in her lap.

"As a matter of fact, I've been thinking maybe I was a little too quick to jump into housecleaning anyway. In some ways I hate turning jobs already in the pipeline over to Noriko because that's like giving up. But I'm telling myself it's okay because our customers are probably in better hands that way. They'll probably be happier with Noriko."

Aoi rose to her feet. Sayoko couldn't bring herself to look up. *In better hands that way? Happier with Noriko than me?* Aoi was probably right, of course, but it was the last thing Sayoko wanted to hear from her. She felt tears starting to well up and quickly bit her tongue to keep from sobbing out loud.

"Well, I guess I'd better brush my teeth and get to work," Aoi said, turning toward the bathroom. Sayoko held her head down, blinking hard to clear the tears from her eyes. When she was sure all trace of them was gone, she looked up.

"Can I ask you something?" She raised her voice so Aoi could hear her in the bathroom.

"Yeah? Wha-a-at?" a cheery voice came back.

Sayoko took a deep breath and blurted out the question. "What ultimately happened?"

Aoi poked her head out into the hall with her toothbrush in her mouth. "What ultimately happened with what?"

"After you jumped off the roof," she said, fixing her gaze firmly on her. She intended this as payback: payback for asking why Sayoko wasn't using the Family Support Center; payback for blithely suggesting that their customers were in better hands with Noriko. She could think of no stronger riposte.

For several seconds, Aoi held Sayoko's gaze without moving a muscle. Then she pulled the toothbrush from her mouth and burst out laughing.

"I didn't realize you knew about that," she said between laughs. "Who filled you in? Junko? Takeshi? They all get such a kick out of that story. Did they tell you I was gay, or that I had a death wish? Sorry to disappoint you, but I'm just an ordinary girl who likes guys. I just don't have much luck with them is all."

After another burst of laughter, Aoi ducked back into the washroom. Sayoko could hear her rinsing her mouth.

Sayoko looked down at her untouched coffee as she waited for her to reemerge. The black liquid in the middle of the cup looked like a tiny portal offering a glimpse of the darkness beyond.

14

What ultimately happened...

The full weight of what Nanako had been saying finally sank in for Aoi. *None of that stuff scares me. None of that stuff matters to me.... If you don't like it, then just don't be part of it. It's as easy as that.*

It wasn't merely bluff, or empty bravado. She was stating simple fact.

At the start of the new academic year in April, Aoi returned to the school Nanako no longer attended. Her mother had urged her many times to just say so if she wanted to transfer, and Aoi had spent much of her break worrying about how stressful going back to the same school was likely to be after what she'd done. When she finally announced her decision to stay, it was purely out of consideration for her parents. She'd uprooted their lives to come to this school. How could she ask them to go through that again? And besides, even at a new place she'd be holding her breath all the time for fear of attracting the wrong kind of attention. It made her feel faint just thinking about it.

So when school started up again, Aoi simply went back as if nothing had happened. It still felt like everything was taking place on the far side of an invisible wall surrounding her. None of the girls from the nondescript group she used to hang out with came to talk with her, nor did she approach any of them. The meanness that ran rampant the year before had not altogether disappeared, but it had lightened up considerably. Nobody called Aoi names the way they had with Nanako, nor did her possessions go missing or her uniform get trampled on, and no lurid stories about the incident flew back and forth across the classroom. Her classmates kept their distance and that was all. She simply had no one to talk to.

But as she looked around her, she realized it was true: there was nothing that really mattered to her here. She couldn't see a single thing on the other side of that invisible wall that she felt any desire to reach out for.

It was quiet. Encapsulated as she was inside her own solitary cocoon, no ripple disturbed the silence that enfolded her so long as she herself remained still. In fact, that placid quietness was what she treasured most—what mattered to her more than anything else in a building no longer graced with Nanako's presence.

After spending her school hours wrapped in this bubble of silence each day, Aoi raced home as fast as she could, yanking open the gate and leaping for the mailbox. But day after day, the letter Aoi longed to see failed to arrive.

Summer vacation neared and still there came no letter from Nanako. Opening the phone book, she began calling every number listed under Noguchi. But none of the Noguchis she called had a seventeen-year-old daughter who wrote her name "fish child" and read it Nanako.

As she sat in her room staring into space, memories came flooding back. The train on the way to Izu. White sheets fluttering on the line in the Manos' yard. Their little boy's plastic cars. Nanako breaking down in Imaihama Station. The love hotel rooms with their bizarre decors. The discos with purple and pink flashing lights. And each time this chain of images scrolled back through her mind, a single exchange from that day on the bridge with Nanako echoed in her ears afterwards: *We never did get anywhere. What I wonder is where we were trying to go. We never did get anywhere. What I wonder is where we were trying to go.* As those words repeated themselves over and over, all the things they had done, and everything that had followed from them, spun rapidly through her head. Nanako insisted that her moving away had no connection to those events, but if it weren't for those things, wouldn't she still be here now? Wasn't the lack of any communications from her part of the same thing? Why had Aoi been left alone to come home each day and stare at the same unchanging landscape outside her bedroom window?... As she mulled over these thoughts, a white haze seemed to descend on everything inside her head. It was a decidedly unwelcome sensation, for she couldn't help thinking that the white haze spreading inside her was Nanako's absence itself.

Aoi passed the days in her bubble of silence, and she walked for graduation surrounded by that same silence. Having made the cut at her first-choice school, she moved to Tokyo with little more than the clothes on her back. Her first home away from home was a dormitory in Nogata.

The biggest surprise she had when she started college was that everybody talked to her as if it were the most natural thing in the world.

"Say, have you joined any clubs?"

"There's going to be a class party. Wanna go?"

"Ooh, where'd you buy that outfit?"

Men and women alike treated her as a friend from the start. She ate lunch with them in the student dining halls and went along to cheap drinking places after classes. She joined the raucous, drunken crowds at large student mixers, and sometimes crashed at a classmate's one-room apartment afterwards. She soon had friends she met up with on weekends to see movies or to go shopping, and a sorta boyfriend she talked with on the phone every night.

But Aoi found it impossible to fully open herself up to any of her new friends. She could laugh with them, rant with them, even play at falling in love with them. But there remained a certain line she was loath to let anybody cross, and if someone tried to come closer than that, she hastily erected a wall, not answering the phone and staying away from classes until a more comfortable distance reasserted itself. A number of her gal pals eventually drifted away as a result, and her sorta boyfriends never became true boyfriends. She was afraid of getting too close to anyone. To her, closeness represented a loss rather than a gain.

As her nineteenth birthday approached, Aoi secretly fantasized about receiving a delivery from Nanako with the promised present inside. But her mailbox remained empty. Then it hit her that Nanako might not actually be alive anymore. She might have chosen a more reliable means of departure this time, and successfully made her way to another place all by herself. The thought was deeply unsettling, as if the ground were slowly crumbling from beneath her feet.

At the start of what would have been her junior year, Aoi set out on an open-ended trip abroad. She'd heard that one of her classmates had hopped the Ganjin Ferry to Shanghai, and decided to follow his example. Although it was both her first time traveling alone and her first time outside Japan, she didn't feel the least bit nervous.

From Shanghai she flew to Hong Kong, and from there on to Vietnam, Sri Lanka, India, and Nepal. The places she visited and the things she saw kept her in a constant state of culture shock. She realized just how tiny her world had been. Feeling that world grow bigger and bigger as she traveled, she pressed eagerly on from one strange town to another.

Nearly a year after first setting out on her journey, Aoi found herself in Laos. She was waiting at a bus stop along the route leading out of Vientiane toward Vangviang when a young man approached her.

"I have a Japanese friend who looks a lot like you," he declared in fluent English. "I met her when she was traveling along this route last year. You reminded me so much of her, I couldn't help wanting to say hello. I wonder if you might know her."

A constant stream of motorcycles and trucks roared by along the unpaved road of red clay. The dust kicked up from the roadbed gave everything in the vicinity a thin red coating as it settled back to earth. Next to the bus stop stood a food stall offering sandwiches made with French bread and a variety of fillings. Flies swarmed busily about.

Aoi asked the natural question: "What was her name?"

It was hard to catch what the young man actually said, but to Aoi it sounded a bit like Nanako.

"Nanako? You say Nanako?" she exclaimed.

"Yes, Nanako," he said with a big nod, and then repeated as if to reconfirm, "Nanako. Nanako."

"Where you meet her? What she doing? How she look? Where she going? What city in Japan she live?" Though frustrated by her own poor command of English, Aoi bombarded the Laotian youth with questions.

"She was a pretty girl, shorter than you, and she said she came here from Thailand. She went back to Japan from here. She said she lived in Tokyo."

Aoi felt her fingers quivering as she listened to his replies. She couldn't actually believe it was the Nanako she knew, yet somewhere deep inside she was convinced of it.

"At my house, I have a letter and some pictures. Would you like to come see them?"

"Yes!" Aoi replied eagerly. She leaped onto the back of his motor-cycle without a second thought.

After bumping briefly along the dusty road, which despite being an important traffic artery was dotted with only a few scattered shops, they proceeded onto the thoroughfare spanned by the Patuxai Gate, modeled on the Arc de Triomphe in Paris. They passed through the gate and drove on. Soon the shops and food stalls disappeared entirely, giving way to the occasional shantylike dwelling set among the large, unfamiliar trees and dense grasses choking both sides of the road. Aoi could only suppose that this was the way to the young man's home, but when he finally pulled over it was in front of an obviously abandoned structure.

"Give me your money," he said as soon as they dismounted. The friendly manner he'd shown before was gone, replaced by a rough, threatening voice. Aoi's knees quavered beneath her, and she broke out in a cold sweat from her forehead to her armpits. Her mouth went instantly dry, and she couldn't speak. So it was a scam! The realization came all too late. At least he wasn't waving a knife at her; apparently she didn't need to fear for her life. *Don't panic, stay calm,* she told herself. *Just hand over the money without any fuss and get yourself out of here as quickly as you can. Think of nothing else.*

Two younger boys, probably not even high school age, came out of the tumbledown tin shack to stare menacingly at her. Making it clear she had no intention of resisting, Aoi lowered her knapsack, fished out a wallet, and handed all the bills it contained to the mugger.

"You've got more than that," he snarled. The two other boys kept up a constant string of chatter in the local language. The buzz of numberless insects in the surrounding underbrush was like a distant ringing in her ears. She in fact had three wallets in her knapsack. The wallet she'd just emptied was the one she used for local currency; a second one held Japanese yen notes, and the third contained approximately the same sum in traveler's checks. Thinking quickly, she took out only the one with the traveler's checks, which she knew she could get replaced.

The youth reached for the thick stack of checks and briefly flipped through them before wedging them into his pocket. He apparently didn't even know they were worthless without a signature, Aoi noted scornfully, trying to steady her nerves. Although the sun blazed down with painful intensity, the skin on her arms remained cold with goose bumps.

Along with the kip notes and traveler's checks, the three youths relieved her of her camera, her lighter, her Walkman, and some tapes. That was all. The fact that they didn't take her passport or make her sign the checks suggested they were smalltime hoods, not part of an organized ring. The young mugger then ordered her back onto the motorcycle and drove her some distance before dropping her off in a place where nothing but makeshift shanties lined the road. As he was about to ride away, he flashed her a smile and said, "Thank you." His boyish smile made him look like a little kid.

The road stretched out in both directions through a landscape of rice paddies dotted with stands of trees. Having no idea where she was, Aoi made her best guess and started walking. Every time she met someone coming the other way, she tried to ask for directions by saying, "Vientiane?" but the shabbily dressed men and women just eyed her curiously, or in some cases with wariness, and no one would tell her the right direction.

"I don't believe it! I don't believe it! I don't believe it!" Aoi muttered as she marched doggedly on. "I hate this country! In all the time I've been traveling, I've never had anything like this happen to me. Everybody's been so nice. Nobody's ever told me such rotten lies. A friend? Nanako? Letters and pictures? If he wanted my money, why couldn't he just demand it on the spot instead of concocting some stupid story? Hope they catch you trying to pass those unsigned checks, you dumbass!"

As she ranted on out loud, the trembling in her hands ceased, her gooseflesh subsided, and the fear that had tightened every nerve in her body slowly eased its grip. The sun continued to sizzle as it tilted lower in the sky. A dog with a large patch of missing hair came up from behind and slowly overtook her. Gnats flew in silent swirls.

"I don't believe it!" Aoi spat out again, but then caught her breath and stopped dead in her tracks on the red clay road.

It was like a bolt from the blue: she *had* believed. Until this very moment, she had truly believed that she could count on people's good faith. It was a realization both marvelous and dumbfounding. She had also believed without a shadow of a doubt that Nanako was still alive. Almost as if she had been there herself, Aoi had believed that Nanako, with that unguarded sociability she seemed to share with middle-aged country women, had engaged in conversation with the young man, joined him for a cup of tea at some open-air café, commemorated the occasion by taking a picture or two, and then written him a letter after returning to Japan.

A young mother with child in arms walked by, staring openly at the foreign woman standing like a pillar on the dusty clay road. An elderly woman emerged from what looked like a general store several doors ahead and stood staring as well. Suddenly everything before Aoi's eyes became magnified, then wavered gently as if she were underwater, and a moment later she realized she was crying. She resumed her march. The sun's powerful rays burned the top of her head. Tears kept rolling down her cheeks like beads of sweat. Flies buzzed about her arms and her face. Sniffling continually and wiping her tearstained cheeks with sunburned wrists, she walked on.

She heard a sound like the whine of a mosquito coming from behind and turned to see a small pickup truck heading toward her, still some distance away. She wondered if she should flag it down and ask for a ride into the city, but stood there, unable to move. She had no way of knowing who would be in the truck. Would they agree to take her to the city? The trembling that had gone from her hands a short while before slowly crept back up from her fingertips.

The truck approached, kicking up thick clouds of red dust in its wake. Children came running out of the shacks along the road to wave at the passing vehicle.

There was no assurance that the driver would take her where she asked. He could easily carry her off to some secluded spot again and force her to hand over the rest of her money. Or even if he did take her into the city, he might demand some outrageous amount in pay-ment. And yet...still...in spite of that...

Taking a deep breath and willing her rigid limbs to move, Aoi lunged out into the path of the oncoming pickup, waving her arms high and wide over her head to get its attention. The truck blared its horn and screeched to a halt several meters away. Clouds of dust bil-lowed up around it, momentarily obscuring it from view. Aoi stepped forcefully forward.

I've got to have faith. That's how it has to be. Right here, right now, I've made up my mind.

"Vientiane!" Leaning in through the open passenger-side window, she shouted across the front seat at the middle-aged driver: "Vien-tiane! Samsentai! Pangam Guesthouse! Tat Luan!" One after the other she barked out the names of the street, her hotel, and the nearby temple, hoping he would understand what she wanted. The ferocity with which this string of words emerged seemed to bewilder him at first, but he finally nodded with recognition when she said the name of the Tarat Sao Market. He reached over to open the pas-senger door.

I've got to have faith. That's how I've made up my mind. I can't shrink in fear. If there's a world where some jerk hoodwinks me and scares me out of my money, there's another world where a kind stranger sets his work aside and walks all over the place to find me an inexpen-sive hotel room, then disappears without even giving me a chance to thank him. It's all the same. If there's a world where Nanako no longer exists, then there must also be a world where she still lives and shares a laugh with someone she's never met before. And in that case, I choose to believe in the latter. Just as I choose to believe this pickup truck will take me where I want to go.

The driver glanced at Aoi from time to time as he drove. Their eyes met and an awkward smile came to his lips. "Vientiane," he said quietly with a nod.

The cries of insects. The smell of the dust. Women walking bare-foot. The unrelenting glare of the sun. The unchanging landscape. It all flowed by at breathtaking speed outside the window. The dusty wind blowing in on Aoi's face soon dried her tear-dampened cheeks.

When she graduated from college, Aoi launched a travel business catering mainly to students. The operation was like a glorified student activity group at first, with earnings so meager she had to take on side jobs to make ends meet. Students she'd gotten to know through her university's Rail Society and Travel Club dropped in frequently at her office, which was also her home. Young people she'd met on her travels would sometimes stay with her for several weeks while they looked for a place to live after getting back to Japan.

Far from finding it stressful to have all these people constantly hanging around her home-slash-office, Aoi enjoyed the company. She liked sharing her days with others, sleeping and waking and working together, then partying over dinner after their work was done. Quite simply, it was what she called fun.

As subcontracting requests from other travel companies increased and her cash flow stabilized, she moved to new quarters in Okubo and incorporated as a limited liability company. When she won a major contract to represent a consortium of hotels, she purchased a condominium unit nearby and reorganized as a joint stock company. The students who'd hung around the office gradually stopped coming, and the rooms filled up instead with office desks, computers, and a large copier and fax machine combo.

She felt like she spent her days tallying up what she could do herself and what she just wasn't up to—with the latter always winning by a large margin. She wasn't very good with numbers or complicated calculations, she frequently forgot appointments she'd made, she had no idea how to manage a filing system, and she generally lacked office skills. But her long list of deficiencies did not particularly trouble her. If there was something she couldn't handle herself, all she had to do was hire someone who could. There were still bound to be things she could do that the people she hired couldn't.

As the years went by, the boom in student travel came to an end, clients she counted on for work fell on hard times and closed up shop, world events made people reluctant to travel abroad, and suddenly Aoi found herself past the midway point of her thirties taking home less than her employees. She experienced a sense of foreboding she had never known before as the ground shook precariously beneath her feet.

Aoi realized she had grown tired of dealing with people. Hiring employees and working shoulder to shoulder with them wasn't simply a matter of dividing up tasks according to each person's skills. One person goofed off when she could and otherwise contributed nothing but complaints. A second would disarm you with a friendly smile and make off with your work. A third remained blind to her own shortcomings but never missed a chance to remind others of theirs. Although it should have been nobody's business, word somehow got around and staff members began prying into Aoi's past with prurient fascination. People came and went, one after the other. One day it dawned on Aoi that dealing with people belonged on the list of things she wasn't equipped to do, and it sent a chill down her spine.

It was at this juncture that she interviewed a housewife from her alma mater for a new venture. She became convinced as soon as Sayoko started work that the decision to hire her was not a mistake. The way she immersed herself in meticulous detail, as if she were painstakingly ironing each fold of a pleated skirt, in some ways seemed like a shell she crawled into because she wanted to shut other people out. But speaking strictly in terms of performance, Aoi could have asked for nothing more.

Through snatches of conversation here and there, Aoi sensed that

Sayoko had begun to crack open her shell and was peering straight at her through the widening hole. It reminded her of herself in high school. As they talked, she sometimes felt like she was now playing the role that Nanako had played back then.

One day when she teamed up with Sayoko to clean a spectacularly grungy apartment, she found herself experiencing strong feelings of déjà vu. Silently scrubbing the tub and splash area in the bathroom. Sweat trickling from temple to chin. The summer sun pouring through the window. Mind empty, face blank, hands unremittingly in motion. Noriko Nakazato's eagle eye. It reminded her so much of Izu. As she and Sayoko went about their separate tasks in separate rooms, Aoi felt her recent sense of foreboding slowly melting away. This was what she had always wanted to be doing: keeping in constant motion, always on the lookout for the next thing she could tackle, and working until she was ready to drop—then, at the end of the day, sharing her exhaustion and a smile with a colleague. Perhaps the future she had longed to find as a teenager existed only somewhere on the far side of days like that. As one whose list of capabilities was probably shorter than most, perhaps what she'd really wanted to do was not to start up and run some fancy company, but simply something like this.

Except for their ages and alma mater, she and Sayoko had little in common. Their situations in life, their perspectives, what they had and didn't have—everything about them was different. To be honest, when Sayoko spoke of her family or her daughter or the nursery school, she might as well have been transmitting some secret code as far as Aoi was concerned. But Aoi also couldn't help feeling that they were ultimately climbing the same hill. Traveling by completely different routes, at times forging ahead regardless, at times sitting down to rest, at times ready to give up the trek altogether, they were slowly but surely ascending the same upward slope. No matter how far apart their situations and perspectives were, and no matter how different the things they had and didn't have might be, Aoi had felt that someday the two of them would clasp hands atop that hill, laughing and cheering together, "We did it! We did it!"

Yet here Sayoko sat, like so many others who had come and gone before, asking, with a hint of scorn tugging at her lips, about what had happened after the big leap.

As she had done with the others, Aoi joked her way lightly through the broader details of her tale, then fixed her eyes firmly on Sayoko.

"Satisfied?"

Sayoko had been listening with her face set in stone. "Yes, I'm glad I asked," she murmured.

"Since we don't have any cleaning jobs on the docket, why don't you just go on home for today," Aoi said with her usual smile. "And let me know as soon as you can about what I proposed a while ago. I'd even say tomorrow, if possible. I've got loads of stuff I'd like to ask you to help with."

"Thank you. I'll be going then." Leaving her coffee untouched, Sayoko stood up and moved into the front hall. After putting on her shoes at the door, she turned. "If you're giving up the housekeeping, I think I'll hand in my resignation, too," she said in a squeak of a voice, then made a quick bow and went out.

Silence filled the room. Aoi lifted her feet onto the chair and cradled her chin on her knees, staring at the closed door. When the sound of Sayoko's footsteps on the stairs died away, she got up to open the kitchen window and lit a cigarette. Standing in the light of the midday sun, she inhaled deeply. The smell of spices and cooking oil from a nearby restaurant filled the air.

Like Junko and Misao, Sayoko had probably gone out that door never to return. Yuki was scheduled to leave for Canada with her husband, and Mao would not be staying long either. Recruiting new staff would take some time, so meanwhile she needed to figure out what she could and couldn't do by herself. What she could and couldn't do... Stubbing out her cigarette in the sink, she slid down the wall to the floor and buried her face against her legs. Once she started contemplating all that had to be done before she could actually begin working with a new team—placing ads and interviewing applicants and teaching them what they needed to know for their jobs—it seemed like all she had in store was headaches.

Wanting to cry, Aoi hunched her back and put her face in her hands. When tears failed to come, she tried to prompt them by raising her voice in a childlike wail, *Waaaah!* Still the tears refused to come. She lay face down and peered through her fingers at the kitchen floor. All of a sudden she was remembering the moment on that red clay road in Laos when she stepped into the path of the oncoming pickup truck and waved her arms high over her head. The burning sun. The colors. The smell of the dust. The quaking of her knees from still fearing the worst.

"I quit!" she exclaimed, and quickly got to her feet. She strode into her office to pick up the cell phone she'd left on the tatami and began scrolling through her phone book.

"Hello. Hana? What're you doing tonight? You're free? Great! Let's go drinking. My treat."

As she cheerfully made plans with the person on the other end, Aoi glanced about the former two-bedroom apartment.

Boy, am I pooped! How would you rate today? A sweet-tooth five? Welcome back! You must be tired. Cakes? Oh, goody. That's exactly what I need! The voices of the women who'd worked in these rooms echoed in her ears. The sun on its way to the top of its arc quietly beamed down on the dining table surrounded by empty chairs in disarray.

15

The end of the year drew near and the nursery school closed for its winter break. With Akari at home every day, it was easy for Sayoko to feel she'd made the right decision.

Since quitting her job at Platinum Planet, she'd spent all her time at home, never going anywhere but the grocery store. She filled her days cleaning the house, polishing every surface to a spotless sheen. Since it was the season for the customary year-end cleaning anyway, she felt no pangs of guilt; she simply told herself that giving the house a thorough buffing-up for the new year took priority over taking Akari on outings to the park or the children's museum.

She'd started work at the beginning of June, so the house had suffered more than six months of neglect. Her quick, weekly once-overs had missed many pockets of accumulating dust and grime. Now, between frequent interruptions from Akari for attention, she degreased the vent fan and scoured the stove, waxed the hardwood floors, shined the dish buffet, washed all the window screens, and scrubbed the bathroom from top to bottom. She cleaned and cleaned and cleaned, and yet she still found more dirt lurking about. Even after going methodically through the house, checking room by room and taking care of each problem she found, she was sure there must be other spots she'd missed, and continued to wander about with her cleaning rag poised at the ready.

At about four o'clock each day she bundled Akari up for a trip to the supermarket, where she threaded her way slowly through the crowds of other young mothers with small children in tow to pick out what she needed for the elaborate dishes she prepared each night. On days when Shuji was out late, she put Akari to bed and then busied herself sewing things for when her daughter would go back to school. The simple tote bag and shoe pouch she'd slapped together in those hectic days before Akari's first day betrayed the rush in which she had made them. Now she pored over the manual for her sewing machine and learned how to use the embroidery functions, trying her hand at Peter Rabbit and Winnie the Pooh and neatly spelling out Akari's name on her towels and handkerchiefs. She knew she would have to withdraw Akari from school unless she found another job, but she felt she had to be doing something.

From time to time she thought of Aoi. Or more precisely, of the story Aoi had told her on that last day at the office. Aoi had said she and the girl she leaped off the roof with never saw each other again. The girl had promptly transferred to another school, and they had neither written nor called each other after that. Hearing this gave Sayoko a certain satisfaction: she'd been correct to imagine Aoi quickly forgetting the friend she ran away with. But having once been envious of the unknown girl from Aoi's past, Sayoko also felt a measure of disappointment in this ending. "That's too bad," she had said quietly, to which Aoi had twisted her lips in a self-deprecating smile and replied, "What can you expect? We were only kids."

She was probably right, Sayoko thought as she cleaned house and embroidered handkerchiefs. No matter how close they may once have been, when two friends go their separate ways the relationship quickly ends. No doubt she herself would soon forget about the offbeat little company called Platinum Planet and the woman her own age who ran it. And that woman would forget about her as well. Even though they weren't "only kids" anymore—maybe, in fact, all the more because they weren't—their memories of the time they had spent together would quickly be lost amidst the day-to-day minutiae of their lives.

When Sayoko told her husband she had quit her job, he didn't seem the least bit surprised. "Yeah, I figured you would," he'd said matter-of-factly. "I think it's better that way."

If Sayoko wasn't working, she would have to withdraw Akari from school by the end of January. But partly because the girl was almost at kindergarten age and now completely used to school, and partly because Sayoko herself enjoyed the friendships she had struck up with some of the other mothers, she really wanted to keep Akari enrolled. That meant she needed to find a new job right away, so she spent time going over the want ads and recruitment inserts in the newspaper, folding down page corners and circling items of interest with a pen. But Shuji's voice saying *I figured you would, I think it's better that way* kept echoing through her head. Unable to make up her mind one way or the other, she simply went back to cleaning the house, and so the year came to an end.

According to their annual custom, they all went to visit Shuji's mother on New Year's Day. As usual, nothing Sayoko did seemed to please Grandma Tamura.

"I don't suppose you cook for New Year's, do you, Sayoko? But really, New Year's isn't the same without the traditional treats, don't you agree? I stayed up late last night making all these things, and I'm completely bushed, so maybe you could make us a salad or something."

As Sayoko set to work in the tiny kitchen, her mother-in-law hovered over her shoulder offering a constant stream of instructions. "Don't use the cabbage," she said as soon as Sayoko opened the vegetable compartment. "And I'll need those carrots, too."

Sayoko took out some *komatsuna* greens and began rinsing them.

"My goodness, a salad with *komatsuna*? That'll certainly be different," her mother-in-law said dubiously. After a pause she went on: "I'm thinking we really ought to have some sashimi, too. The supermarket by the station is open, so maybe you could go pick out a few things, whatever you like."

Here we go again, Sayoko bristled, but then in a sudden inspiration she raised her voice and called out to Shuji, who was draped lazily across the sofa in the living room: "Honey, your mom says we need some sashimi. Could you go to the store?"

"Hunh?" he grunted, sluggishly pulling himself to his feet. "What'd you say you wanted me to get?"

"Some sashimi. Pick out whatever you like. And take Akari along, if you don't mind. I'm getting ready to fix these greens, so I'll have my hands full for a while."

Sayoko braced herself for a sharp rebuke, but to her surprise her mother-in-law grabbed her purse and quickly shuffled over to Shuji.

"Tuna or sea bream, maybe. Or flounder would be okay, too," she said, then added, like a mother sending her child shopping for the first time, "Do you even know what sea bream and flounder look like?"

Shuji laughed his mother down and turned to Akari. "Come on, kiddo! We're going to the store!"

The girl had been bored and starting to fuss, but she leaped to her feet. "We're going to the store!" she echoed.

Sayoko went back to the refrigerator and promptly began removing anything she thought she could use in a salad, including the cabbage and the carrots. *How hard was that?* she thought in pleasant surprise. *I don't always have to be the one to do everything. I just have to ask.* As she checked on the water she was heating for the greens, she realized she was humming—here in the house where she always got nothing but grief.

Dinner was ready at six. Grandma's traditional New Year's foods arranged in lacquered boxes shared the center of the table with the sashimi Shuji and Akari had brought back from the store and the salad and boiled greens prepared by Sayoko. On TV a raucous New Year's talent show was in progress.

"These New Year's specials are all so noisy," Grandma said.

"Oh, that reminds me, Mom," Shuji said, getting to his feet. "I brought a video. From Akari's first Field Day. I thought maybe we could all watch it together. I've been looking for a chance to show it to you."

He got the tape from his bag and squatted in front of the TV to load it into the VCR.

"I got to be a ninja, Nana! I danced the ninja dance!" Akari said, leaning forward eagerly in her chair.

"Oh, my, you don't say," Grandma replied. She didn't sound particularly enthusiastic.

The loud voices on the TV abruptly broke off as the screen went blue for a moment, and then the video started to play. Sayoko cast a glance toward the screen but turned right back to her food and continued eating, not saying a word. She had watched the part showing Akari's dance a few times, but nothing more. The video inevitably brought back other memories of the day Aoi had shot it.

Music crackled from the speakers, and a teacher yelled a cheer into the microphone. Each time the scene changed, Akari piped up with a comment, and Shuji explained to his mother what was going on.

Sayoko reached for a prawn from one of the lacquered boxes and deftly peeled off its shell. Leaving that for later, she picked up a piece of tuna sashimi with her chopsticks and dipped it in the soy sauce on her small dipping plate.

"The picture's so clear," her mother-in-law observed.

"Yeah. Just like real TV, isn't it? Oh! There's Sayoko."

"Well, look at that! But, who's filming then?"

"Mommy danced with me, Nana. 'Yo-he-ho, the peach tree...'" Akari started singing the dance song.

"A friend of mine came," Sayoko explained. "Unfortunately, Shuji couldn't make it."

"I said I was sorry. You know I hated having to miss it."

"Oh, dear. That little girl's crying. Look at her, the poor thing." In a rare show of amusement, Grandma laughed out loud.

"Sakura's a crybaby," Akari said, also laughing.

"My goodness, how old are these kids that just came on? They look a whole lot bigger than the last group."

Sayoko looked up from the table to see. The video had changed from the parent-child dance to a group of older kids gathering at the starting line for their dash around the track. Aoi had even filmed events Akari wasn't in. All of a sudden, the children at the line took off running.

"I think they're the five-year-olds," Sayoko said, her eyes lingering on the screen. Lively music played in the background as the children raced around the track. Suddenly one of the boys took a nasty tumble and landed on his face. Making no effort to pick himself back up, he burst into tears.

A teacher's voice came over the loudspeakers. "Run, Naoki! You're almost there! Get up and run!" The camera zoomed in on the fallen runner. Another boy a few steps ahead turned to look, and his legs did a funny little dance step as he tried to make up his mind whether to continue his dash for the goal or double back to give some help. Finally he decided to turn back, and a cheer went up. He flopped down on the ground and said something to comfort or encourage his classmate. As he spoke to him, he took the boy's hand to help him to his feet, and together they began walking slowly toward the goal. The one who fell was still bawling, his face turned toward the sky. Leading him by the hand, the other boy reached back now and then to wipe the tears from his cheeks.

After following the pair across the goal line, the image on screen broke up momentarily and then Sayoko appeared, waving and walking toward the camera. Almost right away the image broke off again, and the camera gave a little jolt as the next scene came up. The kids in Akari's class were assembling in the middle of the playground. The picture zoomed in on Akari.

Sayoko watched with a slice of tuna poised between her chopsticks in midair.

The camera pulled back as teachers led Akari and her classmates by the hand to their places. The loudspeakers struck up a bouncy new tune. A flawless blue sky stretched overhead. All around the playground parents with cameras and camcorders could be seen leaning over the ropes, straining to get the best shot of their child. Now Akari returned to the middle of the picture, standing there motionless, with only her eyes darting back and forth. Sayoko and Aoi could be heard near the camera, first laughing, then shouting words of encouragement: "Dance, Akari! You can do it! Go, Akari!" Finally Akari began moving awkwardly to the music.

As her eyes followed the action on screen, Sayoko was picturing instead the figure of Aoi with the video camera in her hands, eyes puffy from lack of sleep. She pictured her intently pursuing Akari's movements. She pictured her zooming in on the boy who turned back to help his fallen friend.

"Goodness, Sayoko! You're dripping! You're dripping!" Grandma's high-pitched cry brought Sayoko back to reality. Several drops of soy sauce from the tuna had fallen onto her skirt.

"Oh dear!" she exclaimed. "And I just bought this skirt brand new for New Year's!"

Hurrying to the bathroom, she soaked a towel in hot water and began dabbing forcefully at the stain. For some reason she was reminded of when she'd chanted *Damn it all! Damn it all!* as she pedaled her bicycle. In the image that came to her she was dripping with sweat, yet in odd contrast to the words she chanted, the pedals spun around quite effortlessly and a hint of a smile tugged at her lips. The outlines of the stain soon blurred and its color faded, but Sayoko continued dabbing at it with more vigor than necessary. She could hear Shuji and his mother and Akari laughing at something in the dining room.

Sayoko wasn't sure she was in the mood, but she accepted Mrs. Motoyama's invitation and tagged along to the coffee klatch of kindergarten moms that met at a nearby family restaurant. As they slipped into their seats in a nonsmoking booth by the window, the ladies called out their orders for coffee or tea. Sayoko had only recently gotten to know these women, so she couldn't yet match all the faces with names.

Mrs. Motoyama was the one who'd introduced her to the group. Sayoko had made her acquaintance in the elevator one day by asking about her little boy and learning that he was in kindergarten. Since the time to withdraw Akari from nursery school was rapidly approaching, she'd immediately taken the opportunity to ask some questions about the boy's kindergarten. After that they began speaking together quite regularly, and Mrs. Motoyama soon suggested she meet the other kindergarten moms who gathered at the family restaurant each day while waiting for their children to be let out of class. The ladies knew Sayoko well enough now to stop and chat with her when she ran into them in the neighborhood of her apartment building.

As they settled into their seats, they all began chattering at breakneck speed about their children's teachers and upcoming events at school. These were topics to which Sayoko could not contribute, but she preferred it that way: it was easier just to smile and nod than to try to be part of the conversation.

The waitress came with their orders, and the ladies interrupted their talk while they waited for her to finish serving the drinks. As soon as she was gone, they picked up right where they'd left off.

"I really think testing for private schools is the way to go."

"Is that what you're doing? Oh, that's right. You said the other day you were putting your boy in exam-prep classes come April."

"I figure the public school should be fine."

"I'm not so sure. It worries me when I see some of the kids who come up through the nursery school system."

"No kidding. So many of them seem like they've never been taught any manners. There's this one boy in my apartment building who glares at you and shouts 'Shut up!' if you try to say anything to him. He cheerfully goes around saying things like 'dumbass' and 'drop dead.' It's shocking!"

"Mrs. Tamura, don't you find that a lot of your daughter's friends in nursery school are poorly behaved?"

With the conversation suddenly coming her way, Sayoko just smiled ambiguously.

"You'd do best to get your girl out of there as soon as you can. Little Akari's a real sweetie, but little ones her age are so impressionable."

"Come to think of it, the boy I was talking about who says 'dumbass' and 'drop dead,' I'm pretty sure he and his brother go to Akari's school. He's with the three-year-olds. Ren Kurata."

"Oh, yes, I know Ren," Sayoko nodded. In her mind she pictured the boy's round-faced mother, who worked for a life insurance company.

"He's a complete terror. Even though he's only three, he knocked my boy down and made him cry."

"That's the problem with nursery school kids."

"It's different for you, Mrs. Tamura, because you quit your job, but basically, when kids get put in nursery school, it means their mothers are working outside the home. Kids like that don't get enough time with their mothers, and they wind up badly behaved and rowdy. You can tell the ones who've been raised in nursery school right away."

"And heaven forbid you say anything to their mothers about it. They'll bite your head off with some fancy talk about making a contribution to society. They're all so full of themselves."

"That's for sure. I met this woman the other day who . . ."

Sayoko pretended to be interested by interjecting the occasional "Uh-huh" or "Oh my!" or "Really?" but her eyes drifted out the window. Murky, leaden clouds hung low in the sky. She had known since first meeting these ladies that every one of them, including Mrs. Motoyama, was a full-time homemaker, and it had been immediately apparent that they all disapproved of mothers who worked outside the home. Even so, Sayoko rarely turned down an invitation to join them for their daily coffee klatch. Quite simply, she welcomed the chance to pick up tidbits about life in kindergarten, as well as their experiences with periodic checkups.

She felt a sense of déjà vu coming over her as she gave noncommittal responses to the working-mom bashing that had suddenly taken over the conversation. Yet almost right away she realized it wasn't only an impression but an actual memory. In spite of all the years that had passed between then and now, what she was witnessing here was no different from what had gone on back in high school, when she had pushed desks together with her girlfriends to eat lunch: a group uniting for the moment to vilify some imagined bugbear. But Sayoko knew how astonishingly short-lived such unity could be. Give these women a few months, and the brunt of their disapproval would perhaps fall on the one who sent her child to exam-prep classes, she speculated somewhat arbitrarily.

What are the gathering years supposed to be for, Sayoko wondered vaguely as she gazed out the window at the leafless ginkgo trees lining the street. It would be easy enough for her to claim she was too busy and turn down these invitations to the coffee klatch. Since she didn't have a child attending their kindergarten anyway, they would probably soon stop asking her. And at her age, she wouldn't feel particularly hurt by this. Unlike in high school, she had no time to be fretting about such things. She had her own family to take care of, her own life to live, and they had theirs.

"There's a lady in my building who takes in work at home. Some kind of design work, I guess, but I don't really know. She thinks nothing of sending her boy over to play and not coming to get him till six and seven in the evening. Of course, all that time, she's doing her work. Talk about brazen!"

"That's some nerve—using you as a free babysitter while she's pulling in the dough. And so blatantly."

"Too bad she had to move into your building."

"And the boy's such a terror. He leaves cookie crumbs all over the tatami room, and the other day he tore a hole in one of our shoji screens."

"Oh dear. You really need to say something about that!"

"I'd think you might get the same thing with the kids in your daughter's class, Mrs. Tamura. Do their moms sometimes dump them on you because they know you stay home?"

A woman not much younger than Sayoko sitting diagonally across the table thrust her chin toward her as she spoke. She looked rather like Takeshi Kihara.

Sayoko glanced down at her watch. "Oh, look at the time!" she exclaimed, getting to her feet. "My daughter's out any minute now. Sorry to rush off, but I have to go."

"My goodness. You're right. You'd better hurry."

"Oh dear, we should have noticed."

A chorus of voices followed Sayoko as she started to walk away, but she quickly turned in her tracks and came back. "Sorry, I almost forgot to pay," she said, placing money for her coffee on the table. "Well, see you." She smiled and hurried away again.

As she raced toward the nursery school, the thought crossed her mind that the discussion may well have turned from Work-at-home

Mom to Akari's Mom as soon as she left, but she immediately shrugged it off. She really didn't care.

Pausing as she came through the gate, she looked for her daughter's figure among the children in the schoolyard. Akari was playing house in the sandbox with Ren, the boy who'd been the topic of conversation just a few minutes before. Sayoko started toward the sandbox but stopped short and stood watching as the two carried on their game.

What had she been using her "gathering years" for lately? To conveniently escape into her own private world as soon as she grew weary of being mixed up with other people? To make excuses that she had to go to the bank, had to pick up her daughter, had to make dinner, and then push the door shut behind her?

The boy accused of pushing an older child to the ground and making him cry took the bowl of sand Akari was holding out to him.

"Aah, we're having sushi tonight," he said, putting on his best grown-up air. "Do we have any beer?"

"No, dear," Akari replied. "You mustn't drink beer."

Sayoko burst out laughing.

"It's your mom," Ren shouted.

Akari turned and was immediately on her feet racing toward Sayoko. Ren got up and came running behind her.

"You're going home already," Ren said with a pout.

"What time will your mother be here, Ren?" Sayoko asked.

"I dunno."

"We were playing house, Mommy," Akari said.

"I'm afraid we have to go, Ren. Come play sometime, okay?"

"I dunno."

"Bye-bye. See you tomorrow."

"Bye-bye," Akari waved, but Ren turned away and deliberately ignored her.

Walking toward the gate with Akari's hand in hers, Sayoko found herself remembering the video Aoi had shot here. She saw the boy falling on his face, and the other boy flopping down beside him to offer comfort. Aoi had instinctively zoomed in to capture it all on tape.

Suddenly it came clear to Sayoko why the two teenage girls who leaped hand in hand off the roof of the apartment building had never seen each other again. It wasn't simply that they'd drifted out of touch, or that they were young and quick to forget. They were afraid. Afraid to learn that the friend with whom they'd shared so much was now in a different place. Afraid to reach out to someone who'd been changed by the utterly different path she had taken since high school and the utterly different set of experiences she had had. Afraid of being asked, "Don't you have any new friends?"

"Bye-bye!"

They heard Ren calling after them and turned to see him pressed against the inside of the fence waving at Akari.

"See you tomorrow!" Akari shouted.

"Yeah, see ya," said Ren, still sounding a little cross. He promptly turned back toward the sandbox.

Sayoko thought back to the day when "Bye-bye!" signified for her an unchanging tomorrow. A tomorrow when she would see her same friend in that same uniform again. A tomorrow when they would hang out together in the same world as today, bantering back and forth with the same phrases, sharing the same looks. She thought back to the day when she counted on that sameness.

"See ya!" Akari called after Ren's receding figure one last time.

As Sayoko lowered her eyes to look at her daughter, she found the question from before going through her mind again.

What are the gathering years supposed to be for?

After riding the creaky old elevator up to the fifth floor, Sayoko stood in front of the rust-spotted door and drew in a deep breath.

She lifted her hand toward the intercom installed at eye level. Her index finger trembled. This could mean being greeted with icy silence, or even driven away. She might only be making a fool of herself by coming here. After all, she was the one who'd walked away, muttering what could be taken as a parting shot. But she had made up her mind. It was something she had to do, even if she wound up getting the door slammed in her face.

A few days ago Sayoko had received a phone call from Noriko Nakazato. In the crisp, no-nonsense style Sayoko remembered so well, Noriko explained that she was creating a registry of homemakers who would provide housekeeping services through her agency. Would Sayoko like to have her name listed? Not immediately sure what to say, Sayoko changed the subject by asking how Noriko knew she'd gone back to being a full-time housewife.

"Well, you know, I heard about what happened at Platinum Planet. To be honest, I pretty much figured the place was on the skids. But I understand that, thanks to you, things were actually starting to get back on track. Aoi was really sick about that, kicking herself for letting it all go to waste. I would be, too. I mean, I remember from the first day I started training you, I could see right away you were a find. Not very many come along who apply themselves the way you do. I even thought about maybe trying to lure you away."

"Are you saying Miss Narahashi asked you to give me a job? Is that why you called?"

"No, no, no. All she could talk about was how sorry she was for blithely telling you to forget about the cleaning business. She said she was just too desperate for help keeping Platinum Planet afloat after everybody else left, you know. Well, she *should* be sorry. She makes you go through all that training and then, just when you finally get down to business, she lets everything fall apart. Anyway, you might say I called to steal a march on her. Since I know it'll be a while before she can even think about the cleaning business again, I figured I'd better snap you up while I have the chance."

Sayoko listened with her ear pressed hard to the handset. She remembered Aoi telling her she was putting the cleaning operation on hold, her face pale without makeup as she stared down at the contents of the coffee mug in her hand. She wondered why she'd been so incensed with her for not knowing all she'd been going through—butting heads with Shuji, holding her self-doubts at bay, and chanting *Damn it all! Damn it all!* as she pedaled her bicycle along.

Sayoko asked Noriko what had happened to Platinum Planet after she'd gone out the door that day.

Aoi had been left with just one employee, Yuki Yamaguchi—and at the end of the year she quit as well, to prepare for her move overseas in March. The company premises were owned, not rented, so Aoi sold the property to scrape together enough money for everybody's severance, and moved the business to her own apartment in Shimokitazawa. She now ran a much-reduced operation from there, all by herself.

"People quit on you all the time," Noriko went on. "The trick is to replace them quickly and get back up to speed. But instead, Aoi dawdles around, giving up the office and stuff and going practically into retreat to carry on quietly by herself. Anyway, what do you say? Can I put you on my list?"

Sayoko thought of Aoi's apartment, which she'd visited just that one time.

"I need some time to think about it," she said, and put down the phone.

Now, taking another deep breath, she pressed the button on the intercom. The sound of the chime inside rang out through the door: *ding-dong.* There was no answer. She pressed the button again.

"Darn, she must be out."

Sayoko felt all the strength drain from her body. What should she do now? If she simply went on home, she doubted she would ever come again. One day she'd have to wash a blanket, the next she'd have to embroider Akari's name on a towel. She'd probably find one excuse or another to put off coming from day to day, until in the end she decided she didn't care anymore and pushed the whole idea from her mind. But there was one thing she knew: walking around the house with a cleaning rag in her hand wasn't going to turn up any more dirt she'd overlooked.

"Maybe I'll wait downstairs," she mumbled, returning along the dim walkway to the elevator and jabbing at the call button.

She listened to the irritating creak of the elevator as it came up to the fifth floor and opened its doors. There stood Aoi.

"Oh!" cried Sayoko in surprise.

"My goodness!" Aoi exclaimed at the same time, staring wide-eyed.

As they both stood frozen to the spot, the doors started to slide shut between them. Sayoko hastily raised her arms to stop them, while Aoi thrust out her foot. They both burst out laughing at the other's awkward posture.

"Wow. You gave me a real start," Aoi said, stepping out of the elevator. In her hand was a grocery bag from the convenience store. She seemed to have lost a lot of weight. Behind her the elevator creaked for a while again as it made its way back down to the first floor, then fell silent.

"Sorry to drop in out of the blue like this," Sayoko said. Their brief burst of laughter had momentarily loosened her taut nerves, but now they were nearly choking her again.

"Out of the blue is right. What is it? You're not here to hit me up for severance, are you?" Slipping past Sayoko, Aoi strode to her front door and inserted the key.

"I do have a request," Sayoko forced out as she followed along the walkway. Aoi looked at her with her hand on the doorknob. "I'd like to work for you. I'll do anything. Answer the phone, enter data, stuff envelopes, clean—really, anything. Training wages will be fine. In fact, no, I'll work for nothing until I've learned the business."

"Maybe you should keep it down a bit, Chief," Aoi cut her off in a low voice. "Talk any louder and the neighbors'll wonder what in the world's going on." She stepped inside and beckoned to Sayoko, who slipped through the door behind her.

"It's a terrible mess, but come on in."

Sayoko stepped out of her shoes and followed her inside. The private apartment now doubling as an office was in such chaotic disarray that Sayoko could not remember what it had been like before. The walls of the main living-dining room were almost completely hidden behind teetering stacks of cardboard boxes; the floor was littered with collapsing piles of pamphlets, page proofs, photocopies, magazines flagged with sticky notes, and sundry other items. Even the window with the view Aoi so loved was blocked two-thirds of the way up with boxes; a narrow strip at the top offered only a glimpse of the clear winter sky.

In the kitchen off the dining area, a mountain of empty noodle cups and box-lunch containers filled the sink, with flies buzzing about even in the middle of winter. The sliding doors to the tatami room had been removed, and Aoi's low round table from the old office, the massive fax and copy machine, and bookshelves crammed untidily with reference materials left little space to maneuver around the twin-size bed. Cardboard boxes covered at least half the window in there, too, leaving the room quite dim.

"Like I said, it's a mess." Aoi quickly moved mounds of clothing and laundry from the sofa to the floor and motioned to Sayoko. "Have a seat. I haven't had lunch yet, so you'll have to excuse me." She plopped down on the floor, took a sandwich and rice ball from the grocery bag, and started eating without another word.

Sayoko stole furtive glances at her as she chewed, trying to read her expression and guess what she might be thinking. But Aoi's face offered no clues. *I've got to say something*, she thought. *I've got to make my case.* She searched for the right words.

"I've been feeling terrible about the way I quit. After everything you did for me, and also just when I was finally getting into the swing of things."

No, she thought, *that's all hogwash; nothing but handy clichés.* She looked at the piles of clothes on the floor, glanced at Aoi peeling the wrapper from her rice ball, then gazed up at the narrow strip of blue sky visible through the window.

"Remember that Family Support Center you mentioned?" she finally resumed. "The truth is, I never bothered to look into it seriously because I always hate having to deal with people I don't know. But I went to sign up the other day, and they introduced me right away to a family in my neighborhood. Just like that. I couldn't believe how easy it was. Really, I can't imagine anymore what I could have been so afraid of, it was so simple, so routine. So I'm all set now. I can even work late when I need to."

Aoi broke off a bite-size piece of the rice ball and shoved it into her mouth. She sat gazing at the floor as she chewed.

Sayoko had decided to go to the center and see about a caregiver in her neighborhood as soon as she got off the phone with Noriko. They referred her to a couple in their fifties whose two grown children had moved out of the house. They said they'd only recently registered with the center.

"It'll be such a joy to have a child to take care of again," the woman beamed when they met to get acquainted.

"No more empty nest syndrome for you," the husband teased with a laugh. "She got hit pretty bad after the kids left," he explained. "She'd spend whole days sitting blankly at the kitchen table."

"Maybe this isn't really the sort of thing you should admit to someone you've only just met, but I felt like I must have failed my children somehow. I was sure that was why they never came around. Then my husband heard about the center and how it worked. I hesitated a long time. If I thought I'd failed my own children, what business did I have taking in somebody else's? But I'm so glad to meet you. I only wish we'd signed up sooner." She smiled gently at Akari. "I could have gotten to know a darling little girl like you a long time ago."

"She reminds me of Eiko when she was little," the husband added. Eiko was apparently their daughter's name.

"You know, I was thinking," the wife said, turning to her husband. "How about if we have them to dinner this weekend? We can invite Eiko and Masashi, too. I bet they'll come. How would that be, Mrs. Tamura? If this week doesn't work for you, we can make it next. Or if that's no good either, it could even be next month. Oh, it'll be so much fun!"

Watching this happy woman already starting to plan her menu, Sayoko felt like she'd finally found the answer. What were the gathering years for? Not for escaping into your own tiny existence and closing the door behind you, but for going out to meet the world. They were for seeking out new encounters, and for striding toward your objectives on your own two feet.

"Didn't Noriko Nakazato call you?" Aoi said. "I'm sure you'll get much better terms working for her than for me."

"No, I have to work for you," Sayoko said emphatically.

Aoi's eyes remained fixed on the sandwich in her hand.

"You know how Mrs. Nakazato forbade us to wear rubber gloves," Sayoko went on, a faint smile on her lips. Her voice was barely above a whisper, almost as if she were talking only to herself. "You'd start with a layer of grease so thick it grabbed at your scouring pad, but if you kept scrubbing and scrubbing until your mind went numb it would gradually give way, and then finally the moment would come when you could slide your bare fingers smoothly across the surface without feeling the slightest resistance. You'd go at the caked-on grease with a pad and cleanser and your two bare hands, and it'd vanish without a trace. Except somehow, ever since I quit, I've had this sour taste in my mouth, as if I came back from a job without getting rid of all the grease. And I'm pretty sure signing on with Mrs. Nakazato to clean houses again isn't going to make that go away."

When Aoi failed to respond, Sayoko grew uneasy. Perhaps she was asking too much. Or perhaps Aoi simply didn't need anybody to work for her anymore.

Aoi looked up. In an instant reflex, Sayoko lowered her eyes and began studying her fingers. Thanks to all the scouring she'd been doing at home, her skin was chapped and her nails were splitting.

"Of course it isn't," said Aoi, popping the last of her sandwich into her mouth. "Unlike me, Noriko's a woman who knows how to keep things neat." She looked up and fixed her eyes sharply on Sayoko. "So you're saying you're ready to take anything I throw at you? Think you're up to making this disaster area spick-and-span in just one day?"

That's not what I meant, Sayoko almost blurted out, but she bit back the words and rose to her feet. She realized that Aoi had indeed understood exactly what she meant.

"Just one day?" she said, surveying the room.

"We'll call it your employment test," Aoi said. "Finish in a day and you're hired. We may have come down a notch, but this is still Platinum Planet, and I'm still the president."

"One day for all this clutter is a pretty tall order. But I accept the challenge. I shall do my best," Sayoko said, bowing deeply.

Aoi returned the bow. "I'll be very much obliged," she said with a note of mock formality.

Sayoko let out a snicker, and Aoi burst into a laugh.

"The first thing is to do something about this window. We need to get some light in here—it's way too gloomy. You just go on about your business. I'll ask if I have a question about throwing something away or how you want things sorted."

Sayoko moved to the large window and started lowering boxes onto the floor, briefly glancing inside each one as she went. Aoi headed into the tatami room, where she sat on the floor in front of the small round table and switched on her laptop. The fax machine clicked and whirred as it automatically picked up an incoming call and began printing.

One box contained stacks of folders and magazines carrying Platinum Planet ads, along with some snack tins and computer disks. Another held travel guides and transportation maps and timetables for various countries, as well as a jumble of office supplies like scissors and glue. Sayoko rolled up her sleeves and concentrated first on getting everything out of the boxes and onto the floor. What little open space remained quickly disappeared, and when she turned to look, piles of magazines and boxes filled the entire room. It was a daunting sight.

Relax. You can do this. Just take it one step at a time, she told herself and set to flattening the boxes she'd emptied. The next box she opened contained a large number of books and a snakes' nest of cables and cords. She sorted the books into stacks, then worked at untangling the cables. One of the stacks at her feet started to topple. With a click of her tongue, she managed to sweep the teetering books into her arms before the whole thing fell, but one pocket paperback tumbled to the floor. When she reached to pick it up, a yellowed piece of paper fluttered from between its pages onto the tangle of cables. She instinctively looked to see what it was.

It was a letter. The little piece of paper was crammed full of characters written in blue ink. Still cradling the books she'd rescued in one arm, Sayoko reached for the note. She knew she wasn't supposed to look at anything like this when cleaning; it was one of the cardinal rules Noriko Nakazato laid down on her very first day of training. Even if she found a bankbook lying open on the floor, under no circumstances was she to peek at its contents.

But Sayoko found herself unable to resist because the handwriting she'd glimpsed might almost have been her own. The overly rounded, rather foreign-looking characters reminded her very much of the way she used to write when she was in high school.

Hi, Aokins, the note began. Sayoko immediately guessed that it was a note addressed by some unknown school friend to Aoi. She could no longer tear her eyes from the page, and quickly scanned the rest of the message.

Hi, Aokins. We just talked on the phone, but here I am already writing a letter. What'd you have for supper tonight? Nobody was home at my place, and I couldn't be bothered making anything so I just had some cookies. Kaola's March. I'm really into them right now.

In world history today, Matsubara amazingly let the class drift way off topic. Did you know he's traveled all over the world? Who'd a thunk? So Ritsuko asked him what's the prettiest place he ever went, and guess what he said? Some place called Machu Picchu. I have no idea where that is, do you? It's supposed to be some kind of phantom city way up high in the sky. Like Laputa, maybe? I don't know.

Anyway, that got him started, and after that he just kept talking on and on about his travels. Listening to him, I got to thinking. How'd you like to go on a big trip together sometime, you and me? To France, maybe, or Australia, or someplace like that. I don't really care where, I just want to go. I wonder where we'll think is prettiest. It'd be fun to find out.

If we did that, do you think we might actually get homesick for this boring dump? Like we'll be sitting in gay Paree and suddenly we're saying, Man, I wish I could see the good ol' Watarase right now! That would reek, but it'd be sort of nice, too, don't you think? I know that sounds weird, but I'm just saying, I think it'd be a happy thing if you could actually feel that way—like you wanted to come back to this place.

See you at our usual spot by the river. I'll bring Fist of the North Star *and the latest issue of* Olive. *How about we stop at the office supply store near the station to look at a globe on our way home? Maybe we can find Machu Picchu. Unless you don't want to.*

All of a sudden I'm getting a powerful craving for a tuna and cheese crepe. I guess I'm still hungry. Maybe I'll go make something.

Sorry for rambling on and on about a bunch of nothing. Why didn't I just wait till tomorrow? What an idiot.

Anyway, see you at the river. Bye!

Nanako

Sayoko looked up from the letter.

A scene from a place she'd never been to rose up before her as vividly as if it were a true memory.

A road runs along the banks of a river. Summer grasses grow tall and thick beside it. Two teenage girls are walking on the far bank, skirts rippling in the breeze, hair flickering in the sun, something funny making them double over with laughter. Suddenly they look across the water and spy the teenage Sayoko standing on the opposite shore. They throw their arms high into the air and wave, shouting something at the top of their lungs. She waves back, and they shout something more. *Wha-a-at? I can't hear you!* They start jumping up and down and pointing along the river in the direction they've been walking. She looks the way they're pointing and sees a bridge spanning the river. They beckon to her and dash for the bridge. She kicks up her skirt and races for the bridge, too, as if chasing after the girls on the other shore. The current flows quietly between them, reflecting the sky above.

The ringing of a phone startled Sayoko back to reality. She quickly slipped the letter back between the pages of the book.